Ralph Compton:
West of the Law

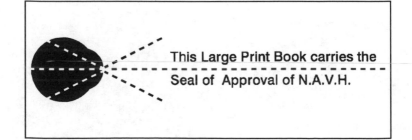

This Large Print Book carries the
Seal of Approval of N.A.V.H.

A RALPH COMPTON NOVEL

RALPH COMPTON: WEST OF THE LAW

JOSEPH A. WEST

THORNDIKE PRESS
A part of Gale, Cengage Learning

GALE
CENGAGE Learning

Detroit • New York • San Francisco • New Haven, Conn • Waterville, Maine • London

W
LP
Fic
Wes
Cl

082397

GALE
CENGAGE Learning™

The publisher does not have any control over and does not assume any responsibility for author or third-party Web sites or their content.
Thorndike Press® Large Print Western.
The text of this Large Print edition is unabridged.
Other aspects of the book may vary from the original edition.
Set in 16 pt. Plantin.
Printed on permanent paper.

LIBRARY OF CONGRESS CATALOGING-IN-PUBLICATION DATA

West, Joseph A.
    West of the law : a Ralph Compton novel / by Joseph A. West.
    p. cm. — (Thorndike Press large print western)
    ISBN-13: 978-1-4104-0922-5 (alk. paper)
    ISBN-10: 1-4104-0922-8 (alk. paper)
    1. Large type books. I. Compton, Ralph. II. Title.
PS3573.E8224W47 2008
813'.54—dc22   2008021254

Published in 2008 by arrangement with NAL Signet, a member of Penguin Group (USA) Inc.

Printed in the United States of America
1 2 3 4 5 6 7 12 11 10 09 08

THE IMMORTAL COWBOY

This is respectfully dedicated to the "American Cowboy." His was the saga sparked by the turmoil that followed the Civil War, and the passing of more than a century has by no means diminished the flame.

True, the old days and the old ways are but treasured memories, and the old trails have grown dim with the ravages of time, but the spirit of the cowboy lives on.

In my travels — to Texas, Oklahoma, Kansas, Nebraska, Colorado, Wyoming, New Mexico, and Arizona — I always find something that reminds me of the Old West. While I am walking these plains and mountains for the first time, there is this feeling that a part of me is eternal, that I have known these old trails before. I believe it is the undying spirit of the frontier calling, allowing me, through the mind's eye, to step back into time. What is the appeal of the Old West of the American frontier?

It has been epitomized by some as the dark and bloody period in American history. Its heroes — Crockett, Bowie, Hickok, Earp — have been reviled and criticized. Yet the Old West lives on, larger than life.

It has become a symbol of freedom, when there was always another mountain to climb and another river to cross; when a dispute between two men was settled not with expensive lawyers, but with fists, knives, or guns. Barbaric? Maybe. But some things never change. When the cowboy rode into the pages of American history, he left behind a legacy that lives within the hearts of us all.

— *Ralph Compton*

CHAPTER 1

The sky was on fire and death stalked the darkness.

John McBride, until that night a detective sergeant, one of New York City's finest, pressed his back against the side of a freight car, the Smith & Wesson .38-caliber self-cocker in his right fist up and ready at shoulder level.

Beside him he heard Inspector Thomas Byrnes curse the rain, the gloom and the lightning that scrawled across the sky like the signature of a demented god.

"John, where is the damn . . . ?" Byrnes' final word was lost in a crash of thunder.

"Train?" McBride finished it for him, a faint smile tugging at his lips.

"Yeah, the train, damn it. I paid the guard ten dollars just to wave a lamp from the back of the caboose as he pulled out of the yard. Well, I don't see a caboose, I don't see a lamp and I sure as hell don't see a train."

The inspector's anxious gaze searched the rain-lashed darkness around them. "You see anything?"

"Nothing."

"At least there's no sign of Sean Donovan's hoodlums. That's good."

"Yeah," McBride said, his bleak eyes lost in darkness, "that's good. But the fact that we can't see them doesn't mean they're not out there."

The big cop saw only a sea of wet, gleaming rails and the hunched, black silhouettes of motionless boxcars. Here and there rose the looming bulk of water towers, standing on four skinny legs like creatures from a child's nightmare. Shadows pooled everywhere, mysterious and full of menace, the torrential rain talking among them in a voice that rattled like black phlegm in the chest of an ancient coal miner.

Beyond the train yard, unseen in the darkness, sprawled a warren of warehouses, slaughterhouses and cattle pens, and behind those the teeming, pestilence-ridden tenements of Hell's Kitchen. The rickety buildings, infested by rats and slyer, more dangerous two-legged vermin, were inhabited by poor Irish immigrants, starving paupers, orphaned children, whores, pickpockets and criminal gangs, the most vicious of them big, laughing Sean Donovan's Forty-fifth Street Derry Boys.

Donovan, six feet four and 250 pounds, all of it bone and muscle, had come up the hard way. He'd begun his criminal career as an enforcer for Dutch Heinrich's ferocious Nineteenth Street Gang. On Dutch Henry's orders he'd used brass knuckles, boots and skull to smash and destroy all those foolish or brave enough to defy the gangster. Donovan had killed eight men with his fists and several more with a gun or knife before he finally forced out the Dutchman and took over his protection, prostitution, gambling and opium rackets.

For all his well-cut suits, his diamond pinkie ring and his cynical, self-serving generosity to the poor, Sean Donovan was a bad man to cross, a born killer with a long memory. It was Detective Sergeant McBride's misfortune that he'd been forced to kill one of the big Irishman's sons . . . and that was a thing Donovan would not forgive or ever forget.

McBride stepped to the corner of the freight car and stared into the flame-streaked night. Sizzling like water on a hot plate, lightning flashes lit up the train yard, scorching the darkness with bolts of scarlet and gold. Nothing moved in the searing light that flickered like a gigantic magic lantern before dying into blackness. There was no sound but the crash of thunder and the dragon hiss of the rain.

"See anything, Sergeant?" Byrnes asked again, a faint note of hope rising in his voice.

"Nothing." McBride let his gun drop to his side. With a toe he pushed his wet carpetbag farther under the freight car, then turned and stood by the inspector. "This doesn't sit well with me," he said. "I mean to cut and run like this. It's sticking in my craw like a dry chicken bone."

Rain ran in rivulets off the black oilskin capes both men wore, and drummed on their plug hats. Around them the raging night was on fire.

Byrnes spoke slowly, as though he were talking to a child. His eyes tried and failed to meet McBride's in the gloom. Thunder crashed, lightning flared and the air smelled of ozone and the rubbery tang of wet oilskin.

"John," he said, "Donovan vows he'll pay the man who brings him your ears a thousand dollars in gold."

"I know that, Inspector," McBride said, a small, stiff anger rising in him. "Isn't that the reason we're here?"

"So I'm telling you something you already know, but it won't do you any harm to hear it again." He waved a hand. "Back there in the Kitchen, there's no lack of toughs who will cut any man, woman or child in half with a shotgun for fifty dollars. The word is out, John. You're a brave man and a good officer, but you're in over your head. For a thousand dollars they'll come at you in the hundreds. There will be no end to them. And finally they'll get you, someday, somewhere, with a bullet or a knife in the back."

"I could go after Donovan," McBride said. He'd moved even closer to Byrnes and the hard planes of his face seemed cast in bronze. "If he's out of the way, there's no one to pay his blood money."

Inspector Byrnes shook his head, a motion McBride heard rather than saw. "John, you know we can't touch Donovan, at least for now. He covers his slimy tracks real well. Even if we did arrest him, his battery of high-priced lawyers would get him out within the hour, and later they'd make sure we never got a conviction." Byrnes' laugh was bitter. "Add to that the fact that he's got half of city hall in his pocket, and right now Mr. Donovan is well-nigh untouchable."

McBride stepped closer to Byrnes, a gusting wind slapping rain into his face. "He's not untouchable, Inspector. I can get to him."

It took a few moments for the implication of what McBride had just said to sink into Byrnes' consciousness. He put his hand on the taller man's wet shoulder. "Sergeant McBride, you are an intelligent, brave and resourceful officer, but if you killed Sean Donovan, it would be my unpleasant duty to charge you with murder. That means either the rope or forty years in Sing Sing. Either way, Donovan would have won because you'd be dead or buried alive in the penitentiary." Byrnes made a fist and punched McBride lightly on the chest. "You think about that now, boyo."

A sense of utter defeat weighing heavy on him, McBride turned his face to a black sky cobwebbed with lightning, thunder roaring like gigantic boulders being hurled along a marble hall. He said nothing. He could not find the words.

"John, you will leave for the Western lands just as we planned," Byrnes said, his tone cajoling. "A man can lose himself out there in the wilderness. After that, let me deal with Donovan. Let the law deal with him."

"The law hasn't dealt with him so far," McBride said. "What makes you think things will change?"

"He'll make a slip, John. His kind always do. We'll get him in the end and lock him away for a long, long time."

"And then I can come running back," McBride said. His voice was flat, the words tasting bitter as acid on his tongue.

"Yes, John. Then you come back."

"The prodigal returns," McBride said. "Welcome home, Detective Sergeant, the man who fled the city with his tail between his legs. The man big Sean Donovan ran out of town."

"It won't be like that, John." Byrnes heard the uncertainty in his own voice and immediately said it again, more confidently this time as he attempted to repair the damage. "It won't be like that." He thought for a few moments, then added, "Besides, you're not running. You're obeying a direct order from your superior to get out of New York."

Byrnes couldn't see McBride's face, but he felt the man's accusing eyes burn into him. The inspector turned away, cursed under his breath, then said aloud, "Where is that damned train?"

The thunderstorm had encouraged the wind and now it blew stronger, slapping the oilskins around the legs of the two men, driving the hard, raking rain straight at them, stinging into their faces. The freight car provided little shelter and McBride felt it rock on the rails, its wooden walls creaking in protest.

His hand wet on the handle of his gun, McBride used his wrist to wipe rain from his eyes. His years as a detective had given him an instinct for danger, and now he felt it strongly. The darkness drew around him, pressing on him, giving him no peace. Out there in the train yard, somewhere, death was drawing close. McBride did not need the candle of reason to read the signs, for there were none. It was enough that he felt the approaching threat, smelled it in the wind. It existed.

Inspector Byrnes drew closer to McBride and reached inside his oilskin. He produced a thick envelope and shoved it into the younger man's hand. "I almost forgot, John. This is for you."

McBride studied the envelope for a moment, then opened it and looked at the contents.

"Eleven hundred dollars," Byrnes said, his voice rising against the keening wind and the relentless rattle of the rain. "A year's salary in advance. Mayor Grace gave his full approval. As far as he is concerned, you are still on the police payroll." The inspector

14

hesitated, then added, "Don't be stiff-necked about this, John. Take the money. You'll need it to help you get settled when you reach the Western territories."

Angry and sick at heart as he was, McBride had it in his mind to refuse. But, a practical man, he knew to arrive exiled and penniless in a strange land would add a new set of problems to the ones he already had.

After some thought, he capitulated. "Thank you, sir," he said, shoving the envelope into the inside pocket of his coat. "And please thank the mayor."

"I will, John," Byrnes said. "God knows, no one deserves that money more than you do. You —" The inspector glanced wildly around him. "Wait! I hear a train!"

McBride heard it too. He stepped away from the freight car and his eyes scanned the night. A few lights burned over at the warehouses and one by one he saw them blink out as they were obscured by a hulking black shape. The locomotive's bell clanked and steam jetted from between its wheels, the *huff-huff-huff* of the venting smoke from the chimney drowning out the sound of the rain.

Byrnes shoved McBride's carpetbag at him. "It's the train. Go now, John!"

McBride felt it then, an overwhelming

sense of dread. The men who stalked him were close. They were here.

A bullet smashed into the side of the boxcar, inches from McBride's head. Another whined viciously off the iron rail close to his feet. Suddenly Byrnes was firing into the darkness, a .38 bucking in his right hand. He turned his head slightly. "Go, John!" he yelled. "I'll hold them off!"

Lightning branded the sky, flashing bright. McBride caught a glimpse of four men running toward him, one of them with a shotgun slanted across his chest. McBride fired at that man, very fast. The light flickered and died as a wild scream split the night.

"You got one of them!" Byrnes yelled. "Now run for the train. That's an order, damn it!"

Desperately, McBride cast one final look at Byrnes, then turned and ran. The caboose was right ahead of him and he saw a red lantern waving from the rear platform.

Behind him, he heard Byrnes' gun. Then the man was pounding after him, running between the rain-slicked rails. Another shot and Byrnes stumbled and fell, clutching at his right leg. McBride stopped, looked back, but the inspector waved him on. "Get to the train!" he hollered. "I'll be all right."

"Inspector, I —," McBride began, standing uncertainly, his gun in one hand, the carpetbag in the other. Now the caboose was off to his left and the train of boxcars was gathering speed, rattling into the darkness. McBride could see the guard now, frantically waving the lantern, yelling words he could not hear against the crash of thunder and roar of rain.

"Go, John, before it's too late!" Byrnes yelled.

McBride ran for the caboose. He heard Byrnes call out, "John, write to me when you get to where you're going." A pause, then: "Confide in no one! Trust no one! Sean Donovan reaches far."

A sickness in him, McBride ran. "Hurry!" the guard yelled.

The big cop threw his bag onto the caboose platform, then leaped for the rail. He swung himself up beside the guard and saw that the man's eyes were wide with fear. A bullet smashed into the glass of the door behind the guard and he yelped, dropped his lantern and ran inside.

The train was moving faster, the boxcars and caboose hammering along the rails, plunging into the darkness.

Fear coursing through him, McBride put his hands to his mouth and roared into the night: "Inspector!"

He heard a flurry of shots. Then an echoing silence mocked him.

CHAPTER 2

Days, nights, melting into a blur of land-
scape, changing weather and the pale, shifting faces of his fellow travelers, rushed past
John McBride at the speed of a steam train.
He had no final destination, no place of rest
in mind. He kept to himself, spoke to no
one and was content to ride the iron rails to
wherever they might lead.

But one thing he did know — his direction was west, always west, toward the Divide.

Two weeks after he'd left New York,
McBride stood on the platform of a train
station . . . he knew not where.

Over the past hour it had grown dark and
the sky was ablaze with stars. Lanterns hung
on each side of the door that led to the waiting room and ticket office, casting dancing
pools of orange light, flecked with tiny white
moths.

His carpetbag at his feet, McBride looked

19

around him. The station was small, but it had been built with care. Elaborate ginger-bread carving adorned the edges of the slanted roof, and expensive, wrought iron benches were placed at strategic intervals along the platform for the convenience of travelers. A water tower stood by the tracks, leaking fat drops as they all did, and close by sprawled a rickety cattle pen.

Beyond the station he saw the lights of a town, tiny by McBride's standards. He was a man who had been born and bred in the big city. But where there was a town, there would be a hotel, and he was looking forward to stretching out on a real bed.

After he'd left the freight he'd ridden the cushions, but had spent long, boring hours kicking his heels at stations in the middle of nowhere, often just an old boxcar on a sid-ing, where he drank coffee made from alkaline water and ate fried salt pork the few times it was available.

There were other stations, farther west, where he looked over the town and judged what it had to offer. But all of them seemed too small, smaller than this one, and in such towns a man as tall and muscular as Mc-Bride would be noticed and be a source of much speculation and talk.

Inspector Byrnes had told him to confide

in no one and trust no one, warning him that Sean Donovan's reach was long. So far none of the towns along the Santa Fe track had offered him the kind of anonymity he sought, and he'd kept on rolling.

At first the country McBride had passed through had been a patchwork of wheat fields, flat country formed by the retreat of ancient glaciers, and a few stretches of pastureland. As the days passed, the land had changed. The villages had disappeared, giving way to rolling prairies that went on forever under the vast blue dome of the sky. The only trees in sight were the cottonwoods and willows that lined the creeks. Once, the train had stopped to allow the passage of a herd of buffalo. Seeing McBride's interest, and pegging him for a pilgrim, one of his fellow passengers, a wiry old man in a buckskin shirt who held a brass-framed rifle between his knees.

"The buffs are all but gone now," the old man had said, a faint touch of sadness in his smile. "Maybe we're seeing the last of them. So remember this, boy, because you'll never come upon their like again, not in your lifetime or in any other."

Only when the old man told him that the Rocky Mountains were directly ahead of them, and beyond the peaks lay the dry, desert lands of the Arizona Territory, did John McBride decide to leave the lurching, smoking misery of the train and find a place where he could settle.

But for how long? A month, a year, longer? He had no answer to this question and the realization of that made him sick at heart. He was a stranger in a strange land, far from the stone canyons and teeming streets of the great city he loved. Maybe there would be no going back as long as Sean Donovan lived. In that case he was doomed to be forever a wandering exile and no one, man, woman or child, would look forward to his coming or regret his leaving.

Unbidden, a sigh escaped McBride's lips. He shook his head slowly, picked up his carpetbag and stepped into the station. A ticket clerk sat behind an iron grille, a small man with a lined face, a visored cap set straight on his head. He looked up when McBride entered.

"No other trains tonight," the clerk said, waving a dismissive hand, " 'cept the Denver cannonball, an' she don't stop."

McBride nodded, a tall man in an ill-fitting brown suit, looking hot and uncomfortable in his high celluloid collar and dark green tie. His black derby hat showed signs of hard use and was frayed around the brim.

The shabby suit coat, cut generously in the style of the time, concealed the Smith & Wesson in the shoulder holster under his arm.

"What is this place?" he asked.

The clerk looked surprised. "Hell, man, you mean you don't know?"

"If I knew, I wouldn't be asking," McBride said.

At first the clerk had tried to slap a brand on the tall man, taking him for a drummer headed for the gold diggings or maybe a cattle buyer. Now, looking into a pair of blue eyes that were the coldest and hardest he'd ever seen, he wasn't so sure. His tone changed.

"That there iron road outside belongs to the Santa Fe, but you already know that." He waved a hand. "The town is called High Hopes an' this is the great state of Colorado. To the west are the Spanish Peaks, to the south the Picketwire and to the north there's miles of nothing until you reach the Platte." The man smiled. "Enough for you, stranger?"

"What's to the east?"

The clerk shrugged. "More nothing until you get back to the place you came from."

McBride allowed himself a smile. "What manner of town is this?"

"It's a town like any other west of the Mississippi, 'cept it's booming on account of the railroad and the gold in the Spanish Peaks. High Hopes caters to miners, cattlemen, whores and gamblers. We got thirty stores, two hotels, three saloons, and I'm betting that nary a man jack of us has ever lived within the sound of church bells."

"That apply to the women as well?" McBride asked, another smile tugging at his lips.

"Especially the women."

McBride thought through what the clerk had told him. Even back East he'd heard of the Western boomtowns with their constantly shifting populations of footloose miners and those who preyed on them, whores, gamblers and saloonkeepers.

A man could lose himself here. He'd just be another face in a constantly changing crowd and no one would notice or care as he came or went.

"What's the best hotel?" McBride asked.

"If you got the money, two dollars a day, the best is the Killeen. If you don't got the money, you can bunk at Charlie Ault's place for two bits a night. Of course, you'll have to share your bunk with another feller and a passel o' bedbugs."

"Then the Killeen it is," McBride said. "I

24

suppose it doesn't have bedbugs?"

"No, no bedbugs," the clerk said. "It's got clean rooms." The man had answered the question absently, obviously thinking about something else. Now he said what was on his mind.

"How long you plan on staying in High Hopes, mister?"

"I don't rightly know," McBride said. "Why do you ask?"

The clerk was suddenly uncomfortable. He rose to his feet, opened the door of the ticket office and stepped beside McBride. "I have some advice for you, if you're willing to take it." His previous bantering tone was gone, replaced by something more serious.

"Advise away," McBride said. "I'm listening."

The clerk nodded, smiling. "Good, because it's been my experience that advice is seldom welcome, and them who need it most, like it the least."

"Like I said, I'm listening."

As though intimidated by McBride's size now that he was standing next to him, the clerk gulped down a breath and said, "The way to keep on living in High Hopes is to see nothing." He glanced fearfully over his shoulder, then back at the tall man. "Just mind your own business, you understand?

You might see things, hear things, but you just walk away and say nothing. Out here you're west of the law, west of most everything. Nothing in High Hopes is as it seems. Everything is upside down, higgledy-piggledy. You get my drift?"

McBride nodded. "That sits fine with me. I'm not hunting trouble, here or anywhere else." He touched the brim of his hat. "Obliged to you. Now I'll look up that hotel."

The clerk shot out his hand and grasped the big man's arm. "There's one more thing."

Slightly irritated, McBride nevertheless held his temper and asked, "And what's that?"

"There's a man in town, goes by the name of Hack Burns. He's poison-mean and fast as chained lightning with a gun. Since he's been here, he's killed three men, and a fourth, the town marshal, is right now lying at death's door with Hack's bullet in him. Now, if you come across this here Hack Burns, just step around him real quiet an' respectful-like and you'll be fine."

All this was nothing new to McBride. Even as a child on the mean streets of the Kitchen he'd been warned about hard cases and over the years he'd come up against quite a few. As things had turned out, he'd proved himself to be a harder case than most of them.

"Sounds like a good man to avoid," he allowed, playing the rube a little longer. "I'll be sure to give Mr. Burns a wide berth. How will I know him?"

"You'll know him when you see him. Wears two guns in crossed belts real low on his hips and right here" — the clerk's fingers strayed to his left cheek — "he's got a stain on his face, looks like spilled port wine. Whatever you do, mister, don't mention it. Hack killed a cowboy last week who funned him about it."

"The mark of Cain," McBride said.

"Huh?"

The big man shook his head. "Nothing. It's something I read one time."

"Well, don't call him Cain either. If you have to talk to him, you say 'Mr. Burns,' and you say it real polite-like. If you don't, he might gun you quicker'n scat."

McBride let the smile that threatened to come to his lips die stillborn. "I'll remember," he said. "Call him Mr. Burns and don't mention the mark."

"See that you do remember," the clerk said, his face stiff and parchment-yellow in the glow of the oil lamps. "Just see you do."

His smile was faint. "You'll live longer that way."

CHAPTER 3

McBride left the station and crossed the street, picking his way through a noisy throng of bearded, profane miners, townspeople hurrying about their business with downcast eyes, lawyers and land speculators in black broadcloth, a few booted and spurred punchers astride wiry cow ponies and a scattering of Chinese who chattered incessantly in a tongue nobody else could understand.

The saloons were roaring, interior oil lamps' hazy halos of orange light lost in a fog of blue cigar smoke. Men bellowed, made loud and bold by whiskey, and the sudden, strident laughter of hard-eyed women rang false, chiming wild like cracked crystal bells.

The town was booming, bursting at the seams, its sea of lights holding back the night. The hour was yet early and High Hopes was just hitting its stride, a seething, shifting mass of humanity eagerly seeking to commit one or all of the seven deadly sins in a place where such transgressions came easy, but never cheap.

For his part, born and raised amid the swarming squalor of Hell's Kitchen, McBride felt right at home and forced a path for himself by elbowing his way through the crowd to the lobby of the Killeen Hotel.

A prominent sign on the wall opposite the door read:

The majority of our rooms are without transoms, ventilation being obtained by the use of adjustable windows. Guests may therefore lie down to peaceful slumbers undisturbed by apprehensions of getting their heads blown off or having their valuables lifted by burglars.
— *The Management.*

Smiling, McBride signed the register as John Smith, apparently a common name in those parts, since the disinterested desk clerk didn't even raise an eyebrow. Then he climbed the stairs to his room on the second floor.

As the man at the station had promised, the room was clean. The bed had fresh sheets and there was a pitcher of water and a basin on a small table. The dresser had a mirror, a rare luxury in the West, and there was a pine clothes closet. Lace curtains hung in the room's only window and an oil lamp stood on the bed stand.

McBride closed the curtains, lit the lamp, then unpacked his few belongings — shirts, socks and a supply of celluloid collars. He took off his high-buttoned coat and sat on the bed, hearing it creak under his weight. He broke open the Smith & Wesson, ejected the shells and thoroughly cleaned and oiled the gun before he reloaded and slid it back into the shoulder holster. The .38 had been a considerable investment on McBride's part, almost a month's salary, and he lavished much more care on the revolver than he did on himself.

A restlessness in him, McBride stepped to the window. He pushed back the curtain, raised the window a few inches and looked outside. A hollow moon was rising and the night was hot, heat lightning flashing to the west over the Spanish Peaks, an electric-blue radiance throbbing in the dark sky. The air smelled of dust, horse dung, cigar smoke and sweat. Pianos played in the saloons, their competing tunes tangling in a calamitous cacophony of jangled notes that fluttered aimlessly in the air like stricken moths.

He was about to close the window and walk away when McBride's attention was attracted to a freight wagon drawn by a couple of sturdy Morgans that had just pulled up at the entrance to the shadowed alley beside the Golden Garter. Normally, he would have glanced at the wagon, then dismissed it from his mind. But there was something different, even sinister about this one. An iron cage had been built into the bed, and in the uncertain light McBride thought he could make out the huddled shapes of several women.

The driver, a tall, heavy man with a red beard that spilled over his chest, jumped down from the box. He was joined by a smaller man carrying a Henry rifle, his thin cheeks pooled with shadow. The red-bearded man, a miner, judging by his battered hat, plaid shirt and mule-eared boots, held a coiled bullwhip in his right hand. He stepped to the back of the wagon, clanked a key in a lock and opened the door of the cage.

McBride watched the man motion with the whip, and a tiny woman rose and crouched hesitantly at the door. Red Beard cursed, then angrily waved the whip again, and the woman dropped lightly to the ground. Now that McBride could see her better, he realized that this was not a grown woman but a young, slight girl in her early teens. She was Chinese and her round face held a mix of fear and apprehension.

Red Beard swore again, motioning with his whip, and three more girls joined the first. They were just as young, just as slight and equally frightened. The big miner made another irritable motion with the whip, pointing it toward the alley. The four girls clung to one another and, their long, blue-black hair gleaming in the light of the oil lamps outside the saloon, shuffled into the alley. Red Beard and the man with the rifle followed. Soon they were swallowed by darkness and McBride could see them no more.

He closed the window, letting the curtain fall back into place, and as he stepped away he shed his shoulder rig. He slid the gun from the leather, placed it on the stand by the bed and stretched out, staring at the ceiling.

What he had just witnessed disturbed him deeply. The oldest of the Chinese girls had looked to be about fourteen and the three others were even younger. There was no doubt in McBride's mind that the girls, children really, had been terrified, cowed into obedience by abuse they'd already suffered. Maybe Red Beard did more with that bullwhip than use it as a pointer.

John McBride swore, telling himself angrily that the fate of four Chinese girls was no concern of his. His orders from Inspector Byrnes — and they had been orders — were to lose himself in the Western lands, lie low and wait until told that it was safe to return to New York. He was young, not yet thirty, and he could resume his police career where he left off. With hard work and a bit of luck he might well end up as an inspector of detectives himself. It was possible. More than possible, it was very likely.

Yes, he was still a law officer. But in New York, not here, not in this wooden shantytown in the middle of nowhere. What happened in High Hopes was hardly his business. Hadn't the railroad clerk told him that the way to stay alive in the town was to see nothing, hear nothing, say nothing, like the three Chinese monkeys?

McBride shook his head in irritation. Now, why did he have to go and think about the Chinese again, even if it was only monkeys? He undid his tie and celluloid collar and laid them on the bed stand with his watch. Then he heeled off one of his elastic-sided ankle boots but had to sit up and remove the other. Wiggling his toes in his socks, he blew out the oil lamp, stretched out on the bed again and closed his eyes.

But sleep would not come to him.

No matter how hard he tried to clear his racing mind, the scared faces of the girls kept coming back to haunt him and an iron fist twisted his heart in his chest.

Outside the boisterous town was as noisy as ever, the saloons going full blast and the street still crowded with people, and once he heard a flurry of shots followed by a woman's scream. Whatever had happened, a killing or some drunken rooster shooting at the moon, High Hopes ignored it and the free-spending miners led the festivities as before.

Tired as he was from his long journey west, McBride gave up the unequal struggle. There would be no sleep until the dawning sun told the town it was time to turn off the lamps and seek the blankets. McBride rose and padded in his stocking feet across the floor to the window. The cage was gone, but now there was something else to attract his interest — a woman.

A woman like no other he'd ever seen.

She stood on the boardwalk outside the saloon, and even in the darkness her beauty burned like a flame. Thick auburn hair was piled high on her head and she wore a low-cut dress of vivid red silk. A thin ribbon of the same color encircled her slim neck, and her shoulders were bare, revealing the swell of her breasts and the deep, shadowed V of cleavage. Her face was oval in shape, and her eyes were large and set wide apart, her lips full, scarlet and inviting.

She was, McBride decided, the most beautiful woman he'd ever seen. Even back in New York, a city renowned for its exquisite women, she would have stood out from the rest.

Like a rose among thorns, McBride thought, pleased that he could still wax poetic, despite the life he'd led, a life where nothing had come easy and the pursuit of criminals and the probing of their often terrible deeds had calloused his soul. In that moment, in a single, blinding flash of realization, he knew he must have this woman, that somehow, some way, she must be his.

There were ominous signs to be read, but blinded by the woman's breathtaking beauty, McBride did not read them. He would pursue the woman in the red dress clean, with no predetermined notions or conditions.

He was new to the West and did not know that among the Sioux, Cheyenne and many other Indian tribes, red is the color of conflict, wounds and violent death.

He did not know it then, but it was a thing he was destined to learn.

Two men stood with the woman, close enough to her that they shaped up to be at least acquaintances. The man at her elbow was tall and as big as McBride himself, but much more handsome in a cheap, flashy way. He sported a thick mane of yellow hair, obviously pomaded, and a trimmed, full mustache calculated to set female hearts aflutter. He was dressed in a well-cut suit of gray broadcloth and a diamond stickpin glittered in his cravat. Whoever he was, self-assured and relaxed even in the company of a beautiful woman, the man projected an image of wealth and raw, arrogant power.

Beside him, his face lost in shadow under a wide-brimmed hat, stood a smaller man that McBride decided could be only Hack Burns. He wore two guns in crossed belts, hung low on his hips, but unlike the bigger man, he was not in the least relaxed. McBride saw his head slowly turn this way and that with the icy menace of a cobra as he studied faces in the passing crowd. There was a readiness about Burns that reminded McBride of a tensed spring about to violently uncoil. He had seen the gunman's like before, back in the Four Corners, sudden, cold-eyed men who would kill for money without emotion or a pang of conscience.

McBride made up his mind that he wanted no part of Hack Burns. Not then, not ever.

He stepped away from the window, lit the oil lamp, then sat on the bed and pulled on his boots. He rose and slipped his suspenders over his shoulders. The night was hot and he decided to forgo his coat and collar. A glance in the mirror told him that he badly needed a shave. He rasped a hand over his lean cheeks, but decided the razor could wait. Right now he had to see the woman again — up close and personal.

John McBride slipped his gun into his right pants pocket, settled his plug hat on his head and left the hotel . . . stepping into a roaring night streaked with lamplight.

CHAPTER 4

The Golden Garter Saloon was packed wall-to-wall with people, gold miners mostly, in from the Spanish Peaks to spend their dust, a sprinkling of flushed punchers with their wide-brimmed hats tipped back, spurs chiming on their heels, and a few women in short dresses of vivid yellow, blue or green silk.

As he made a place for himself at the bar, McBride's eyes scanned the smoke-filled room, but he saw no sign of the woman in the red gown.

The bartender, his pomaded hair parted in the middle of his head, slicked down shiny and flat on either side, asked McBride to name his poison. The product of a drunken, violent father, McBride had long ago sworn off alcohol, but he ordered a beer and let it sit, the foam settling as its tiny bubbles popped.

He saw her then.

A momentary parting of the crowd revealed the far corner of the saloon. She was sitting at a table with four miners, studying the playing cards in her hand. Stacks of poker chips stood on the table in front of her and surprisingly, given her surroundings, a small silver tray holding a steaming china teapot and a cup and saucer.

The woman's eyes met McBride's for an instant — dark hazel, he noticed — then dropped to her cards again, long lashes lying on her cheekbones like spread black fans.

The throng crowded together again and she was once more lost from his sight.

McBride turned to the man at his side, a young miner wearing a plaid shirt, a seaman's woolen cap on his head.

"Can I buy you a drink?" he asked.

For a moment the man looked surprised, but then he shrugged and said, "Sure, why not? Whiskey." He stuck out his hand. "Name's Jim Palmer, harpooner, late of good old Nantucket Town. Now I'm here at the diggings."

McBride shook Palmer's hand, gave his name as John Smith, then motioned to the bartender to fill the miner's glass. When the man had his drink he asked, "There's a woman over there at the corner table, playing cards. Who is she?"

Palmer gave McBride a knowing smile. "Sooner or later every stranger who sets foot in High Hopes asks that same question." He tried his drink, grimaced and set his glass back on the bar. "Her name's Shannon Roark. She's the house dealer for the owner of the saloon." The man nodded to the end of the bar. "That's him over there. Name's Gamble Trask and he cuts a wide path around these parts."

Trask was the handsome man McBride had seen outside the saloon with Shannon. Their eyes met and McBride was burned by the challenge in Trask's eyes, that and the arrogance of money and power.

McBride had no quarrel with Gamble Trask. He had nothing to prove and did not want to draw unwelcome attention to himself. He looked quickly away, missing the cruel smile of triumph on the man's face.

Palmer was talking again, smiling as though at some inner thought. "I know what's on your mind, John Smith, but let it go. A lot of well-set fellows have tried to dab a loop on Shannon, as the cowboys say, but she's sent them all packing with their tails between their legs and shrunk to about three feet tall. I believe Miss Roark is a woman who will choose her own man in

41

her own time and on her own terms." He nodded, still smiling, wistfully, like a man watching a fairy gift fade in the morning light. "Yup, that's what I believe all right."

"I want to meet her," McBride said.

Palmer shrugged. "Easy enough. If you're a gambling man, just sit in on the game at her table. If you're not, she takes a break two or three times a night. You could ask her if you can buy her a drink."

"Champagne?" McBride asked, making a snap judgment.

Palmer shook his head. "Tea. She never touches the hard stuff."

"Then I'll do —"

McBride never finished his sentence. Suddenly Palmer, a small man, was jerked backward by the collar of his shirt and sent sprawling on the floor.

"Just makin' room at the bar is all," the man who stepped into Palmer's space laughed. Those around him who were within earshot laughed with him, uneasily, shifting their feet or suddenly finding something of great interest at the bottom of their glass.

John McBride didn't laugh. Growing up hard as he had done, he'd met his share of bullies and he detested the breed. He had not wanted to draw unwelcome attention, but he could not let this go.

The man who stood arrogantly beside him, purposely crowding him, was the red-bearded man he'd seen from the hotel window who'd driven the young Chinese girls into the alley like livestock. Up close, Red Beard was huge, big in the shoulders and arms, and he shared Gamble Trask's arrogance, his cruelty plain in his thin mouth and pale blue eyes. The man had fresh scratches on his left cheek, the marks of a woman's fingernails. Remembering the little Chinese girls, McBride did not want to think about what had caused them to be there.

A white-hot anger building in him, Mc-Bride bent slightly and offered Palmer his hand. The miner shook his head, making no attempt to rise from the floor. "Let it go, Smith," he said. His frightened eyes went to Red Beard, who was watching him and McBride with faint, contemptuous amusement. Palmer said, "Nolan didn't mean nothing by it."

The man called Nolan grinned, his teeth long and yellow as piano keys. "That's right, tin pan, I didn't mean nothing by it. Just cleared myself some room." He looked around at the men at the bar, his grin widening. "Ain't that right, boys?"

A chorus of approval by intimidated men

followed and a few loudly banged their glasses on the bar. McBride's voice, cold and flat, cut across the noise.

"This gentleman" — he bent and hauled Palmer to his feet — "and I had not finished our conversation. Now, Nolan, if that's your name, step away and clear a space."

Nolan looked like he'd been slapped. He stood staring at McBride in stunned wonderment for a few long seconds, then said, shaking out the bullwhip in his right hand, "Mister, nobody talks to Jim Nolan like that. Just to be sure you remember, I'm going to cut some of the hide right off'n you."

The man carried a Colt in a cross-draw holster on his left hip and McBride had no doubt he was a practiced fighting man. He had not wanted to step into the limelight, but now it was being forced on him and if he tried to back off, he knew Nolan would kill him.

A hush had settled on the saloon, the last few notes of the piano faltering to a ragged stop. McBride was aware that down at the other end of the bar Trask and his gunman Hack Burns were watching him intently. Smiling.

Nolan stepped back, giving himself room to swing the whip. Above his beard, the man's face glowed with a triumphant, vicious light. He was a man who looked like he enjoyed killing and he was enjoying it now, like a glutton anticipating the first bite of a feast spread before him.

"You're making a big mistake, Nolan," McBride said, his eyes cold. "I'm a man grown, not a little Chinese girl you can push around."

Stung, Nolan roared and swung the bullwhip.

McBride moved — very fast for a big man. His fingers curled on the beer mug in front of him and he hurled it with all his strength into Nolan's face.

The glass hit Nolan high on the forehead, opening a cut, and beer splashed over his face and beard. The big man roared his fury, and swung back his arm again, readying the bullwhip for a slashing strike at McBride's face that could tear out his eyes.

McBride did not let him get set. He moved in on Nolan and stabbed a straight right into the man's mouth. Nolan was sobered by the unexpected power behind that punch and he stepped back, shaking his head, blood and saliva flying from his smashed lips. He dropped the whip, realizing the big man would not give him room to swing its ten-foot length, and waded into McBride, punching hard to the body with both hands.

McBride fought back, standing his ground. He took a swinging right to the jaw from Nolan and pretended to stagger, hoping the man would come after him. Nolan did and McBride closed with him again. He hammered the front of his skull onto the bridge of Nolan's nose and felt the crunch of bone. Nolan went back, gasping, blood staining his red beard scarlet. But he was far from beaten.

Nolan rushed in, swinging both fists at McBride's face. Solid blows smashed into McBride's chin and he staggered for real this time, his hat flying away as his head snapped back. His legs were threatening to buckle under him, and in that instant McBride knew he was fighting for his life. If he dropped to the floor, Nolan would use his boots to kick him to a bloody pulp.

"Now you got him, Jim!" somebody in the crowd yelled. "Put him away."

McBride hung on, wrestling now as Jim Nolan tried to throw him to the floor. He felt steel in the man, the roping muscles along his spine as big as a ship's cables. For the first time since the fight began, McBride realized this was a knuckle, boot and skull battle he could easily lose.

He arched as Nolan's enormous arms

circled his waist, trying to break his back. The pain made McBride gasp and he felt the bones of his lower spine grind. Nolan's shattered face was very close to his own. He smelled blood on the man's breath as his grip tightened. "I'm going to snap you like a twig," Nolan taunted. "You'll scream like a woman."

McBride's strength was fading fast. Nolan's arms were an irresistible force, like steel hawsers crushing the life out of him. He knew his backbone could soon shatter, leaving him paralyzed and helpless on the floor.

Desperately McBride chopped a short right to Nolan's chin and then another. The man shook off the blows and laughed. "You won't hurt me with those punches!"

The crowd was cheering wildly now, their blood-lust surging. Judging by the sound and the cries for Nolan to end it, McBride figured that a stranger had mighty few friends in the Golden Garter.

McBride suddenly went limp and hung his head. He heard Nolan's triumphant yell and for a moment the terrible pressure on his spine eased a little as it dawned on the big man that the battle was won.

It was all the time McBride needed.

Straightening, he stabbed his thumbs into

47

Nolan's eyes, thrusting hard. The man screamed and jerked his head away, but he again immediately applied pressure to McBride's weakening back.

Fear spiking at him, McBride again went for Nolan's eyes. His powerful thumbs dug deep. He roared like a wounded animal, every last shred of civilized behavior fleeing from him. McBride rammed his thumbs even deeper, trying to blind Nolan.

Finally the man had enough. He broke his hold and stepped unsteadily back, dashing away blood from his eyes with the heel of his hand. Maddened by the pain in his spine, McBride went after Nolan, no mercy in him.

A killing rage welled in him and exploded in his skull like a million pieces of shattered glass reflected in fire. He slammed a wicked right hook to Nolan's chin and followed up with a fist to the belly. His face gray under a grotesque mask of blood, Nolan backed up, his mouth hanging open and his knees like rubber. McBride kept after him, hooking short, punishing blows to the man's head. Nolan started to go down, but McBride, his blood up, would not let him off the hook. He dug his fingers into Nolan's hair and held him up as he hammered a smashing right into the man's chin, then another.

McBride opened his fingers and Nolan dropped to the floor, his busted jaw hanging loose.

Used up, McBride stood where he was, his chest heaving. His left eye was swollen shut and he tasted the raw iron tang of blood in his mouth. It hurt to breathe, his ribs and lower back pounding spasms of pain at him. Finally he turned and walked back to the bar, the crowd of stunned miners and saloon girls opening a path for him. McBride was aware of the tangled combination of wonder, fear and apprehension in their eyes, like children watching a caged tiger at a traveling circus.

Even the bartender, who had seen much of violence, was wary when McBride leaned on the bar and ordered a beer. Palmer, his eyes as guarded as the others', stepped beside McBride and opened his mouth to speak. He didn't get the chance to utter a word.

"Look out!"

A woman's voice.

McBride spun and saw Nolan on his feet, staggering a little as he drew his Colt. The man had made a reputation in the town as a bully and a hard case, good with his fists or a gun. If he lost that reputation now, he knew he was finished in High Hopes.

Nolan fired as McBride yanked his Smith & Wesson from his pocket. The bullet burned across the heavy meat of his left shoulder as he assumed the duelist's stance as his firearms instructors had taught him. He held the revolver at eye level, his arm straight, the instep of his left foot behind the heel of his right. He and Nolan fired at the same time.

The big .45 slug from Nolan's gun plowed across the top of the bar, inches from McBride's waist, showering splinters. McBride's bullet parted Nolan's beard, thudding into him square in the middle of his chest. Hit hard, the man stumbled back, but he was still trying to bring his gun into line. McBride fired his self-cocker again, and once again, scoring both times.

Nolan went to his knees, pumping bullets into the floor. Then his eyes rolled up white in his head and he fell flat on his face as all that was alive in him fled.

A sickness curling in his belly, McBride let his revolver drop to his side. In the echoing silence that followed, gray gun smoke drifted through the saloon and he was aware of a young girl in a yellow dress at his side, her shuddering breasts rising and falling as, shocked by what she had just witnessed, she fought for breath.

"Well done, that, man!"

McBride turned to see a man striding toward him, a beaming smile on his handsome face. He paused momentarily when he drew abreast of Nolan's body, then motioned to a couple of men. "Wilson, Reid, get that out of here. It's staining my floor."

Trask stepped beside McBride. "Let me shake your hand, gunfighter. My name is Gamble Trask and I always figured that big Jim Nolan was one of my best men. Now I know differently."

Reluctantly McBride took the man's hand. "John Smith," he said. "I'm not a gunfighter and I'm just a traveler passing through."

He pocketed his gun as Nolan's body was carried past, and heard Trask say, "You'd better get that eye seen to, Smith — it's badly swollen. Believe it or not, we have an excellent doctor in town." The man grinned. "Now let me buy you a drink." He turned his head and yelled, "Hell, I'm buying everybody a drink! Piano player — music!"

The piano player, maybe with the killing of Jim Nolan in mind, started up a spirited rendition of "Bury Me Not on the Lone Prairie," and men cheered and women laughed as they crowded up to the bar.

Trask, smiling, leaned closer to McBride so he could be heard. "I think you're feeling bad, but don't be. Nolan wasn't much, so his was a small, meaningless death. Look around you, Smith — he's already gone and forgotten. Now, how about that drink?"

"I have a beer," McBride said, his dislike for Trask growing. The cheap price the man had just put on Nolan's life served only to twist the broken shards of glass already lacerating his conscience.

"Then I'll join you," Trask said. He ordered a beer, then said, "I have a proposition for you, Smith."

"What kind of proposition?"

"Why, man, I'm offering you a job."

"Not interested."

"The least you can do is listen, especially since you just gunned one of my men," Trask said. He was wearing the sly smile of a hungry lobo wolf.

McBride nodded. "All right, I'm listening."

CHAPTER 5

Gamble Trask led McBride to an unoc-
cupied table in a corner, where there was a
full view of the saloon. "Take a seat," he
said, waving. "This table stays reserved for
me."

McBride sat and Trask took a chair opposite him. Hack Burns appeared out of
nowhere, handed McBride his plug hat,
then took his place behind his boss' chair.
When the gunman's pale eyes fell on Mc-
Bride they revealed nothing, neither interest
nor hostility, but his thumbs were hooked
in his gun belts and he stood ready. The
livid purple stain on Burns' left cheek
seemed to McBride a living thing that
threatened to spread and consume him, a
grotesque mask that concealed the man's
innermost thoughts and feelings. His legs
straddled, hips thrust forward, his cobra
eyes roamed the crowd, missing nothing.

For the first time, McBride noticed that

Burns wore a town marshal's star on his black leather vest.

"Now, John —" Trask smiled. "May I call you John?"

The man was as smooth as silk, polished to a brilliant sheen, poised, confident and seemingly willing to be friendly. But there was a thin-lipped hardness about his mouth, and scars covered the knuckles of his big hands. The sixth sense that every good detective possesses told McBride that here was a man who would kill without compunction and never lose a night of sleep over the doing of it.

He made no answer to Trask's question.

"John?" A slight note of irritation.

"Sure," McBride said. "That's fine by me." Around him people were watching. He was now full in the glare of the spotlight, a place he never wanted to be. A place, he knew, that could well get him killed.

Trask was talking again. "Do you want to hear about the job I'm offering?"

The safest course was to go along with it. At least for now. "Like I told you earlier, I'm listening," McBride said.

Trask clapped his hands. "Excellent! I like a man who listens." He turned his head and glanced up at Burns. "John is true-blue, isn't that the truth of it, Hack?"

Burns nodded, his face expressionless. "Whatever you say, boss, whatever you say."

Trask turned to McBride again. "Now, John, here's the deal. I liked how you handled yourself against Nolan. You're good with your fists and a gun and I need men like you. I want you to serve as one of Marshal Burns' deputies. A hundred and twenty a month, and that's just for starters. And I'll pay a substantial bonus every time I think you've done a good job for me." The man smiled. "How does that set with you, Deputy Marshal Smith? Think of it, man — you can get rich in High Hopes. I can make you rich."

McBride nodded. "It's a tempting offer, but I believe I'll pass."

Throwing up his hands in mock exasperation, Trask said, "Well, what more can I do? John, I can tell by your accent that you're new to the Western lands and unfamiliar with our ways. Trust me, you'll never get such an offer again, not from me or anyone else. Remember, I'm the big man in town and I plan on getting a sight bigger. You can grow with me."

"I appreciate it, Trask," McBride said, knowing the use of the man's name without the "Mr." would sting. "But I'm not for sale."

082397

Ice formed in Trask's eyes. He was a powerful man, a man well used to getting his way and now this . . . this nonentity had the impertinence to thwart him. "All right," he said, "I planned on giving you a fair shake and you turned me down. No harm done." He rose to his feet. "Marshal Burns, see that . . . ah . . . Mr. Smith is out of town by noon tomorrow."

Now Burns showed his first sign of interest. The mark on his cheek stood out in stark relief as he smiled at McBride with all the warmth of a hungry panther. "I'll see that it's done, boss," he said.

"You're making a mistake, Trask," McBride said, his voice level. He did not look up, studiously turning his beer glass on the table. "I plan on staying around for a while."

Trask had been about to walk away. Now he stopped. "Smith, get out of High Hopes by noon tomorrow or you'll die," he said. "The choice is yours."

After Trask left, Hack Burns lingered. "You made the boss look small in front of everybody, Smith," he said. "I'll kill you for that if I see you around town after noon tomorrow."

McBride's gaze lifted to the gunman. "He is small, Burns. I didn't make him that way." He felt his battered face stiffen. "And I don't plan on going anywhere."

"Just remember what I told you," Burns said. "I saw you gunfight Nolan, and mister, you ain't near good enough. If you're on the street" — he pointed directly upward — "after the sun is that high, you're a dead man."

John McBride smiled inwardly as Burns walked away. Back in New York what the gunman had just told him would be considered a sure conversation stopper. But it was true that Burns' talking was all done. Tomorrow he'd act, and he'd be almighty sudden and deadly.

Common sense told McBride that now was the time to cut and run, just like he'd done in New York. Inspector Byrnes had ordered him to lie low and not attract attention to himself. Bitterly, he realized he'd disobeyed that order. By morning the whole damn town would be aware that Gamble Trask had told him to get out of High Hopes and that Hack Burns had promised to shoot him on sight if he did not.

He was now a marked man, and as such, he'd be the focus of much talk and speculation. His cover was blown. It was high time to pick up and leave.

Yet McBride was tired of running. The way he'd been forced to flee Sean Donovan and his hired assassins still rankled, eating at him like a cancer. The bottom line was he could swallow his pride and get out of High Hopes or stay and face Hack Burns. Neither option had much appeal for him. And even if he killed Burns in a gunfight, and that outcome was in doubt, what then? He would attract even more attention, becoming a named man, a gunfighter, and his fame would spread.

Notoriety like that might even reach New York by way of the newspapers and dime novels and the eager ears of Sean Donovan. Of course, his name would be told as John Smith, but his description would be written in detail. Donovan was not a stupid man. He might put two and two together and start asking questions. And had not Byrnes told him that the man's tentacles reached far . . . maybe as far as the town of High Hopes, west of forever?

Like a man groping his way along a dark tunnel, McBride could see no way out and there was no light. Suddenly he felt trapped with nowhere to turn. . . .

Then Shannon Roark walked into his life.

He saw her step toward him, moving through the crowd of drab miners like crimson fire.

McBride rose to his feet, his heart pounding, as the woman reached his table. Her smile was dazzling, her lustrous beauty breathtaking. "May I sit?"

"Yes," McBride stammered. "Yes, of course."

"My name is Shannon Roark," the woman said as he helped her into a chair.

"Yes, yes, I know that." McBride knew he must look a sight with one eye swollen shut in his battered face, blood staining the sleeve of his shirt where Nolan's bullet had burned him. And now he was sounding like a shy, awkward teenage boy at his first cotillion. "My name is" — he hesitated a moment, then finished — "John Smith."

The brilliant smile flashed again. "And I also know that. Gamble . . . Mr. Trask . . . told me." Shannon leaned across the table, her fingertips resting lightly on the back of McBride's hand. "I heard about the unpleasantness between you and Gamble. I'm so sorry. He's terribly upset."

"Is that why he ordered me out of town?"

"Oh, that . . . it's just Gamble's way. He didn't mean a word of it."

"He sounded pretty convincing to me."

The woman's perfume filled McBride's head and his eyes lingered on the slim, ivory column of her neck, her naked shoulders and the swell of her breasts barely confined by the crimson silk of her dress.

He was falling in love, moment by moment, devastated by a longing that was almost a hunger. He had no idea where it would end . . . but he fervently hoped this was the beginning.

"John," Shannon said. She smiled. "I like that name, John. It has a rare solidity to it. John, Gamble won't tell you this himself, but he needs a man like you. He needs a strong right arm he can depend upon. He confides in me and he has told me that many times."

With a tremendous effort of will, McBride fought back to sanity. He was glad his voice held steady as he said, "He has Hack Burns for that."

The woman shook her head, a glossy tendril of auburn hair bouncing at the back of her neck. "Burns can't fulfill that role, nor can the rest of Gamble's men. Hack Burns is a killer and I believe he might be insane. As for the others . . . well, they're big on brawn but light on brains." Her brilliant hazel eyes found McBride's. "Gamble needs you, John. One day he'll be the biggest man in the state of Colorado and he won't forget those who helped him. I can make everything all right again, let bygones be bygones. You only have to say the word."

"Shannon, I told Trask that I'm not for sale. That answer still stands." McBride shook his head. "I just don't like the man."

"Then I can't convince you to change your mind?"

"No, Shannon, I won't change my mind."

The woman stood, her back stiff, and McBride knew he was losing her. She was slipping through his fingers like mist.

"Then I can do no more for you," she said, turning to leave.

Desperately McBride tried to keep her there, close to him. "Shannon!"

She stared at him, her face a beautiful, porcelain mask. "Yes?"

The raucous racket of the crowded revelers was closing in on him so he could hardly hear his own voice above the clamor. "Earlier tonight I saw Jim Nolan and another man walk into the alley alongside the saloon with four young Chinese girls."

That was bad. He knew that much as soon as he said it. It was a policeman's flat statement, not the soft, winning words of a suitor.

For a single moment of time Shannon Roark's mask slipped and McBride caught a flicker of surprise in her eyes. "What is so strange about that?"

"There was a steel cage on the wagon that

brought them here and Nolan had his bull-whip."

"They were probably visiting the Chinese fortune-teller's shack behind the saloon," Shannon said. "The Celestials do that maybe once or twice a year." Her smile was not as bright as before. "I suppose they want to know when they'll meet their future husbands."

"Why Nolan and the whip?" Keep her talking. Keep her here.

"Those Chinese miners out at the Spanish Peaks are very jealous of their women-folk," Shannon said easily. "They often hire men like Nolan to guard . . . ah . . . their virtue. The steel cage is another precaution. It keeps passing cowboys at arm's length." The woman shook her lovely head. "I would imagine the other man you spoke of has taken the girls home already."

She waited. But when McBride did not speak she said, "Any other questions, Mr. Smith?"

He smiled in turn. "Sorry, Shannon, I'm a questioning man, I guess."

"Then ask yourself this — do you still want to be alive at this time tomorrow?"

McBride opened his mouth to speak, but the woman stopped him. "You still have time to change your mind about Gamble. If

62

you do, come talk to me. I'll be here until daybreak."

She left then, and only the whispering memory of her perfume remained.

CHAPTER 6

John McBride stepped out of the Golden Garter and onto the boardwalk. He stood in the shimmering glow of an oil lamp that touched his shoulders and the top of his hat with orange light.

Now, more than ever, Shannon Roark seemed an unattainable prize and her beauty haunted him, causing him more pain than pleasure. Did he have any chance with her? He knew he did not. It would be easier for him to reach up and try to grab a handful of stars.

McBride cupped his swollen eye with a scarred hand, feeling its heat. Well, he'd been punched in the eye a few times before and the swelling would eventually go down of its own accord. He had no need to see a doctor. His back and ribs were aching, but nothing seemed broken. He would live.

At least for a while.

The humor of that thought made him

smile and suddenly, to his surprise, he was hungry. He turned to his left and stepped along the crowded boardwalk, past the alley where he'd seen the Chinese girls.

The night was oppressively muggy, damp heat lying over the town like a shroud. The air was thick, hard to breathe, smelling rank from rotten vegetation and the dead dog that lay in the street, its back broken by the wheels of a freight wagon. Fat black flies buzzed everywhere and each oil lamp had its attendant swarm of scorched, tattered moths.

McBride stopped a staggering miner who was sucking on a whiskey bottle, and asked about a restaurant.

"The Bon-Ton," the man slurred. He jerked a thumb over his shoulder. "That-away."

The restaurant was crowded when McBride stepped inside, and he turned some heads. He didn't know if word of his gunfight with Nolan had gotten around or if it was his battered face, bloody shirt and swollen eye that had drawn their attention.

A little of both, he decided as he found an empty place at one of the four benches in the room. The Bon-Ton was anything but elegant, but McBride guessed that few frontier eateries were. A pretty and clean enough waitress took his order — steak, potatoes and a couple of fried eggs — then returned and poured him coffee.

The clientele was mostly miners, rough, bearded men in woolen shirts, their canvas pants stuffed into scuffed mule-eared boots. All carried knives and a few wore holstered revolvers on their belts. No one looked at McBride directly, but he knew by the excited, whispered talk that he was the focus of much conversation. He had killed a named gunman in a fair fight, and that made him a subject for discussion and speculation wherever Western men gathered. If gunfighters of reputation, the likes of John Wesley Hardin or Ben Thompson, had walked into the Bon-Ton, they would hardly have elicited more interest.

And no doubt all present were aware that Hack Burns had threatened to kill the big man who was now bent to his food if he was still in town after noon tomorrow. That was an event to be eagerly anticipated.

McBride was using a piece of bread to sop up the last of the gravy on his plate when a small, stocky man in a shabby suit of black broadcloth, a soft felt hat on his gray head, walked inside. The newcomer, who looked to be in his early seventies, glanced around the restaurant for a few moments. Then his

66

eyes lit on McBride.

"Mr. Smith, I presume," he said.

McBride nodded. The man tapped a miner who was sitting opposite McBride and said, "Do you mind?"

The miner looked up, opened his mouth to speak, then thought the better of it. He shrugged and slid farther up the bench. The gray-haired man took the vacated place and smiled benignly at McBride. "My name is Theodosius T. Leggett, owner and editor of the *High Hopes Tribune*." He stuck out his hand. "Honored to make your acquaintance, sir."

McBride took the proffered hand, then said, "I don't talk to the newspapers, Mr. Leggett."

"Ah, but that is no longer a problem," Leggett said. "You see, I don't have a newspaper anymore, not since" — he looked around and raised his voice so everybody in the restaurant could hear — "not since Mr. Gamble Trask destroyed my press and shut me down for suggesting that he was behind the shooting of Marshal Lute Clark."

A buzz of comment ran around the Bon-Ton, but McBride detected very few voices sympathetic to Leggett.

"What can I do for you, Mr. Leggett?" he asked, only half-interested in whatever the man might have to say.

"Perhaps nothing. Perhaps everything. And, please, call me Theo. Everyone else does, when they call me anything." Leggett waved to the young waitress. "Mattie, coffee here, if you please."

"Hold your horses, Theo," the waitress yelled. "You're not the only customer in the place, you know."

"A delightful girl, just delightful," Leggett muttered. He waved at Mattie again. "And bring a raw beefsteak with the coffee."

The two men sat in silence for a few minutes, Leggett smiling slightly as he studied McBride's face. Miners came and went, each one aiming a measuring glance at McBride as he passed.

Mattie brought the coffee and laid a raw steak on the table. Leggett reached into his pocket, produced a pint of bourbon and held it up to McBride, his face framing a question.

McBride shook his head and Leggett asked, "No?" then shrugged and poured a generous dollop into his own cup. "The beefsteak is for your eye, you know."

"I don't think I want to sit here holding a chunk of beef to my face," McBride said.

"Afraid these men will laugh at you? Trust me, after what you did to the late, unlamented Jim Nolan, they won't." Leggett picked up the steak. "Now, here, hold that to your eye. It will help with the swelling."

McBride looked around the restaurant, then held the steak against his eye. "Thank you," he said.

"No trouble at all, my boy."

"You still haven't told me why you're here."

"Here? Why, to drink coffee. Later you and I will take a little stroll. I want to show you something."

"A bit late for a stroll, isn't it?"

Leggett laughed. "My dear boy, the night is young. It's not yet midnight and High Hopes is only now hitting its stride."

McBride started to rise, leaving the steak on the table. "Well, Theo, if it's all the same to you, I believe I'll pass on the stroll." He grinned. "And the steak."

Leggett's eyes lifted to the tall man. "Even if a walk in the dark is the means of saving your life?"

"I don't understand," McBride said.

The older man glanced around him. "Not here. There are too many ears. We'll talk when we're outside."

Leggett insisted on picking up the bill for McBride's meal, waving off his protests, then led the way to the door. They walked along the boardwalk until Leggett suddenly stopped under a hanging sign that said, TRAVIS RAMSEY & SON — GUNSMITHS.

As though the sign had stirred something in his mind, the old newspaperman looked directly into McBride's face and said, "You can't beat Hack Burns in a gunfight, you know. He'll put two or three bullets into you before you even shuck your gun. He's the best around, maybe the best there is."

"I have no intention of meeting Burns in a gun battle," McBride said. "I've got nothing to prove."

"He'll come after you. You'll have to prove yourself then."

McBride felt trapped. The logical thing to do was to catch the first train out of town and go somewhere else. But his stiff-necked pride would not let him run away again. He knew it was a weakness in him, his pride, but he acknowledged it and accepted the limitations it placed on his future actions. And then there was Shannon. His feelings for her also conspired to keep him in High Hopes. There was no escaping that. What she was and what he hoped they might become was holding him in place, like a butterfly pinned to a board.

"Leggett, what do you want from me?" McBride asked, his patience with the man wearing thin.

"Soon. Trust me, I'll tell you soon." Leggett's shrewd eyes made a study of McBride, from his battered plug hat to the dusty toes of his boots. He tapped the side of his nose with a forefinger. "Do you know what this is, John? It's a nose, a nose for news, and right now it's telling me that you're a lawman of some kind. A Pinkerton maybe?"

"I'm not a Pinkerton," McBride said. This old man was no fool.

"But a policeman nevertheless. Or you were. From back East somewhere, Boston or Philadelphia perhaps, but more probably New York."

Leggett read McBride's startled expression and raised his arms above his head. "Yes! *Formosa facies muta commendatio est!* For those among us who know no Latin . . . ahem . . . that means, 'Your handsome face is a silent testimonial.' "

The old man cocked his head to one side, his eyes as bright and inquisitive as a bird's. "Look, no notebook, no Faber. Do you want to tell me about it?"

"I was a police officer, in New York, as you guessed."

The boardwalk had cleared as the miners crowded into the saloons and the more respectable sort of townspeople had sought their beds. The moon was riding high in a starless sky, hazy from the rising heat, and out on the rolling plains the coyotes were talking.

Leggett had stirred McBride's memory. My God, had it been only a few short weeks? It already seemed like a lifetime ago.

Strange, that . . . very strange . . .

The Honey Heaven had been the worst kind of brothel in the Four Corners, one of big Sean Donovan's lesser establishments where he sent his worn-out whores to be finally worked to death. Only the poorest, most drink-sodden male denizens of the slums that made up Hell's Kitchen ever went there. The women's cheeks were pockmarked, their skin mottled, cavernous canker sores all over their toothless gums. Their rented lovers took them in beds crawling with lice, bedbugs, crabs, fleas and other vermin. The men kept their shoes on lest the gibbering rats chew on their toes before they were finished, and the brothel stank of ingrained filth, vomit and disease and the stench of the rank barrels placed outside the doors of the rooms to collect human waste. Among all this ran swarming, naked children with the sly, feral eyes of wild animals, starving, their ribs showing in bodies covered in sores and as white as the bellies of fish.

Here, one dark, rainy night, young, handsome Patrick Donovan came to collect his father's dues. He flashed his diamonds, pretending not to notice the vile hell around him. As his father had told him many times, "Money doesn't stink." Patrick himself believed in that implicitly.

Here too, that night, came Detective Inspector Thomas Byrnes, Detective Sergeant John McBride and a dozen uniformed officers. They had come to raid the place, the shot, stabbed or just plain dead bodies thrown on the sidewalk outside the Honey Heaven most mornings having finally become too much for even the most hardened residents of the Kitchen.

Perhaps when young Patrick Donovan spotted McBride and drew his gun, he believed, as the son of a rich and influential man, the big cop would quail before him and let him go. In this he was wrong. Fatally wrong. McBride, a man who was fond of children and was already incensed at how they were abused at the Honey Heaven, saw Donovan slide the .44 Colt from a shoulder holster and fired, instinctively, without thought. His bullet smacked into the middle of Patrick's handsome forehead and the young man suddenly looked old and he dropped. Inspector Byrnes later noted, with grim satisfaction, that he had been dead when he hit the ground.

From that moment on, big Sean Donovan, ravaged by grief and possessed by a terrible rage, declared John McBride a marked man, saying that he would bestow riches on the one who brought him his ears.

"Why did you leave the city?" Leggett asked.

"I killed a man," McBride told Leggett, the details of that night a lifetime ago lingering like ghosts in his memory.

"And you had to flee New York."

"Something like that. The father of the man I killed put a price on my head. I was given a leave of absence and told to head West and lie low."

Leggett laughed. "You just killed a known gunman and you face another at noon tomorrow. John, my boy, you have a strange way of lying low."

"That thought has occurred to me," McBride said, irritated at the man for telling him something he already knew.

"Let's walk," Leggett said.

"I don't think —"

"It's not far."

They walked to the edge of town, past a scattered collection of tar-paper shacks and tents, to the spot where the town lights faded and the darkness began. Here the stars were visible and the air smelled cleaner. The moonlight touched the crests of low, rolling hills with a silver sheen, pooling the hollows with purple shadow. There was no wind and nothing moved or made a sound.

"Not much farther," Leggett said. "In fact I do believe we'll soon see the lights of the place."

McBride, a man of the city, found the darkness disturbing. "Where are we going?" he asked.

"Hell," Leggett said.

CHAPTER 7

After a quarter of a mile, Leggett led McBride along the bank of a narrow creek that curved to the west and then opened up to a width of about ten feet, a few scrawny cottonwoods growing along its bank. Beyond the bend McBride saw the lights of a large cabin glowing dimly in the gloom.

"This place used to be a stage way station before the railroad got here," Leggett said. "Now it's owned by Gamble Trask."

They walked to the door and Leggett asked, "Shall we enter?"

The man looked suddenly older than his years and a strange, yellowish tinge clouded his face. There was a dark air of despondency about Leggett that took McBride by surprise. For a talkative man he had been oddly silent since they'd left the outskirts of town and now he seemed strained, like a man shuffling through yesterday's memories.

"I used to know this place well," Leggett said. "There are times when I still wish I did."

The old man opened the door and McBride followed. Immediately his nostrils were assailed by a sweet, corrupt odor, like the stench of rotting flowers. He recognized it for what it was — the smell of opium smoke.

Had Leggett brought him all the way out here just to show him an opium den? New York was full of such places, though the authorities were cracking down on them because of the social costs. It was mostly the poor who smoked, seeking to escape lives of degradation and misery, but the toll among families was terrible. Many men spent all their wages on opium, preferring the drug to alcohol, and often the result was that their wives and children died of starvation. Workingmen addicted to opium did not eat and their bodies wasted away until they were living skeletons. Men like that could no longer perform hard manual labor and again it was their families that suffered.

McBride had always hated opium dens and the men who profited by them. Leggett had said that Gamble Trask owned the cabin. In addition to his saloon, was he also in the opium business? McBride could give the man the benefit of the doubt — maybe Trask just rented out the cabin. But he did not believe that, even as the thought had come to him.

The door opened on a long, hastily constructed corridor, and there was a window just beyond the door where addicts could buy the drug. A cheerful young Chinese man wearing a round black cap on his head grinned knowingly at Theo and said, "Good evening, Mr. Leggett."

Leggett waved, his face gray in the light of the single oil lamp that hung from the ceiling. "Good evening, Chang."

"You dream some dreams tonight?"

"No." Leggett shook his head. "No more of that for me, Chang."

The man called Chang scowled. "Then why the hell you here? This place busy. Very busy."

"My friend may be interested in a pipe or two," Leggett lied smoothly. "He wishes first to inspect the . . . ah . . . premises."

"Clean place," Chang said to McBride. "Very clean place, you see." He waved toward a closed door at the end of the corridor where shadows gathered. "Take look, then come back and talk to me."

Leggett made a bow and extended his hand. "Shall we, Mr. Smith?"

The door opened onto a large room, the darkness kept at bay by a few lamps that cast a troubled amber light. A sweet-smelling vapor hung in the air and the only sound was the soft gurgle of water pipes. Two Chinese men, both incredibly wrinkled, yellow and old, moved around silently on padded feet, now and then bending to check on the dozens of men sprawled on the floor like stone statues, pipes to their lips. As McBride and Leggett passed between them, the opium smokers neither moved nor looked up, their eyes either closed or frozen wide open as they drifted like phantoms through their demented dreams. Others smiled, the vague, empty smile of the living dead.

Leggett pointed to a couple of young girls who lay side by side on the floor. They were almost skeletal, skin drawn so tight against the bones of their faces that their cheeks were sunken, mouths open wide in a permanent, painful grimace.

"Look at their arms, John," Leggett whispered, like a man in some dreadful church. "See the track marks? Heroin addicts." His smile was without humor. "There are quite a few of those in High Hopes."

"Who are they?" McBride asked. He'd seen what heroin could do to addicts, but the sight never failed to affect him.

"Does it matter? They'll be dead soon, or so Dr. Cox says." Leggett sighed. "They're twin sisters, Hannah and Margaret Collins. At one time they worked for Gamble Trask at the Golden Garter, but not anymore. They sell themselves to any horny rooster who will give them enough money to come here." The old man shook his head. "It's sad really. They're fourteen and they should be married and keeping their own houses by now. Instead . . . well, you can see the instead for yourself."

"Leggett —"

"Theo, my boy, please."

"Theo, why did you bring me here?"

The old man was silent for a few moments, as though collecting his thoughts. "John," he said finally, "all this, this hell, is owned and operated by Gamble Trask. It's a steady moneymaker and he needs money, lots of it, to finance his ambitions. Trask doesn't intend to remain in High Hopes and see his dreams confined by the wooden walls of a hick town. He has his sights set on Washington, the honorable senator from Colorado, and maybe higher. Trask is a man who desires power every bit as much as he does wealth, and believe me, that he craves like the poor creatures you see around you crave opium."

Leggett led the way to the door, then stopped, his eyes shadowed. "Trask has other ways of making money" — he waved a hand around the room — "just as dirty as this. He traffics in young Chinese girls out of San Francisco, then ships them to the big cities back East. Out here the services of Chinese whores don't bring a premium price, but they do in New York and Boston and other places. They're marketed in big-city brothels as 'exotics,' and are always in demand. Trask's Chinese girls, or slaves or whatever you want to call them, are anywhere from twelve to fourteen years old and when they reach the brothels their life expectancy is about two to four years. They die quickly from grief, disease or opium, and usually from a combination of all three."

McBride remembered the Chinese girls being herded into the alley behind the Golden Garter. Shannon had told him they were visiting a fortune-teller. Was she a part of Trask's schemes? He refused to believe she could be party to anything so vile, and he said as much to Leggett.

"Not here," the man said. "Outside. If I stay here much longer, I'll start to get my old urges again."

The Chinese man was not at the payment window when McBride and Leggett passed. Just as well, McBride decided. After seeing what was inside, he wasn't feeling inclined to be sociable. He followed Leggett through the door into the clean, dark air of the night and the two men walked to the cottonwoods beside the creek.

McBride gulped fresh air and Leggett, watching him, smiled. "There was a time I loved such places," he said. His eyes sought McBride's in the darkness. "John, have you ever heard of Wild Bill Hickok?"

"Yes, even in New York. He'd make the newspapers every now and then, usually after he killed a man, and he was in all the dime novels."

"Bill and his friend Colorado Charlie Utter introduced me to opium when I was running a paper in Deadwood," Leggett said. "Ah, those were good days, smoking opium with Bill and Charlie for two, three days at a time, dreaming the dreams."

"He's dead now, isn't he?"

"Hickok? Yes, shot in Deadwood. That was a few years back."

"Theo, you were going to tell me about Shannon Roark."

"No, I wasn't, because there's really not much to tell. She arrived in High Hopes with Gamble Trask and Hack Burns two years ago. After he built the Golden Garter, the biggest and best saloon in town, Trask put her in the place as a dealer. That's all I know about her."

"She's beautiful," McBride said. "The most beautiful woman I ever saw. I can't believe she's mixed up with Trask."

Leggett shrugged. "From all I hear, the lovely Miss Roark is fond of money herself, as she's not averse to a bottom deal when it means relieving a drunk miner of his poke. She keeps a suite at the Killeen and dresses in the latest Paris fashions. That takes money."

"It doesn't mean she's a part of Trask's crooked dealings."

"No, it doesn't, my boy. But she has Trask's ear and I'd step wary of her if I were you. Especially if you agree to my proposition."

"What is your proposition, Theo? I know it's got to be part of the reason you brought me here."

Leggett leaned his back against a cottonwood trunk. "John, Gamble Trask must be stopped. He's getting rich on opium and slave girls and he couldn't care less about the human suffering he causes."

McBride opened his mouth to speak, but

Leggett raised a hand to silence him. "Hear me out. It's no accident that Trask chose High Hopes for his base of operations. The town is at the junction of two railroads, the Union Pacific and the Santa Fe. Raw opium and the Chinese girls are smuggled into San Francisco, then shipped to him on the Union Pacific. He then sends opium and girls east via the Santa Fe to New York, among other cities. I believe Trask has someone back East who pays him well." The old man searched inside his coat, found a cigar and thumbed a match into flame. "John, you were a policeman in New York. You know what this kind of trade in drugs and girls can do to a town."

McBride watched as Leggett lit his cigar, then said, "What's your interest in this, Theo? Do you really care about the Chinese girls or do you want to make a name for yourself as a crusading newspaperman?"

"I care about High Hopes. This was a nice place to live before Gamble Trask got here and I want it to go back to how it was. Now I see corruption everywhere. Trask gives the miners what they want and directly or indirectly, a lot of people — merchants, bankers, even the railroads — are profiting from his enterprises. If he's not stopped and stopped soon, High Hopes is doomed. Trask will suck it dry, then toss away what's left of it to rot in the sun. We'll end up a ghost town and only the pack rats will live here."

"You've still got the miners. Even if Trask goes, they'll always need a place to spend their money."

"The Spanish Peaks mines are all but played out. Another year, maybe two, the miners will be moving on. There's been talk of another big strike in the Montana Territory and some have already left." Leggett studied the glowing end of his cigar. "John, as I see it, the future of this town lies in cattle. The local ranchers could ship their herds from here instead of trailing west through the mountains to Cimarron and running off tons of beef. High Hopes could become the major shipping center for the Colorado cattle industry and the town would prosper without the slime tracks of Gamble Trask's dirty fingers all over it.

"There are some others who think the same way as I do and so did Marshal Lute Clark. After my press was destroyed, he moved to shut down the Golden Garter and Hack Burns shot him. There were maybe a hundred men in the saloon that night, and every man jack of them swore Burns drew in self-defense. When Trask made Burns the new city marshal few made any objection.

They were too busy counting their money."

McBride stifled a yawn, the late hour getting to him. "And now you want me to shut down Trask?"

Leggett nodded. "That's about the size of it, I reckon. You're good with your fists and a gun. We saw that tonight. We need a man like you to lead us. The men who think as I do — Dr. Cox, Grant Wilson, who owns the hardware store, Ned Barlow, the blacksmith, and a few others — they're all good men, but they're not gunfighters. I plan on taking my case against Trask all the way to the state capital, but you have to buy me some time."

"I may not be around tomorrow," McBride said. "Have you considered that? I'm not a gunfighter and I don't even want the name of one. And I'm no match for Hack Burns, or at least that's what he told me. Chances are, I'll be on the first train out of here in the morning."

Around them translucent moonlight was silvering the smoke-colored leaves of the cottonwoods and the creek babbled nonsense to itself as it ran over a bed of sand and pebbles. Out on the plains the coyotes were again yipping their hunger, lacing the darkness with ribbons of sound.

Leggett stuffed his cigar back in his mouth and puffed furiously. "John, I —"

The racketing roar of a rifle shattered the night and suddenly McBride's face was spattered with blood and brains. He saw Leggett fall . . . and then he was running.

CHAPTER 8

A bullet cut the air next to McBride's ear and a second kicked up a startled exclamation point of dirt at his feet. He dived into thick brush along the creek bank and pulled his gun from his pocket.

How many unfired cartridges were left after his fight with Jim Nolan? He couldn't remember and now was not the time to think about it. Out there somebody wanted to kill him real bad and now his whole attention must be on surviving.

From over by the cottonwoods, McBride heard Leggett groan. The man was still alive. Had the hidden rifleman heard it too? A couple of searching shots rattled through the branches of the trees, answering his question.

McBride noted the flare of the rifle. It was off to his right, but he couldn't tell how far. Whoever the rifleman was, he'd shot at the glow of Leggett's cigar and hit his target.

He'd have to be wary of a man with that kind of gun skill.

It was in McBride's mind to back out of the brush, then work his way to his left and come up on the bushwhacker from behind. A good plan, but as soon as he rose up to walk or even crawl, he'd be out in the open and a dead man. There had to be another way. The man out there was patient, waiting for a killing shot. And he was good at his job. Real good.

Four bullets, fast and evenly spaced, thudded into trees and crackled through brush along the creek bank. McBride knew the man was trying to flush him, like he would a flock of quail. He could try firing at the rifle flash, but hitting his target with a .38 at distance and in the dark was an uncertain thing.

He'd have to get closer. A lot closer.

Then McBride had an idea, or at least the germ of one.

He inched forward, trying to be as quiet as possible. Where was the edge of the creek bank? A few more inches and he stopped, listening. There was only the wind, rising now as the night grew a little cooler. It whispered to the night as it explored among the cottonwoods.

McBride moved forward again, expecting

to draw a bullet at any second. The land around him was flat, he recalled, here and there some shallow, rolling hills. This was rifle country and about then he decided that the Smith & Wesson was mighty poor company for a hunted man.

Even though he was moving forward at a snail's pace, the brush tore at his back and sides and once he almost cried out in pain when a sharp thorn dug its way across his swollen eye.

McBride's head broke through the brush and what he saw appalled him. Here the creek suddenly curved away from him, and the bank was a good twenty feet from where he lay. The land between was flat, covered in short grass dappled with moonlight.

It was a killing ground.

John McBride swallowed hard, his heart hammering in his chest. He set down his gun, wiped a sweaty palm on his pants, then picked the .38 up again. He was scared, more scared than he'd ever been in his life. He felt that the night had eyes, watching him, measuring him, finding him wanting.

Angry at himself for the fear he felt, McBride decided to back out of the brush again and go back to his original plan. He had started to wriggle backward when an idea came to him. Even a blind pig will find an acorn once in a while, he decided, allowing himself a small, grim smile.

He lay on his side and broke open the Smith & Wesson. He extracted three spent shells, held them in his right hand, then rotated the cylinder so that the others would be in line to fall under the hammer.

The skin under McBride's eye was bleeding where the thorn had raked him and it smarted like a dozen wasp stings, adding to his discomfort and growing rage. He felt like a trapped rat and he directed all his irritation toward the man hidden out there in the darkness. Right then, McBride wanted to put a bullet into him so bad he could taste it.

The brush had closed over McBride, but when he carefully turned his head he saw a break a couple of feet behind him where the sky was visible. He eased back, and froze when a twig snapped under his weight. The noise drew a probing bullet that thudded into a tree several yards away.

A minute passed, then another. He did not dare breathe, staying still, listening to the night. The rifleman did not fire again, and McBride resumed his backward crawl. When he reached the break in the thick brush, he rose up enough to get one foot under him. When the time came, he'd have to run faster than he'd ever done in his life and pushing off on the foot would help.

Swiveling from the waist, a motion that instantly stabbed pain into his tortured lower back, he drew back his arm, then threw the empty shells as far as he could. He heard them rattle into undergrowth a few yards away, immediately drawing fire from the rifleman.

Then he was up and running.

McBride crashed out of the brush and pounded across the grass between him and the creek bank. A bullet cracked spitefully past his head and another burned across his neck. He dived off the bank into the creek, hitting the water hard. His right knee thudded into a submerged rock and he gasped in pain. He fell on his back, the rushing water instantly soaking him, then rose and threw himself against the opposite bank.

Shots hammered into the ground above his head, but McBride stayed where he was. When the firing stopped he crouched low and made his way carefully along the streambed. Twenty yards ahead of him, barely visible in the darkness, the creek curved around a dead cottonwood, its trunk split into a V by some past frost. McBride reached the bend, his gun up and ready. Using the tree for cover, he raised his head and looked around the trunk into the gloom. He saw nothing.

Then something moved, a sudden, jerky motion, a momentary flash of white.

McBride touched his tongue to suddenly dry lips. He could hear his heart pounding in his ears. Was the bushwhacker wearing a white shirt or hat? It was possible. A man sure of himself and his skill with a rifle might not have bothered to dress in dark clothing.

There it was again. A quick flicker of white. Then slow, steady footfalls coming toward him, soft on the grass. The wind was making a different sound, no longer whispering, sighing through the skeletal limbs of the dead cottonwood like a sailor's widow.

McBride held his gun in both hands and pushed it out in front of him. Far in the distance the coyotes were talking and from farther away still, he heard the howl of a hunting wolf pack.

"McBride, old son," he whispered to himself, "you're a long way from New York."

The footsteps came closer. McBride steeled himself, surprised that the Smith & Wesson was steady in his hands. His fear was gone, all his concentration on the gunman walking toward him.

A small paint horse emerged from the

gloom. The animal sensed the presence of a human and stopped, tossing its head, the bit jangling. Pent-up breath hissed from between McBride's teeth and for a moment he rested his head on his outstretched arms, his heart hammering. The horse was saddled and could only be the mount of the man who was trying to kill him.

The paint took a few steps closer. It was standing on the bank beside the cotton-wood. McBride had never sat on a horse in his life, but he could use this one. He climbed out of the creek and stepped to the paint, keeping the horse between him and the rifleman out there in the long grass.

The reins were trailing and he gathered them up and swung the horse around so that it was facing the way it had come. The animal would be between him and the bushwhacker and he'd walk the paint into the darkness, trusting that if the man saw his horse, he wouldn't spot an extra pair of legs until it was too late. McBride figured to walk a good distance and then let the horse go and hide out somewhere in the gloom until the man gave up and left.

He stood at the pony's shoulder, the reins in his left hand near the animal's chin. He tried to push the horse forward, but the little paint planted its feet and stubbornly refused to budge.

"Giddyup," McBride whispered urgently. The fear was back and his mouth was dry. The horse shook its head violently, the bit chiming loud in the quiet as it tried to pull away from him.

"Damn it, giddyup," McBride rasped, irritated beyond all measure at the obstinate orneriness of equines.

A long, low whistle came out of the darkness. The horse's head came up, its ears pricked forward, arcs of white showing in its black eyes. Then the paint started to trot, McBride running at its side.

He knew he was heading right for the hidden rifleman. The man must have heard his mount's bit jangle and, perhaps fearing wolves, had whistled the animal closer.

The paint began to canter and McBride could no longer keep up. Suddenly the horse was ten yards in front of him and he was completely exposed.

Flame stabbed out of the darkness. Two shots, close together. McBride heard a scream and the horse went down, its rear legs flailing wildly as it collapsed. A moment later a tall man in a wide-brimmed hat, a rifle slanted across his chest, emerged from the moonlight-splashed gloom. He and McBride saw each other at the same time.

The man shot from the hip and levered his rifle again. McBride fired. Once, twice, three times, triggering the Smith & Wesson very fast. The rifleman staggered, then went to his knees. He shot at McBride and the bullet cut the air above the big man's head. The gunman tried to work his rifle again, but the effort was too much of him. He pitched forward onto his face and lay still.

McBride shoved his now empty gun into his pocket and walked warily toward the fallen man. He kneeled beside the man and rolled him on his back — then cursed loud, long and vehemently.

He was looking at the round, freckled face of a boy. A puncher by the look of him, he couldn't have been any older than sixteen. All three of McBride's bullets had hit squarely in the middle of the kid's shirt pocket, very close, like the ace of clubs on a playing card. The boy's blue eyes were wide open, staring at McBride without expression, and the death shadows were already gathering under his eyes. Quickly McBride searched the kid's pockets and found what he'd expected to find — a few nickels and dimes and five shiny double eagles.

McBride rose to his feet, a hot anger building in him. Bushwhacker or no, the killer of Theo Leggett, this boy was still some mother's son, and she would soon be grieving for him.

Someone had paid the young puncher a hundred dollars to silence Theo Leggett and kill McBride for listening to him. The old man talked too much and was threatening a state investigation. The only one who had an interest in seeing him dead was Gamble Trask. He had paid the blood money, hiring a boy to do his dirty work.

McBride checked on the paint horse. It was dead. He walked back to the creek, splashed across and went to where the young Chinese man was bending over Theo's body.

"Very bad," the man said, looking up as McBride stepped beside him. "Half his skull blown away. He's been asking for you."

McBride kneeled beside Theo. Despite his terrible wound the old man was desperately clinging to life, trying to eke out a few more seconds. "Theo," McBride said, "I'm here."

Leggett's eyes opened, already glazing in death as he struggled to raise his head. "John," he whispered, "listen to me . . . trains . . . don't let Trask . . . trains . . ."

"Theo, I'm not understanding you," McBride said hopelessly.

"Trains . . . orphan trains . . . don't let Trask —"

The old man's eyes were still staring into McBride's, but the life was gone from them forever.

McBride turned to the Chinese man. "Chang, isn't it?"

"Yes, my name is Chang."

"I'll send an undertaker for Theo."

"No, no undertaker. Bad for business have death vulture here. I will bury him, say the Christian words. Real nice ceremony, you'll see."

"Lay Theo away decent, Chang. Bury him in his clothes. I don't want him to meet his Maker naked."

"Decent, very decent. You no worry about that. He was good customer one time, Mr. Leggett. I see to him, bury him in his suit. Say the words."

McBride nodded, his anger scalding him, like he'd swallowed boiling-hot lead.

He turned his back on Chang, crossed the creek again and walked through the darkness to the young cowboy's body. He had never used a Winchester, but he was familiar with the rifle, since every police precinct in New York had at least a few of them. McBride stripped .44-.40 cartridges from the dead boy's belt and fed them into the Winchester. The kid's gun was still in the holster, but that, McBride left alone. His

Smith & Wesson was less powerful than the Colt, but he had trained with the self-cocking revolver and knew it to be the faster and more accurate shooter.

McBride laid the Winchester on the grass, then picked up the dead cowboy and threw him over his shoulder. He was a big man, strong in the back and shoulders, and the kid weighed little. He bent at the knees, picked up the rifle and started walking back toward town.

It was time to call on Gamble Trask.

CHAPTER 9

The wind was blowing much stronger, driving hard and fast off the vast plain between the Arkansas and the Platte, and a cloud of rising dust veiled the moon. Men stepped along the boardwalk, hats pulled low over their faces, now and then stepping in place as they bent against sudden gusts that filled their mouths and eyes with grit. The wind was talking, answered by the creak and bang of the chained signs that hung outside the stores. Scraps of paper spiraled into the air like fluttering white doves, only to disappear from sight as they were borne away over the rooftops.

John McBride trudged along the middle of the street with his burden, the Winchester hanging loose in his right hand. A skinny, yellow dog walked out of an alley, trotted a few steps toward him, then thought better of it and ran away, tail between its legs. The wind teased McBride unmercifully, slapping at his pants, threatening to lift the hat off his head. Yellow dust covered him from the top of his hat to the toes of his boots as he reached the Golden Garter and stepped onto the boardwalk.

The panels of the saloon's batwing doors rattled noisily against each other and the windows vibrated in their frames. From somewhere close a screen door slammed, opening and shutting on the whim of the wind.

McBride stepped inside.

For a moment he stood there, tall and terrible, looking around him. His left eye was now completely swollen shut and blood from the thorn that had caught him had dried into black fingers on his cheek. The wind and dust had taken their toll on him, and his teeth were bared as he fought for breath.

A saloon girl shrieked at the sight of him and men shrank back as though he was a dreadful apparition that had appeared from the darkness.

Gamble Trask was sitting at his table with Hack Burns and a tall man McBride didn't recognize, a whiskey bottle and glasses between them. Trask's puzzled eyes moved from McBride to the dead man on his shoulder and back again. Burns' face showed the sudden awareness of a hunting cougar and the tall man shifted slightly in his chair, clearing his holstered gun for the draw.

McBride walked toward Trask's table and the man smiled and called out, "My, my, Mr. Smith, don't we look a sight?"

A few people laughed nervously, as McBride ignored the man and walked closer. He was conscious of Burns getting slowly to his feet, his hands close to his guns. The tall man, dressed in a black, low-crowned hat with a flat brim and a black broadcloth frock coat, stayed where he was. But he was confident and ready and the mean look in his eyes suggested he could handle himself.

McBride stepped to the table and Trask started to rise. McBride threw the dead cowboy from his shoulder and the body landed flat on its back on the tabletop. The kid had been small, but he was heavy enough to collapse the rickety table, which splintered under him with a crash. As the whiskey bottle and glasses shattered on the floor, Trask, now on his feet, stepped back.

"Are you crazy?" he yelled, his eyes blazing.

There was no give in McBride. "Trask," he said, "next time you try to kill me, send a man and not a boy."

Trask looked wildly around him, trying to gauge the mood of the crowd. Vigilante justice was a force to be reckoned with in a frontier town and not to be taken lightly, even by a man as influential as himself. So far, the miners were just interested bystanders, but their mood could change in an instant. "What the hell are you talking about, Smith?" Trask yelled. "I didn't send this man to kill anybody."

"He's a boy, not a man, but tonight he was grown enough to kill Theo Leggett and then try to kill me." McBride reached into the boy's pocket, found the five double eagles and threw them into Trask's face. "There, take back your blood money."

Trask's voice rose. "I tell you, I didn't send this man to kill anybody." He looked down at the kid's gray face. "I've seen this cowboy around, but I've never talked to him."

"Trask, you wanted to silence Theo Leggett. You wanted him dead because he knew too much and talked too much. Why did you also want me dead? Huh? Was it because Theo had been seen talking to me and you were afraid he told me what he knew?"

"You're insane, Smith," Trask said. "I'm a respectable businessman. I've got nothing to hide." He waved a hand around the room. "Ask any of these men."

A few miners muttered words of agreement, but not all. They knew that any man who got so rich so fast, as Gamble Trask had, had to be shady. Opium and liquor were legitimate businesses and they had no argument with that, but many believed the man's tables were crooked and that his dealers knew their way around the bottom of a deck.

Still, not a man present grieved for Theo Leggett or the young cowboy and as far as the miners were concerned John Smith was just another drifter in town and of no account. If it came to it, they would stand by Trask — and nobody knew that better than McBride.

He turned to Burns. "You've been real quiet. Maybe because it was you who hired the cowboy to kill Leggett."

Trask opened his mouth to speak, but Burns stopped him. "Let me handle this, boss," he said. "It's time I shut this man's big mouth for keeps." He moved his hands closer to the butts of his guns. "Smith, I gave you until noon to clear out of High Hopes. That don't go no more. You're leaving right now. Only difference is that four men will carry you out of here by the handles."

McBride brought up the muzzle of the Winchester. It was pointed right at Burns' belly. "Try for those guns and I'll blow your navel right through your backbone," he said, his voice level.

"And that will be the last thing you'll ever do, mister."

The voice came from McBride's right. The tall man in the black frock coat was within the limits of McBride's vision. He had his coat thrown back and his hand was resting on the ivory butt of his Colt.

"Your move, Smith," Trask said, grinning. "I should warn you that my friend Stryker Allison is a man to be reckoned with."

The saloon was hushed, the only sound the wail of the wind as it bullied its way around the walls of the building. A rat rustled in a corner and a woman yelped and threw herself into the arms of a grinning, bearded miner.

McBride's anger was pushing him into going for it. First Burns, then a fast turn, levering the rifle as he did so, and try to get a shot into the tall man. His chance of success was slim, he knew, but his fury and his policeman's inborn hatred of men like Gamble Trask were raking him like spurs.

His finger tightened on the trigger.

"Stop! Stop that right now!"

Shannon Roark had swept through the crowd and now she stepped between McBride and Burns. She turned to Trask, a frown gathering on her forehead. "Gamble, three dead men is enough for one night. Call off your boys."

Trask thought about it for a few moments. Then he grinned and shrugged. "You're right, Shannon. I believe there's been enough gunplay already. Hack, Stryker, let it go." His eyes went to McBride. "But if you ever come into my place with your wild accusations again, I will think very differently."

"John," Shannon said, "it's over. There will be no more killing, not now or at noon tomorrow." She had placed emphasis on the word "noon." Now she shook her head. "Listen to me, John. Gamble didn't hire that cowboy to kill you and Theo. That's not his style. Maybe the boy just had robbery on his mind."

The woman flashed McBride her dazzling smile. "You look tired, John, and your face is covered with blood. Why don't you go back to the hotel, clean up and get a good night's rest?"

The moment was gone and McBride knew it. If he tried to push it now, the miners would see him as the aggressor and line up against him. One way or another he'd be a dead man, either from a bullet or a rope.

He let the rifle drop to his side.

"Wise choice, Mr. Smith," Trask said. "Now, why don't you toddle off to bed." Before McBride could answer, Trask turned to Shannon. "I'll say this just once, Shannon, and I hope I'll never have cause to repeat myself — you are my employee and I don't want you to meddle in my affairs ever again."

McBride expected a flare of anger and defiance from Shannon, but her face showed only contrition. "I'm sorry, Gamble," she said meekly. "It's . . . it's just that I want no more killing in High Hopes."

"Your concern for our fair town is very commendable, my dear, very commendable indeed," Trask said. His eyes angled to McBride and he made no attempt to conceal the contempt in them. "Now, Mr. Smith, please leave my establishment. You've caused quite enough disruption already." The man nudged the cowboy's body with the toe of his polished shoe. "And take that with you."

McBride knew he'd been backed into a corner, but his anger was cold and hard as polished iron and it would not allow him to bend. "He's yours, Trask," he said. "You bury him."

A few, tense seconds spun out, fragile as a cobweb. Then high-heeled boots and the chime of spurs sounded loud in the hushed saloon. A young, black-haired puncher stepped up to the body and looked down at the dead man. "His name is Rusty Prescott an' he's a rider for the Rafter H over to Apishapa Creek way. I'll take him home." He turned to the watching miners. "A couple of you boys help me get him on my hoss."

The cowboy kneeled beside Prescott's body, then his eyes lifted to McBride. "Mister, something you should know. Rusty has a brother, feller by the name of Luke Prescott. You heard of him?"

McBride shook his head, the killing of the young cowboy still weighing on him.

"You should. Luke's at the Rafter H an' I reckon he'll be lookin' for you."

Trask grinned. "Well, Mr. Smith, it seems your troubles never end. Luke Prescott is a gunfighter out of Pueblo." He turned to the man named Allison. "How good is he, Stryker?"

"He's good," Allison answered. "Real fast on the draw and shoot. Killed Banjo Charlie Whipple in a fair fight down Amarillo way a few months back — and Charlie was considered a mighty dangerous hombre."

McBride opened his mouth to speak, but Shannon stopped him. "John, you'd better go back to the hotel. This is over."

He looked at the faces of the men around him. Hack Burns had a faint smile on his lips, but his eyes were eager and he was ready to kill. Stryker Allison had the calm, studied air of the professional gunman about him. He would draw if pushed, but would see little sense in fighting if there was no money in it. Gamble Trask had a triumphant smile on his handsome face, a man confident of his ability to control this and any other situation. The black-haired puncher's gaze was accusing, tangled up with something else. Pity, maybe.

McBride turned and walked out of the saloon, his stiff face burning as an outburst of loud, mocking laughter followed him, tearing at his soul like a flock of hungry ravens.

CHAPTER 10

John McBride lit the lamp beside his bed, filling the room with a dim, flickering yellow light. Shadows danced in the corners where the spiders lived and the boisterous wind beat at the windows, noisily demanding to be let inside.

McBride stretched out on the bed and stared at the play of the restless lamplight on the ceiling. He felt a mild surprise that New York, with its tall, stone buildings, horse trolleys, streetlamps and forty thousand teeming, crime-ridden tenements, was already fading from his mind's eye.

Did the West change a man that fast?

He had seen the vast, endless land only from a railroad car or while, bored, he kicked around for hours on the platform of an out-of-the-way station. But away from the smells and dirt of the city, he had found room to breathe. A few steps beyond dusty, noisy High Hopes and he could fill his lungs with air scented by tall grass and distant pines. He had read that the Western lands were filling up fast and that the old ways were already fading into memory. The Indians had been cannoned and sabered into submission and only a few Apache, far to the south in the desert country, were making a doomed, last stand.

Should he leave High Hopes on the next train and see all of the West before it was gone forever? He could remember it and in later years tell others about how the land had been.

It would be easy, just pack his bag and go and he would leave his increasing list of troubles behind. Inspector Byrnes had told him to lie low, vanish from sight. All he'd be doing was following orders. He was still on the payroll as a serving New York police officer, a detective sergeant, and it was not in his interest to get involved in the affairs of High Hopes. Theo Leggett had lived here and the town's concerns were his own. But he had no ties to this place. . . .

Then McBride thought of Shannon Roark and one by one all his hollow arguments for leaving popped in his head like bubbles.

He would leave here one day, that was certain, but when he did, Shannon would be at his side as his wife.

His mind made up, McBride rose, cleaned and reloaded his gun and placed it back beside his bed. He glanced at his watch. It was four in the morning. Outside the street had cleared and there was less noise from the Golden Garter — even the ceaseless piano had stilled. Veils of dust as high as a man on a horse lifted from the street and the wind had blown out the oil lamps. The alleys were tunnels of darkness and shadows slanted everywhere. The wind had transformed the night, making it restless with movement as it pushed, shoved, bullied and wailed.

A rap at the door. Soft, almost timid.

McBride picked up his gun and stepped to the door. "Who is it? And remember, I can drill you."

"John, it's me. Shannon."

McBride opened the door and Shannon Roark slipped inside. She wore a hooded, dark green cloak over her dress, dusty from the street.

"What a wind," she said, smiling, showing her wonderful teeth. "I declare, I thought I would be blown over." She undid the cloak and passed it to McBride. "There, that's better."

He laid the cloak over the back of the chair and said, "You know, it's not proper for a young lady to visit a gentleman's hotel room."

Shannon laughed. "John, in High Hopes? I wish I had a dollar for every young lady that's spent the night with a man in this room." She sat on the edge of the bed and patted a spot beside her. "Here, sit right here. We have to talk."

McBride did as he was told. Then Shannon studied his face, a frown gathering between her eyebrows. "Lordy, John, you are a sight. Your poor eye!" She leaned forward. "Let me kiss it better for you."

The woman lightly brushed the swelling under McBride's eye with her lips, then sat back and smiled. "There, that will make it all better."

McBride felt a hot surge of desire, but battled to control himself. "Shannon," he said unsteadily, swallowing hard, "why are you here?"

"Can't a lady visit with a handsome gentleman?"

"Right now, I imagine I look anything but handsome. Are you here to get me to work for Trask?"

"Nothing like that." Shannon shook her head. She hesitated a few heartbeats, then said, "John, I'm frightened."

McBride could see enough in her face to

know that she was telling the truth. "Frightened of what?"

"Gamble. I saw another side of him tonight, the way he acted after you brought in the dead cowboy's body." She laid her small hand on the back of McBride's huge, scarred paw. "I think he did hire that boy to kill you and Theo Leggett. In fact I'm sure of it."

"Why the change of heart all of a sudden? You told me yourself that the kid could have been trying to rob us."

"Even as I told you that, I didn't believe it myself. I think Gamble was afraid Theo would tell you something that could harm him, so he wanted to silence the old man, and you." Shannon's fingers touched her slender throat and her dark eyes were haunted. "John, what did Theo tell you?"

"Only that Trask is trading in opium and Chinese girls and that when he leaves, High Hopes will die because there will be nothing to take his place. The gold mines are playing out and the miners will soon be moving on. Theo said the only way the town has a future is to get rid of Trask and attract the local cattlemen."

"That was it? That was all?"

"As he was dying he said something about Trask and orphan trains. Have you any idea what he meant by that?"

"No," Shannon answered. "Maybe Theo was delirious by the time you spoke to him."

"It could be. But he repeated it twice. He held on to life long enough to tell me about the orphan trains."

"Yes, I suppose it is strange," Shannon said without interest. She moved closer to McBride and placed her hand on his thigh. "John, I told you I was frightened and I am. Gamble told me tonight he plans on pulling out of High Hopes soon and he wants me to go with him. He said we can get married back East, maybe in New York or Boston. Then he said a couple of things that scared me. He said he was planning to make one big score before he left that would bring him enough money to ensure our entry into high society. Then he said he would cover his tracks, that he'd leave no loose ends behind him in High Hopes. If I don't leave with him, I know I'll be one of those loose ends."

"He's in a dirty business, Shannon," McBride said. "Opium, heroin and slave girls. I can see that he'd want to cover his tracks. A past like that won't help his political ambitions."

Shannon nodded. "Tonight, for the first time, Gamble admitted to me he was shipping young Celestials to Eastern brothels. He said when we're in Washington all that will be forgotten by both of us."

Shannon's eyes showed sudden fear. "John, I don't want to marry Gamble Trask."

"Did you tell him that?"

"No. I was too afraid. I told him I'd think about it, and then his whole attitude changed. He said, 'Don't think about it for too long, Shannon. I'm not a patient man.' He scared me, John. The look in his eyes . . . it was . . . murderous."

"Those loose ends you were talking about — I expect that includes me."

"Yes, John, you, and the men Theo Leggett confided in, Dr. Cox, Grant Wilson and a few others. I believe that's why Gamble has hired the Allison brothers. They're professionals who will do Gamble's killing, including Hack Burns at the end. He's someone else who knows too much, another loose end."

"I'd say Stryker Allison would find Burns a handful."

"Maybe, but Stryker isn't the worst of the brothers. The miners say the youngest, Harland, has killed seven men. He has a vile temper, especially when he's drinking, and he shoots first and talks later. Like Stryker, the other two, Julius and Clint, will kill only if the price is right. Last year, up in Wyoming, the Allisons hired their guns to a rancher who wanted to clean out nesters in the Shoshone Basin country. When the brothers left and the bodies were counted, seventeen men and half-grown boys and two women were dead on the ground."

"The big score Trask was talking about, any idea what it is? The Allison brothers might also be involved in that," McBride said.

"I don't know. He didn't confide in me that much."

McBride thoughtfully rubbed the harsh stubble on his jaw, his trained detective's brain working. "Could be it's about what Theo said, something to do with orphan trains."

Shannon laughed. "Maybe Gamble is thinking of starting up an orphanage. It would really impress voters when he gets to Washington."

The two sat in silence for a few moments, busy with their own thoughts. Then McBride said finally, "Shannon, you didn't come here tonight just to tell me you were frightened."

The woman shook her head. "No, I came here to ask for your help. You're the only man I can trust in High Hopes and I'm asking for your protection."

McBride's smile was slight. "I'd be outnumbered. Do you think I'm up to the task?"

"Yes, I do. I've never put my trust in any man before, but I'm doing it now. I need you, John."

"And I need you, Shannon," McBride said, his voice husky with desire.

"Your poor eye," Shannon whispered, kissing him lightly again. Her fingers moved through McBride's hair. "I've never met a man like you. . . . Never . . ."

Their eyes met and held for a long time. Shannon's moist lips were parted as though she was finding it hard to breathe and McBride's entire being cried out for her. He pulled her toward him and felt the swell of her breasts against his chest and he kissed her. Shannon gasped and returned the kiss with an abandoned passion.

"Love me, John," she murmured, her head thrown back as McBride's lips sought her throat. "Love me forever."

"I will," he said, his head filled with the sweet, woman smell of her. "Forever . . ."

An hour later, after they parted ways, McBride lay back on the tumbled bed.

The scent of Shannon Roark's perfume lingered . . . and he saw her everywhere.

CHAPTER 11

John McBride woke to a gray dawn. On bare feet he rose and padded across the floor to the window. The wind had died, and sometime during the night a mist had drifted into town from the plains. Now it was lifting, like a wrinkled and ancient Salome removing the last veil, revealing High Hopes in all its shoddy ugliness.

McBride had harbored a hope, all the while knowing how forlorn it was, that he might catch a glimpse of Shannon. But the street was empty of people and only the curling mist was moving.

He moved to the dresser, poured water into the basin from the jug and washed as best he could. He glanced in the mirror, decided to postpone shaving for one more day, then dressed. He shrugged into his high-buttoned coat but left off the uncomfortable celluloid collar and tie.

McBride slid the Smith & Wesson into the

shoulder holster and settled his plug hat on his head. He stepped out of the room and walked downstairs into the new day.

The warm glow from the time he'd spent with Shannon was still with McBride as he sat at a bench in the restaurant and ordered steak and eggs. The waitress looked much less pretty in the harsh dawn light — pale hair, pale skin and pale eyes — and McBride could not help but compare her insipid look to Shannon's vibrant beauty. Mattie poured McBride coffee, showing little inclination for conversation, and walked back to the kitchen, leaving him alone.

At this early hour of the morning, there were few other diners and McBride ate quickly and left.

He stopped for a while on the boardwalk outside the restaurant and breathed the cool morning air. The mist was all but gone and only a few wisps lingered in the alleys like gray ghosts. A train pulled into the station, the locomotive's bell clanking. Then it hissed to a stop, belching steam.

McBride stepped aside for an unsteady miner who was heading for the restaurant with his head lowered, obviously nursing a hangover. Before he got to the door, Mc-Bride stopped him. "Where does Marshal Clark live?" he asked.

The man looked McBride up and down, the stench of whiskey and foul humor on his breath. "Hell of a thing to ask a man conundrums afore he's had a cup of coffee."

"It's a civil question and I expect a civil answer."

The miner saw something in McBride's eyes he didn't like and it took the edge off his surliness. "Just outside of town, thataway. Yellow house. That is, if'n the old law dog is still alive. He's got lead in him."

McBride nodded his thanks and the miner turned away with a muttered curse and lurched into the restaurant.

The marshal's house was not hard to find. A hundred yards of open, sandy ground separated the place from the town limits and it stood in a grove of mixed piñon and juniper. A white picket fence surrounded the house, and from its polished brass door knocker to the blooming pink flowers in the window pots, the place had obviously been loved and cared for.

McBride rapped on the door and after a few moments it was opened by a thin, careworn woman who looked to be in her early forties. She pushed a stray lock of hair from her forehead, settled it behind an ear and looked at McBride without speaking.

He touched the brim of his hat. "Mrs. Clark?"

The woman shook her head. "I'm not Mrs. Clark. I'm not 'Mrs.' anybody. You here to see the marshal?"

"Yes. The name's Smith, John Smith."

"He's met a lot of those." The woman studied McBride for a moment or two, then decided an explanation was warranted. "Lute and me are not married. We've lived together for the past ten years, so I guess you could say that makes me his common-law wife." She smiled without warmth. "Not that it matters a hill of beans. Lute isn't going to live much longer. When a man's set his mind on dying, there ain't much his woman can do about it." Then, as an after-thought, as though it wasn't important: "My name's Dolly Jakes." She took a step back. "Come in. Lute doesn't get many visitors anymore."

The house was dark and smelled of wax polish and meat baking in the stove. A grandfather clock stood in the hallway and ticked slow seconds into the quiet, its brassy voice hushed. A small calico cat twined through McBride's legs and he bent and rubbed its head, smiling.

"Charlie likes you," Dolly said. "That's a good sign. There are not many he likes."

123

"Kids and animals seem to like me," McBride said. "I don't know why."

"You've got gentle hands. Small, innocent things want to be treated gentle. So do women." She nodded. "Room at the end of the hall. Go right in. You'll be quite safe. Lute doesn't keep his gun by the bed any longer."

McBride rapped on the door of Clark's room and stuck his head inside. The place smelled of sickness, of damp sheets, of the slow decay of a human being and of the laudanum that kept him numb.

"Marshal Clark?"

The room was dark, the curtains drawn. A voice came from the heaped shape on the bed, thin and unfriendly. "What the hell do you want?"

"Name's Smith, John Smith. I'd like to talk to you."

"I've known a lot of men who called themselves John Smith. Ran more than a few of them out of towns from the Pecos to the Picketwire. What do you want with me?"

McBride stepped to the bed. He looked around in the gloom, found a chair and sat down. Clark's face was lost in the darkness, but McBride felt the burn of the man's eyes.

"How are you feeling, Marshal?"

"As well as any man who can't move from

the neck down feels. Man can't stand on his own two feet, he ain't a man any longer. He's nothing." He was silent for a while, then asked, "Dolly send you in here?"

"Yes, she did. I told her I needed to talk with you."

"Good woman, Dolly. We used to have a time, her and me, in bed and out of it. Now that's over, like everything else." A lonely man will often talk freely once he gets past the first few words and Clark did now. "Dolly was working the line in Abilene when I met her. I killed the man who figured he owned her, then a deputy sheriff who figured on stopping us leaving. Then I brung her here. That was ten years ago and she's been a good woman to me since."

Clark groaned and his head moved on the pillow. "Bottle . . . on the table."

McBride found the laudanum, raised the marshal's head and held it to his lips. Clark swallowed a few times, then turned away. "Enough. For a spell."

Now that McBride had become accustomed to the darkness he could make out the pale outlines of the marshal's face. His cheeks and temples were sunken and his eyes lay deep and in shadow. A dragoon mustache, showing gray and obviously kept trimmed by Dolly, failed to hide a wide, hard mouth that showed arcs of humor at the corners. At one time Clark's face had been good, strong, the forehead high and intelligent, his thick eyebrows a sign of strength and determination. But now his face was shrunken, wrinkled, like a withered winter apple.

Clark's head turned until he could lift his eyes to his visitor. "I know your name ain't Smith and you're not pinned onto a tin star but you've got lawman sign all over you."

McBride smiled. "Theo Leggett told me that very thing."

"How is Theo?"

"Dead."

"How did it happen? Opium or the drink?"

"Neither. He was shot."

Briefly, McBride told the marshal about the murder of Leggett, leaving out his own part in the affair. "I believe Gamble Trask ordered Theo killed," he said. He waited, wondering how Clark would respond.

It was a long time before the marshal spoke and for a while McBride thought the laudanum had put him to sleep.

But the man's voice was firm, wide-awake. "Theo and a few others, including me, didn't like what Trask was doing to this town. When he built the Golden Garter he filled it with whores, opium and busthead whiskey. He brought Hack Burns with him too. A combination like that is bad news and pretty soon most mornings we were getting a dead man with breakfast."

Clark paused, then said, "Like its name signifies, me, Theo and the others had high hopes for High Hopes. There was talk of a church and a town hall, even a fire station. We were foolish enough to figure the town would be a good place for families to live, but Trask put an end to all that. His saloon attracts the miners and they spend money in the stores and businesses. Suddenly it seemed that everybody was getting rich and there was no more talk about churches."

"And you tried to shut Trask down?"

"Yeah, that's it, I tried. I walked into the Golden Garter and told Trask to close the place and get out of town on the next train. Then Hack Burns threw down on me and his bullet cut my backbone in two. He's fast, mighty fast on the draw."

"And now he's the new marshal."

"Yeah, he's the new marshal all right, and High Hopes is going to hell in a handbasket even faster."

"Marshal Clark, my real name is John McBride. I was . . . I guess I still am . . . a detective sergeant with the New York Police

Department."

"Figured you for a shadow of some kind, a Pink maybe."

"Gamble Trask is a threat to the life of . . . a friend of mine and I aim to take him down. I plan on asking the others who think the same way as you do about High Hopes to help me." McBride thought for a moment. "Doc Cox, Grant Wilson, the blacksmith . . . I can't remember his name."

"Ned Barlow."

"Yes, him and as many others as I can find."

"There are no others, McBride. And none of those men are gunfighters. Ask them to go up against Hack Burns and you'll kill them, just as surely as if you'd put a gun to their heads."

"There's more, Marshal. Trask has hired the Allison brothers."

Clark's voice had sounded tired. now it became alive again. "You mean Stryker an' them?"

"Yes. He's in town now."

Clark let out a long sigh. "Then it's all over. You ever read the Good Book? The Allison brothers are the Four Horsemen of the Apocalypse — they spread death and destruction wherever they go. McBride, I don't know why you're here, but take my advice and get out of High Hopes before it's too late. Go back to New York, where you belong." He held for a few moments, then added, "And don't call me marshal again. I'm not the marshal. Hell, I'm not even a man anymore."

McBride understood how Clark felt and he could not find the words. He could imagine himself lying in that bed, paralyzed, helpless, waiting only for death.

"Marshal Clark, I —"

"Spare me your pity, McBride. Just . . . just leave me be. It's over, I tell you. Now, go home to the big city."

McBride rose to his feet. He looked down at Clark. The man's cheeks were glistening with tears. "I have to ask you a couple of things more, that's all. Did you know that Trask is dealing in young Chinese girls?"

"Yeah, I knew. He buys them cheap in San Francisco and then sends them East at a big profit. At first he used the Chinese girls in his saloon, in the cribs, but miners don't much care for Celestials, even the women. Pretty soon Trask realized there was more money to be made by shipping the girls to New York and other places."

"Trask has been talking about making one big score, then leaving High Hopes for good. You any idea what that might be?"

Clark shook his head. "No, I don't."

"How about orphan trains? Theo told me Trask was somehow mixed up with orphan trains."

"I don't know anything about that either." Clark's voice was weakening. "McBride, you told me a friend of yours was in danger. Listen and listen good — you have no friends in High Hopes. And anybody who tells you different is a liar."

Another sigh escaped Clark's lips. "Now, let me be and don't come back here again. I want to lie here in the dark and get through with my dying in peace."

McBride walked quietly to the door. Clark's voice stopped him.

"Send Dolly in here. I need her."

CHAPTER 12

Noon came and went but McBride saw no sign of Hack Burns in the street. It seemed that Shannon had prevailed on Trask to rein in his gunman. At least for now.

Shannon had asked for his protection, but McBride was at a loss where to start. When she was in her suite at the hotel, he was close by and could look out for her. But when she was at the Golden Garter he couldn't camp out there night after night, watching over her.

There had to be a better way. And that better way was for Shannon to leave High Hopes with him. They could head back East, to a big city where no one would know them, get married and start a new life together.

But even as he considered that, the dark, ominous shadow of Gamble Trask cast itself over his plans.

Trask wanted Shannon for himself and he

wouldn't stand idly by and let another man take her away from him. If McBride tried to leave High Hopes with Shannon, it would have to be over Trask's dead body. Then so be it. He'd told Marshal Clark that he planned to bring the man down. Now he'd have to make good on his boast.

He was one man against five of the best guns in the West. But no matter, the time for bragging was over. If he wanted Shannon Roark to be his wife, he had it to do.

The light slowly changed in McBride's room. The yellow glow of day shaded into the blue of dusk and then the darkness of night. Out on the street the miners were coming in from the hills, shabby, bearded men with gnarled hands seeking whiskey and female companionship after days of backbreaking labor when injury and death came easy but gold came hard.

The reflector lamps had been lit along the boardwalk, casting long shadows of men as they passed, black, undulating shapes moving across a backdrop of orange light. There was a stillness about the night, a strange quiet that made men talk in whispers and wonder why they did. It was as though the town were holding its breath, waiting for something to happen.

McBride decided it was time to investigate Trask a little further, a first, minor skirmish in his coming war with the man. He lit the lamp in the room and gingerly shaved his battered face by its dim flicker. Then he slid the Smith & Wesson into the shoulder holster, put on his hat and headed outside. He mingled, unnoticed, with the miners crowding the street and stepped into the alley beside the Golden Garter.

Shannon had said that the Chinese girls had been visiting a fortune-teller behind the saloon, but she was probably repeating what Trask had told her. If there was a fortune-teller's shack back there, McBride was sure it was the place where the girls were held before being shipped out on an eastbound train.

Yet how was that possible? Surely the girls would wail and holler and beg passersby for help, attracting unwanted attention. Trask had to have found a way to get them to the train station without causing too much fuss.

The moon had not yet climbed into the sky and the alley was dark, pooled in shadow. Something small squeaked and scuttled at his feet as McBride passed the corner of the saloon and found himself in an open area of ground. A brewery wagon was parked to his right, its tongue raised. A few upended wooden barrels stood close by. About twenty yards ahead of him, he could make out the vague outline of a shack with a crooked tin chimney sticking through the steeply angled roof. There was no light showing in the single window to the left of the door.

On cat feet, McBride stepped closer to the shack. Laughter and loud talk drifted from the saloon and the night spread so quiet around him he could hear the click of the roulette wheel and the rattle of dice.

Above the door of the lathe and tar-paper cabin a crude, hand-painted sign proclaimed:

MADAME HUAN ∼ *Palmistry*

McBride tried the door. It was locked. He walked around to the rear of the shack, found that there was no other entrance and returned to the door. There was no one around and he was invisible in the darkness. McBride leaned his shoulder against the door and pushed. It held firm. He pushed harder. Wood splintered and the door swung open on its rawhide hinges.

It was dark inside and the place stank. McBride took a chance on not being seen from the saloon and thumbed a match into flame. He discovered an oil lamp and lit the wick, alarmed at the amount of light that flooded into the room. If Trask or one of his men happened to be passing by . . .

He forced that thought from his mind. There might be something in the shack that would explain how Trask kept the Chinese girls quiet.

He was standing in the middle of a small room, a narrow door opposite him. The only furnishings were a rusty iron stove, a table, a chair and a cot, enough to convince anyone who glanced inside that someone lived here.

McBride guessed that there was no Madame Huan and that the shack was always locked. He doubted that the miners cared about having their palms read and never came near the place.

Swiftly crossing the room, he opened the narrow door and was immediately hit by a feral stench, the smell of the young women who had been confined there for days at a time.

He raised the lamp. Half a dozen thick posts had been driven into the dirt floor of the tiny room and from each hung a pair of iron shackles. There was a shelf to his right, with several syringes, cotton, spoons, candles, narrow leather straps and bottles laid carefully on it. Only one of the bottles still had a handwritten label, which said, *Citric Acid.*

Desperately McBride tried to recall the lectures he'd attended on heroin addiction. The citric acid was used to break down black tar heroin so it could be injected — he remembered that. The heroin was placed in the spoon and then the acid and a little water were added. A spoon was held over a candle flame until the heroin dissolved and afterward a tiny piece of cotton was used to soak up the liquid. The addict drew the heroin from the cotton with a syringe, hoping to filter out particles of tar and other impurities. The heroin was then injected into the arm or leg, or sometimes directly into the neck.

Injection was the cheapest method of administering opium, but it created a greater dependency on the drug and as the user's tolerance grew, more and more was needed to get the same effect.

The Chinese girls had come from San Francisco, probably from the notorious and vicious Barbary Coast waterfront. After getting off the boat, they would have been raped repeatedly, beaten and forced to endure heroin injections. Once dependent on the drug, they would become compliant and be willing to do anything to get more.

Trask obviously controlled the young women with heroin. The drug made them obedient and docile and they could be shipped east on trains without trouble. On each trip one or two of his men must travel with the girls, a plentiful supply of heroin at the ready.

It was a neat setup and a profitable one. The girls McBride had seen herded into the alley had spent some time chained to the posts and were already gone. It was of no concern to Gamble Trask that all four would be dead within a couple of years.

Cold anger rising in him, McBride knew it was too late to help the girls who'd been here, but he would make sure Trask would never use this prison again. He lifted the oil lamp high, ready to throw it against a wall. But he never completed the motion.

A shot from the direction of the outside door hit the lamp and it shattered apart in his hand, hurling sheets of flame. Burning oil hit McBride on the shoulder and his coat flared. He threw off the smoldering coat as the dry tar-paper walls around him caught fire, surrounding him with raging cascades of flame. Smoke hung thick and black in the air as McBride lurched out of the room.

Another shot slammed, but curling clouds

of smoke obscured McBride and the bullet whined past his head, buzzing like an angry hornet. He drew his gun as he stumbled toward the door. It banged shut just before he reached it, scorching tongues of fire licking at him.

McBride barged through the door, ripping it from the hinges, and ran outside. Behind him the shack was an inferno. A tangle of men was piling out the door of the Golden Garter and he thought he heard someone call his name. He did not wait to find out. Footsteps pounded off to his left and he went after them.

Away from the street it was very dark. Ahead of him the footsteps slowed and then fell silent. Crouching low, his skin crawling as he expected a bullet at any moment, McBride was alone in the night with only the stars watching him. He heard a commotion and the clank of buckets back at the saloon as men fought to put out the fire, but he kept on moving.

Counting Jim Nolan, three men had now tried to kill him and his patience had worn thin. He planned to catch up with the man ahead of him, and shoot him or beat him to a pulp with his fists. Then, as he'd done with the young cowboy, he'd deliver him back to Gamble Trask.

Lamps were lit in the stores along the street and their back windows cast rectangles of yellow light on the ground as McBride passed. A few scattered cabins and shacks also showed gleaming windows, but around them lay canyons of darkness. Off to his left, a dog barked in sudden alarm. McBride turned and stepped toward the sound, his gun ready.

A cabin lay just ahead of him and beyond it, only the inky blackness of the plains. As he got closer McBride saw the dog staring intently into the gloom. The dog started to bark again and the cabin door opened and a man in shirtsleeves came out and looked around him. Hidden by the dark, McBride stayed where he was. Finally the man called the dog inside. The animal walked to the door reluctantly, growling as its eyes continued to search the night.

After the cabin door slammed, McBride holstered his gun. It would be suicide to walk out into the dark after a man who could even now be waiting in ambush. He'd learned that lesson when he went out in the dark after the cowboy who had killed Theo. It was not an experience he cared to repeat.

A sense of defeat weighing on him, McBride made his way back behind the stores, but he stopped at a hand pump at the rear of the restaurant, his face puzzled. The pump stood in the light of a window and around it the ground was muddy. The thing that had caught McBride's eye was a perfect footprint in the mud. He kneeled and looked closer. The only person who would pump water for the restaurant was the waitress, but she would surely have left more than one footprint. In any case this was too wide to be a woman's print. The track was very recent and it was shallow. McBride guessed it had been left by a small-ish man who could not have weighed more than 140 pounds. What intrigued McBride was that it was a shoe print, probably made by a shoe with a leather sole and heel. As far as he was aware, all of Gamble Trask's men wore boots. Hack Burns certainly did. So did Stryker Allison and the miners who helped Trask bring in the Chinese girls.

McBride was convinced the man who'd tried to kill him at the shack and then fled had left this print. He was equally sure it wasn't one of Trask's men. Then who?

Unbidden, a dark memory wormed its way into his mind, of a man back in New York called Gypsy Jim O'Hara. He was nicknamed Gypsy not because he was a Romany but for his swarthy skin and black eyes and hair.

O'Hara was a contract killer, an ice-cold assassin without conscience who was suspected of at least two dozen murders. Inspector Byrnes had many times tried to bring O'Hara to justice, but the man always had a cast-iron alibi and walked free. He also enjoyed the protection of gangsters like Sean Donovan who appreciated his deadly skills and provided him with the best lawyers money could buy.

Jim O'Hara was a small, compact man with the flat, soulless eyes of a basilisk. Extremely vain, he always dressed in the height of fashion and a shoe-shine was part of his morning ritual. He was good with a revolver but would use a shotgun or knife as the occasion demanded. O'Hara was a bad enemy, relentless in pursuit, merciless at the kill, a man to be reckoned with.

McBride stood and looked around him. Away from the glare of the streetlamps the stars were visible, the sky a spangled roof over the world that gradually melted in the distance and became one with the violet darkness of the plain. The coyotes were talking to the night birds and the prairie wind was asleep. Nothing moved among the brooding shadows but hidden things that skittered and screeched and hunted their own kind.

The air smelled of dust and heat as Mc-Bride stood, head bent in thought.

Gypsy Jim here in High Hopes? That was impossible. The man was a sewer rat who would never leave the suffocating brick canyons and swarming, filthy alleys of the city. Yet Byrnes had warned him that Dono-van's reach was long. Was O'Hara here — hunting him?

It was not so improbable as it sounded. Many crooked New York cops were on Sean Donovan's payroll. Could it be that Mc-Bride's message to Byrnes had been inter-cepted, the envelope steamed open and the letter read? Pay O'Hara enough money and he'd track a man all the way into hell.

McBride shook his head. He was thinking like an old lady who hears a rustle in every bush. His dread of Gypsy Jim was based on a single shoe print that could have been left by anybody, a gambler maybe, or a member of the town's broadclothed citizenry.

He breathed deep, fighting his own over-wrought imagination. But the thought lingered, nagging at him like a bad tooth-ache. He had a copper's instinct for danger and now it was telling him to be wary, that the danger he sensed was very close and getting closer.

He would go on the assumption that

Gypsy Jim was in High Hopes, at least until he learned differently. McBride took no joy in that conclusion. It brought him only a great deal of worry.

The shack was still a blazing inferno as McBride walked along the street to the hotel. He smiled when he saw that Trask had organized a bucket brigade. The man was running around in a panic, barking orders to miners who were throwing water on the back wall and roof of the saloon. Fire was always a hazard in a wooden town, and sparks from the burning shack could easily set the Golden Garter alight.

Trask had good cause to be panicked and that pleased McBride mightily. To his relief he saw Shannon standing outside on the boardwalk, a shawl around her shoulders. She saw him, smiled and waved, then went back inside.

McBride lit the lamp in his room and grieved mightily for his lost coat. It had cost him ten dollars at Aaron Goldberg's Clothing Emporium for Gents back in New York and he doubted if he'd find another quite so fine.

He stepped to the window and looked outside. The fire had died down and the bucket brigade had disbanded. There was no sign of Trask.

He heard a soft knock at his door and smiled. Shannon had come to pay him a visit. He stepped to the door and opened it wide, his smile quickly fading as he saw the small, compact man in the doorway — a man who held a gun aimed right at his belly.

CHAPTER 13

"You call yourself John Smith?" the man asked.

McBride nodded. "I go by that name."

The man motioned with the gun. "Inside." McBride hesitated. "Now!"

McBride backed into the room and his visitor followed, shutting the door behind him with his foot. He was wearing boots.

"Shuck the iron with your left hand and lay it on the bed," the man said.

McBride did as he was told. "I didn't catch your name," he said.

"I didn't give it." A moment's pause, then: "Name's Luke Prescott, out of Pueblo and other places."

"Your brother —"

"Was Rusty Prescott. You killed him."

"He tried to kill me."

"I know." To McBride's surprise Prescott holstered his gun. "Move away from the bed," he said. "I'm not what you'd call a

145

trusting man."

McBride stepped close to the window. "Now you want revenge, is that it?"

Prescott nodded. "That's why I'm here."

The man saw McBride's eyes angle to the gun on the bed and he smiled. "Don't even think about it. I'd put three bullets into your belly before you even got halfway there."

"I'd still get a couple into you," McBride said.

"Maybe you would at that." Prescott shrugged. "Then again, maybe you wouldn't."

The man was dressed in dusty range clothes, but his boots, hat and coat were all top quality. He hadn't bought those duds on a puncher's wages, McBride decided, experiencing a momentary pang of regret for his own coat.

"I heard that somebody paid my brother to kill you and another man. Is that the way of it?" Prescott asked, his eyes searching McBride's face.

"That's the way of it. He killed an old newspaperman named Theo Leggett. He missed me. Later I found five double eagles in your brother's pocket. That works out at fifty dollars a man, cheap enough for a human life."

"Rusty always figured on making money

the easy way. He wasn't much on hard work, leastways not punching cows on a half-broke pony eighteen hours a day for thirty dollars a month."

"Too bad," McBride said. "But he should have stayed on the ranch."

"I said them very words when I buried him. He should have stayed on the ranch." Prescott's gaze again explored McBride's face. "You heard my name before?"

"Yes. I was told you're pretty good with that gun on your hip. Of course, that's only what people say. I don't know the truth of it."

Prescott moved. Suddenly, in a motion too fast to see, the Colt was in his hand. He did a border shift, twirled the gun, then sent it spinning back to his right hand. The Colt was still revolving when he slammed it into the holster.

"The people were right, Smith. I am pretty good."

"Fancy work, but it could get you killed if a man was shooting at you."

To McBride's surprise, Prescott laughed. "You never said a truer word. When I aim to kill a man, I leave the fancy work back at the barn."

"And do you aim to kill me? If you do, draw that revolver again and we'll see what happens."

McBride was poised, ready to make a dive for the Smith & Wesson. The rifle he'd taken from Rusty Prescott was standing in a corner, but he'd never make it.

Reading the other man's eyes, Prescott smiled. "Relax, Smith, I'm not going to kill you. You did what you had to do and I have no quarrel with that. I'm here because I want the name of the man who paid my brother the blood money. The way I figure it, that man killed Rusty, not you."

McBride stepped to the bed, picked up his gun and slid it into the holster. Prescott watched, but made no attempt to stop him.

"The man's name is Gamble Trask."

"The owner of the Golden Garter?"

"Yes, the very same."

Confusion showed in Prescott's eyes. "Why would Trask want to kill you?"

"Because Theo Leggett talked to me. Gamble Trask is a small man, but he wants to grow a lot bigger. He has political ambitions, the honorable senator from the great state of Colorado being one of them. Theo wanted to expose Trask's dealings in drugs and Chinese slave girls, and that's why Trask couldn't let him live. Carrying baggage like that, his political career would go nowhere. Now I know what Theo knew, and he sure can't leave me around either."

Prescott chewed on the end of his mustache as he thought through what McBride had just told him. Finally he said, "What Trask does with drugs and Celestials is none of my concern. What does concern me is that he got my brother killed." Prescott touched his hat. "Thanks for the information, Smith. Now I've got it to do."

The man turned to leave, but McBride stopped him. "Prescott, you'll be bucking a stacked deck. A man named Hack Burns is always with Trask, and he's no bargain."

"You mean a man with a purple taint on his face?" Prescott's hand moved to his left cheek. "Here."

"Yes. Do you know him?"

"Our trails have crossed a time or two. We stepped around each other." The man was silent for a few moments, thinking. He said, "I can take Hack Burns."

"Could be. But Stryker Allison will back him, and his brothers."

Prescott was surprised. "The Allison brothers are here in High Hopes?"

"Stryker is. I don't know if the other three have joined him yet."

Luke Prescott looked like a man who'd just been slapped. "The Allisons are men to be reckoned with, Stryker and them. Seen them operate down in Texas one time. They're hell on wheels, leave a lot of dead men behind." He stepped to the window, pulled the curtain aside and looked over at the Golden Garter. "Place is busy," he said, more to himself than McBride. Prescott took a deep breath and squared his shoulders. He turned from the window. "Well, no matter. I still got it to do."

He was a small man, but at that moment he looked tough and hard to kill.

"There's a better way," McBride said. "Or at least another way."

"I'm listening."

"We hit Trask where he can least afford it — in his pocketbook. He hires gold miners to bring the Chinese girls into town. That could mean they spend some time at the diggings in the Spanish Peaks, and I've got a feeling Trask's opium is delivered from there as well."

Prescott shook his head. "I don't get your drift."

"We disrupt the shipments, free the girls and destroy the opium. When Trask's money dries up, guns for hire like Burns and the Allison brothers won't stick around for long."

"And he'll be alone," Prescott said, his mind working.

"Exactly. And there's something else. I hear that Trask is planning something big, so big that after it comes off he'll be able to leave town with enough money to guarantee his entry into Washington high society. I'd say that's why he hired the Allison brothers."

"What does he have in mind?"

McBride shook his head. "I have no idea. Maybe something to do with orphan trains. You ever heard of those?"

"Wagon trains, I have," Prescott said, smiling. "But never orphan trains." He looked long and hard at McBride. "What's your stake in this, Smith? You could avoid getting killed by just leaving town on the next train. What's keeping you in High Hopes? You some kind of law? A Pinkerton maybe?"

For a fleeting moment McBride thought about revealing his true identity to Prescott. But he decided against it. Byrnes had told him to trust no one, and so far he hadn't been making a real good job of it.

"I'm here because a friend of mine is in danger," he said.

"A woman?"

"Yes, a woman."

"I thought so. Only a woman can hog-tie a man and keep him in one place. Have I heard of the lady in question?"

"Her name's Shannon Roark. She works for Gamble Trask at the Golden Garter."

Prescott whistled between his teeth. "You sure set your sights high, Smith. Everybody's heard of the beautiful Shannon Roark. They say she's never taken up with a man, though plenty have tried."

McBride shrugged. "She seems to like me well enough."

Prescott was grinning. "Could be you found the secret, have her feel sorry for a man." He circled an eye with his forefinger. "I mean, did she take one look at that swollen peeper and swoon into your arms?"

"The man who gave me that is dead," McBride said, stung. Then, by way of turning aside any more of Prescott's comments: "I believe Shannon loves me as I love her and I intend to make her my wife."

"Then good luck to you, Smith, and I hope I didn't speak out of turn."

"No harm done," McBride said. "Now, what about my plan to bring down Trask? Are you willing to draw the line?"

"I'll go along with it, at least for now. Like any other feller, I don't want to die on the sawdust after trying to outshoot half a dozen men." Prescott stepped to the door. "Meet me at the livery stable at first light with your horse saddled. We'll ride out to the Peaks and take a look-see."

After Prescott left, McBride lay on the bed trying to work through a major problem — he'd never sat on a horse in his life.

CHAPTER 14

The T. J. Williams Livery and Feed Stable was the only adobe building in High Hopes. Just before sunup McBride stopped and read a notice painted on the wall beside the door.

CITY TRANSFER AND HACK LINE ~
EXPRESSING AND HAULING
*Fine saddle horses let
by the day, week or month*

That, McBride told himself, was what he needed, a fine saddle horse. If it was nice and quiet.

He opened the livery door and stepped inside. The stable was in darkness, but from somewhere in the gloom he heard a horse stamp a foot and blow through its nose. The noise did nothing to reassure him, but he had little time to think about it as a door opened to his left and an old man stepped out of the office. He was wearing red long johns and slippers, and a battered black hat sat on his head.

"What can I do fer ye, mister? Kinda early, ain't ye?"

"I guess. I need a horse."

"Purchase or let?"

"Let."

The old man scratched his belly, spit and wiped his bearded mouth with the back of his hand. "I got a real good buckskin back there will suit ye fine. Cost ye fifty cents a day and two bits extry fer saddle an' bridle."

"Sounds reasonable," McBride allowed.

"Then I'll saddle him up for ye." The old man hesitated and stuck out his hand. "That will be seventy-five cents in advance, plus a ten-dollar deposit on the hoss."

"Not a trusting man, are you?" McBride said.

The old man shrugged. "You mought be honest, but then again you mought be a hoss thief. Well, young feller, does the ten-dollar deposit go?"

"It goes." He paid the old man.

"Name's Ebenezer Keble, fer them as likes to know. There's coffee on the stove, if'n you've a mind to drink some."

McBride laid his carpetbag and the Winchester on the floor, then stepped into the office. He found a tin cup and poured himself coffee. He was draining the last of it as Ebenezer led a tall, rawboned horse to the door. McBride's heart leaped into his throat. "Kind of big, isn't he?" he said.

"Yup, he's a big un all right. Some folks say 'Admire a big hoss, but ride a small one,' but I don't hold with that. This big feller will take you to where you're goin' and back again without breaking a sweat."

A tense minute ticked past, then another. "Ye gonna climb into the saddle or no?" the old man asked, growing puzzlement in his eyes.

"Sure," McBride said. He could hear the hammer of his heart. He stepped to the horse.

"If'n I was you, I'd mount from t'other side," Ebenezer said. "At least that's how it's done around these parts."

McBride nodded and walked to the left side of the horse. The buckskin whinnied, rolled its eyes and sidestepped away from him.

"Jes' grab on to the horn with your lef' hand and put your foot in the stirrup," the old man advised. He watched the proceedings for a few moments as McBride hopped around on one leg, then said, "If'n I was you, I'd put my lef' foot in the stirrup. You'll find it's a sight easier that way."

The prancing horse led McBride around in circles. He was now hopping on his right leg, his other foot in the stirrup. Thick clouds of choking dust swirled, making him cough.

"Hoist yerself up now," Ebenezer hollered. "That's it. There you go."

McBride was belly down across the saddle, the bouncing, snorting buckskin giving him no help. "What do I do now?" he yelled.

"Th'ow yer leg over the saddle nice an' easy an' sit up. There's a good gent."

McBride could hear from the tone of the old man's voice that he very much doubted his equestrian abilities. The irritating thing was that he was right.

Finally McBride got to a sitting position and he slid his right foot into the stirrup. Suddenly the buckskin went quiet, and pleased, he relaxed.

"Git ready now," the old man said.

"For what?"

"Oh, nothin' much, he'll just buck a few times to let ye know he's awake an' ready to go. He don't mean anything bad by it. All ye have to do is show him who's boss."

Those dire tidings did not have time to sink into McBride's consciousness because the horse suddenly uncoiled like a spring, arched its back and started to crow-hop around in fast, tight circles.

"Hold on, feller!" Ebenezer yelled. "Ye got him" — the end of the sentence faded away into a whisper, directed at McBride lying facedown in the dust — "on . . . the . . . run."

Stunned, McBride lay where he was for a few minutes, then rose painfully to his feet. He took off his hat and slapped dust from his pants as the old man asked, "Here, are you one o' them city fellers?"

McBride nodded, grimacing as his lower back punished him.

Ebenezer scratched his whiskered cheek. "Well, sir, it seems to me we have a problem here."

"A smaller horse might help." McBride was irritated at himself, the old man and above all the buckskin, now standing head down, its eyes shut, as it dozed.

Ebenezer slammed a fist into his open palm. "An' by jiminy I've got the very thing. You stay where you are — I'll be right back."

"I'm not going anywhere," McBride said.

The dawn was shading into the tarnished silver light of morning. Ribbons of scarlet and jade streaked the sky, melting into rose pink at the horizon. Jays were quarreling among the branches of a scrub oak at the rear of the barn and the air smelled of the clean, newborn day.

McBride turned and saw Luke Prescott walking toward him. The gunfighter carried a rifle in one hand, a bulging burlap sack in the other. He glanced at the buckskin. "I see you're all ready to go, Smith. I'll saddle up." He raised the sack. "I got us some grub, hardtack, salt pork and coffee. Got a pot and fry pan as well. We could be out for a few days."

A few minutes later Prescott walked out of the barn, leading a magnificent black. "Well, let's go," he said. He tied the sack onto the horn, then swung into the saddle with effortless grace. He looked down at McBride. "Mount up."

"I can't," McBride said miserably. "I don't know how to ride." He felt like he was confessing to a crime.

And Prescott took it as such. His face shocked, he asked, "You can't ride?"

"Damn it, isn't that what I just said?"

"How do you get around?"

"Usually, I take a streetcar."

Prescott threw back his head and laughed. "Hell, I was right. I had you pegged as a city boy." The laughter glow was still in his eyes as he crossed his hands on the saddle horn and leaned forward. "And I figure your name isn't John Smith either."

"It's McBride. The John part stays."

"Well, John McBride, in this country a man without a horse has two choices — stay home or walk."

"How far to the Spanish Peaks?"

"Sixty miles, give or take. Your feet would be mighty sore by the time you got there."

Defensively, McBride said that the man called Ebenezer was bringing him a smaller and tamer horse. "I think I can manage that," he said.

"Let's hope so." Prescott grinned. "Where we're going is rough country and a man on foot isn't going to put a scare into Gamble Trask and his boys."

Later, Ebenezer did lead out a small, mouse-colored mustang — but it was between the shafts of a two-wheeled trap.

"Got what you need right here," the old man said. "Cost you the same as the buckskin."

Prescott's laughter was a joyous thing. "Hell, John, even you can't fall off that!"

His face burning, McBride asked the old man, "What do I need to know?"

"Not much. Jes' slap his back with the reins to go, and pull back on them to whoa." Ebenezer nodded toward Prescott. "This little pony will still be going when that big

American stud of his is lying dead beat on the trail."

"Could be," Prescott allowed, fighting back a grin. "Nothing like a pony and trap to take a man where he wants to go in comfort."

McBride ignored the man, got his carpetbag and rifle and tossed them on the seat. He climbed onboard, took up the reins and slapped the mustang's back. The trap lurched forward and Prescott swung beside him.

"This," McBride said, pleased, "is much better."

Prescott smiled. "Yeah, until we hit the mountains."

CHAPTER 15

McBride and Prescott headed north across broken, hilly country, then swung west along the bank of Apishapa Creek.

"Lead us right to the Peaks," Prescott said. He turned in the saddle and looked at McBride. "You ever been in this country before?"

McBride was bouncing on the trap's seat springs and his voice jolted as he answered, "First time."

"The Comanche, Ute and Apache figured the Peaks were sacred and named them Wahatoya. That means 'Breasts of the Earth' in plain American. Before that, the Aztecs came up this far, hunting for gold and slaves."

McBride looked around him. Deer were feeding among the cottonwoods lining the banks of the creek, their sleek coats dappled by the sunlight filtering through the leaves. Trout leaped in the sun-spangled water and far off a small herd of antelope merged into the shimmering horizon and disappeared from sight.

Ahead, a rocky plateau rose above the plain, as yet just a ribbon of blue in the distance. Prescott told him the Spanish Peaks rose to the north of the plateau in high, big-pine country. To the south lay the bend of the Picketwire and, thirty miles south of that, the New Mexico border.

"Kit Carson, Wild Bill Hickok and a bunch of mountain men traveled this country," Prescott said. "And a lot of outlaws still do." He smiled. "Myself included."

"You on the run from the law?" McBride asked.

Prescott nodded. "Yeah. Sometimes after you kill a man all you can do is run. It's either that or face a vigilante necktie party." He hesitated a heartbeat, then said, "And you, John, what are you running from?"

McBride was taken aback. "Is it that obvious?"

Prescott shrugged. "You claim you're not the law, so you got to be running. You didn't come to High Hopes to save a woman. You came because you figured you'd run far enough."

"I killed a man," McBride said.

"Back in the city?"

"New York."

"I'd say you've skedaddled a fair piece off your home range."

"Could be I haven't run far enough," McBride said, remembering Gypsy Jim O'Hara. "The father of the man I killed has a far reach."

"Then watch your back trail, John. Them's words of wisdom."

They camped that night in a grove of mixed juniper and piñon, beside a stream that bubbled clear from between a cleft in a sandstone parapet that stood taller than a man. The wall, shaped like the prow of a ship, jutted from the side of a hill and it had been undercut by centuries of floodwater, forming a deep hollow.

"I reckon we'll be glad to sleep in the cave tonight," Prescott said. He lifted his head and tested the wind. "I smell lightning."

"All I can I smell is the salt pork frying," McBride said sourly, hurting from the jolting misery of the poorly sprung trap.

"Maybe so — but listen."

Prescott, possessing the instincts of a hunted animal, had heard the thunder long before McBride. But now, as he stepped away from the sizzling fry pan and crackling fire, McBride heard it too.

The storm was blowing in from off the

rocky backbone of the Sangre de Cristo range, and by the time McBride squatted by the fire to eat, the sky to the west was flashing silver.

"Be here in an hour or less," Prescott said. "And it sounds like a big one. Summer lightning storms in Colorado can put a scare into a man. After we eat we'll bring the horses into the cave."

Thirty minutes later the wind began to blow strong. It tossed the branches of the juniper, tattered the flames of the fire and threw up crimson sparks that rose bright into the darkness, then winked out like dying stars.

As McBride and Prescott moved into the meager shelter of the cave, thunder bellowed like a monstrous bull as lightning branded the sky. Rain hammered down, hissing like a snake, and around them the fragile, crystal air shattered into a million shards, catching the lightning flare, shimmering with fire.

The night was being torn apart to a mad symphony of thunder and lightning and the demented counterpoint of the howling wind.

And John McBride did not like it one bit.

"Not like the big city, huh?" Prescott said, raising his voice over the din. He was grinning, building a cigarette, a man completely at ease with his environment.

"I've never seen it real close like this," McBride answered. "In New York the thunder was always above the rooftops, up where the pigeons live."

Prescott thumbed a match into flame and lit his cigarette, the blue smoke he exhaled immediately snatched away by the wind. "We'll be safe enough so long as we stay right where we are."

McBride smiled. "Luke, at this moment wild horses couldn't drag me out of this cave."

The storm was directly above them now, a colossal, scarlet-scaled dragon that roared and breathed blue fire.

McBride was blinded by the searing intensity of the lightning strike, deafened by the accompanying bang of thunder. Beside him he was aware of Prescott jumping to his feet, a curse on his lips as he ran to the horses. His stud recoiled from him, reared and backed out of the cave. The big horse then swung around and ran into the night.

The trap was upended, the wheels blasted away. A few feeble flames fluttered on the woodwork like yellow moths, then died in the rain.

Prescott cursed long and loud. He turned

and looked at McBride, his eyes blazing. "It will take me all day to round up that damned stud. He'll keep on going until he outruns the storm."

"The trap's done for," McBride said, realizing he was piling misery on misery.

"See that," Prescott said without interest.

The little mustang was standing head down, seemingly oblivious to the thunder and the loss of its companion. "We still have a horse," McBride said.

Prescott nodded. "You could call it that."

McBride could see that the other man was seething mad, and he let it go. He sat down, wrapped in a cocoon of gloomy silence as the storm raged around him. At some point in the night he fell asleep. He dreamed of Shannon and horses.

When McBride woke, Prescott was gone. He stepped to the trap and saw to his chagrin that it was wrecked beyond repair. Ebenezer would charge him dearly for the lost wagon, he knew, and it would put a big hole in his dwindling supply of money.

The sky was clear, the color of washed-out denim, tinged with red. The air smelled fresh of rain and piñon, and water hung on the leaves of the junipers, a point of morning light captured in each drop.

But McBride took little joy in the dawn, the loss of the trap and the prospect of being forced to walk weighing on him.

The ugly little mustang had left the cave and was grazing on bunchgrass as McBride filled the coffeepot at the stream and added a handful of Arbuckle.

He had forgotten about the fire.

Two hours later, when Prescott rode into camp astride his stud, McBride had used up his matches and all he had to show for his efforts was a few charred twigs.

The little gunfighter sat his horse and grinned. "Coffee smells good."

"The wood is wet," McBride said defensively, irritated that the other man sounded so cheerful. "Damn it, everything is wet."

Prescott slid off the stud and stepped to the ashes of the fire. He gathered up some twigs and leaves and within a few minutes had a fire blazing. He set the coffeepot on the flames and built a smoke, smiling, but saying nothing.

"In New York," McBride said defensively, "when I want coffee, I say to a waiter, 'Bring me coffee,' and he brings it."

"Good way," Prescott said.

"I never had to light a fire," McBride said, even more irritated at having to justify his city ways.

"Out here a man should know how to make a fire," Prescott said. "He just never can tell when he'll need one."

The implied criticism stung and McBride opened his mouth to make a sharp reply, but the other man headed him off, his eyes suddenly serious. "Saw something that might interest you, John."

"What was that?"

"I started out to track my horse just after the storm passed, while you were snoring."

"I don't —"

"Anyhoo, he headed west, into the storm, knowing it would follow him otherwise."

"Real smart horse," McBride said drily.

"Well, thank you. I reckon he is." Prescott checked the coffeepot. "We'll let it bile for a spell longer." He set the pot back on the fire. "There's a wagon road a mile to the north of where we are. It's well traveled because the gold miners use it to haul out ore to High Hopes and bring in supplies. But about a mile west of here, a trail cuts off the main road and swings to the northwest. La Veta Pass is in that direction, but I don't believe that's where the trail is headed."

"I'm not catching your drift," McBride said.

Prescott grinned. "Good! You're learning

the lingo." He was again busy with tobacco and papers. "What I'm saying is that the trail will eventually meet up with the Union Pacific road. If memory serves me right, there's a watering stop for their engines around there. The rails come down from Denver, through Pueblo, then meet the Santa Fe road at Trinidad, just north of the New Mexico border. But that's by the way. The main thing is that Gamble Trask's Chinese girls and his opium could be loaded onto a Union Pacific freight in Denver, then off-loaded at the watering stop east of La Veta Pass."

"But wouldn't the train crew notice what was happening?"

Prescott smiled. "It's been my experience that railroaders like money as much as anybody else. Trask can buy their silence."

"Then the girls aren't held at the mines?"

"I don't think so. There are some decent men at the gold mines who wouldn't hold with what Trask is doing. There would be talk, something he doesn't want."

"Then the girls and the opium must be taken to somewhere near the Union Pacific line. Either that or they're driven straight from the watering stop to High Hopes."

"That's my thinking," Prescott allowed. He picked up the pot, thumbed open the lid and glanced inside. "Coffee's ready. Let's have your cup."

They drank coffee in silence, each man busy with his own thoughts. Then Prescott said, "I propose we go scout around that watering stop. That is, if my memory is correct and it's really where I say it is."

"I was thinking that myself," McBride said. "Only we have a problem."

"What problem?"

"How the hell do I get there?"

CHAPTER 16

"Your charger is ready, Mr. McBride," Prescott said, trying to hide the grin that flirted with his mouth. "I even fixed you up with a saddle on account of how the mustang has a backbone like the High Sierras."

There was nothing about the ugly little horse that filled McBride with confidence.

Prescott had cut back the reins to a manageable length and stripped off an undamaged portion of the trap's seat cushion. He'd tied the scorched cushion to the mustang's back with the remainder of the leathers.

"Just be careful how you get up on her," he said. "The saddle is a mighty uncertain thing. It could slip and slide."

Prescott read the lack of enthusiasm in McBride's eyes. "Beats walking, John."

"Maybe." McBride stepped to the horse. It looked taller now that he was close. "How do I get up there?"

"Easy." Prescott bent from the waist and laced the fingers of his hands together. "Put your foot in there and I'll boost you up. Then ease down real slow into the saddle." McBride lifted a foot. "Probably better to use the left one, John."

Angry at himself for making the same mistake twice, McBride changed feet and Prescott, revealing surprising strength for such a small man, hoisted him effortlessly onto the mustang's back.

The gunfighter stepped back, rubbing his chin like an artist admiring his work. "Well, so far, so good, and you sure don't have far to fall, John. Your feet are only about six inches off the ground." He swung into the saddle of his prancing black. "Now, what say you, should we hit the trail and see if we can do some damage to Gamble Trask?"

McBride nodded and gathered up the reins. "Giddyup," he said. The mustang stood where it was, its blunt hammerhead hanging.

"Two things," Prescott said. "First, squeeze the horse with your knees when you want it to go. Second, lay the reins against the right side of its neck when you want to turn left, left side when you want to go right. Got that?"

"I would have figured that out for myself,"

McBride said, annoyed at being spoken to like a child. He kneed the horse and it walked forward, making him lurch ungracefully on the seat cushion.

"Crackerjack!" Prescott said. "We'll make a rider out of you yet." Irritated as he was, McBride was oddly pleased. Compliments of any kind from Luke Prescott were rare.

The man handed him his rifle. "Here," he said. "I have a feeling you might need that . . . sooner than later."

They reached the wagon road and headed west, riding through hilly, broken country, much of it forested with piñon and juniper. Here and there ironwood and catclaw grew on the slopes of the rises, surrounded by streaks of pink daisies and bright scarlet paintbrush.

After a mile Prescott found the cutoff and they swung northwest, the elevation climbing, piñon and spruce gradually giving way to aspen, fir and ponderosa pine on the slopes of the higher hills.

McBride had finally relaxed, moving easily with the mustang's choppy gait. The little horse was teacher and he student, and he accepted their relationship as such.

By noon, after they crossed the reedy shallows of Apishapa Creek, the day grew hot, the sun a burning gold coin in a sky free of cloud. The two riders followed the wagon trail through a series of narrow arroyos, where the air hung still, the only sounds the creak of saddle leather and the soft footfalls of the horses.

When they topped a shallow rise, Prescott drew rein. "If you look westward, you can just see the Spanish Peaks, John," he said. "It's beautiful country around there."

McBride stared into the vast distance of the lonely land, stunned at its beauty, by the far blue mountains and the play of light and shadow among the hills. City born, city bred, he had grown accustomed to vistas reduced to the crowded clamor of dirty streets and tall brick buildings that rose so high they blocked the sun.

This was so different, all that surrounded him. For a few moments he took delight in what he was seeing, breathing clean air, scented by pines.

With a start, McBride realized he was swallowing hard. He had fallen in love with Shannon — was he now falling in love with the land that nurtured her?

Luke Prescott was a perceptive man, his instincts honed to razor sharpness by the years he'd lived by the gun. Now he smiled at McBride. "Gets to a man, doesn't it?"

McBride nodded. "I've never seen its like."

"When this is all over and Gamble Trask is dead, you should spend some time in the mountains with your lady. Then you'll really see something."

McBride smiled. "Trask dead? Right now, that seems almost impossible."

Prescott was not smiling and his eyes were cold. "It's not impossible. If this little jaunt of ours fails, I'll still get to him and kill him."

"Then we'd better not fail. To save Shannon, I want him to lose all he has. I want him isolated and alone so he looks around and realizes he's come out on the far end of what he'd once been."

The little gunfighter nodded, his hard face grim. "So be it. Then let's get it done."

McBride's eyes fell on a hawk riding the air currents in the far distance ahead of him. They rode in that direction.

But McBride had no way of knowing that at the exact moment he'd seen the hawk, the bird's sharp eyes were looking down on a scene that had transformed a very small part of the enchanted land into a place of unbelievable horror.

For the most part the wagon trail skirted the aspen groves. Only once had trees been hacked down to clear a path over a humpbacked ridge that led down to a broad and pleasant meadow strewn with wildflowers. A stream bordered by cottonwoods and willows angled across the flat, bubbling clear over a bed of pebbles.

McBride and Prescott sat their horses at the top of the ridge and looked down at the valley. "Good a place as any to stop and boil up coffee and eat," Prescott said. "There's some salt pork left, but after that, we'll have to shoot our own grub."

They rode down the slope and reached the creek.

That was when the smell hit them. "Something dead," Prescott said, his nose lifted to the tainted air. "Maybe an antelope. Now and then coyotes can pull one down that's old or sick."

"Where the hell is it coming from?" McBride asked, talking through pursed lips, the cloying sweetness of death in his nostrils.

"Further ahead of us. I only hope wherever the critter is, it's not in the water."

McBride's mustang, which up until now had taken little interest in its surroundings, lifted its head, ragged ears pricked forward. Prescott's big black was up on its toes, tossing its head as it fought the bit.

Prescott's blue eyes scanned the tree line along the creek, his face showing concern.

With a wild animal's instinct for danger he slid his Winchester out of the scabbard and racked a round into the chamber.

"I think we've got a dead man ahead of us," he said, turning to McBride. "And where's there a dead man his killer might still be close by."

"Indians?" McBride asked.

"Only the Apache are still hostile and I doubt they'd come this far north." Prescott fought his nervous horse, then said, "Keep your rifle ready, but if the work is close, toss it aside and shuck your revolver. Fast."

"Could it be Apaches?" McBride asked, the words coming dry as sticks from his parched mouth.

"Could be. Sometimes they torture a man so long, his body starts to rot."

McBride wiped suddenly sweaty palms on his pants, then levered his rifle. The mustang's head was still up, but it was standing pat.

"Probably just an animal," McBride said hopefully.

"Probably. But don't count on it." Prescott smiled. "You ever fit Injuns before, John?"

"Never."

"Well, I reckon there's a first time for everything."

McBride sighed. "And this could be the time."

"Seems like."

Prescott kneed his mount forward and McBride followed. He knew his seat on the mustang was a precarious thing, and he resolved to dismount and fight on foot if he found himself surrounded by hordes of feathered savages. Back in New York he'd once read a dime novel about Apache who massacred a regiment of U.S. Cavalry. Nothing he recalled about the book provided him with the slightest reassurance.

The two riders splashed across the stream to the far bank, then followed its meandering course, keeping close to the sun-dappled cover of the cottonwoods. The afternoon was very still, without a breeze. Crickets made their small sound in the grass and once a marsh rabbit bounded away from them, bouncing across the meadow like a rubber ball.

The stench of death grew stronger.

McBride saw Prescott ease his Colt in the holster, his eyes roaming far, searching for whatever lay ahead. The black reared, attempting to turn away from the nearness of a thing it feared. A skilled horseman, Prescott fought the stud and pushed it forward.

McBride followed. The heat of the day

crowded uncomfortably close to him, like the naked body of an unwanted lover, and sweat trickled from under his hat brim. He was surprised that he wasn't afraid, a city boy about to take on the dreaded Apache, sitting a horse he couldn't ride, holding a rifle he couldn't shoot.

The thought, unsettling though it was, made McBride smile . . . until he heard Prescott's wild curse.

CHAPTER 17

Luke Prescott swung out of the saddle and started to run, yelling at McBride to come after him.

McBride swung his leg over the mustang, got his foot caught up in the seat-cushion saddle and fell flat on his back. The black cantered past him as he climbed to his feet and pounded after Prescott.

Ahead of him the stream bank formed a sharp arc around a sandbar, a tall cottonwood standing at its center. Close by, a willow trailed its branches into the water, but McBride's eyes were fixed on the ruined cabin that lay beyond the trees — and the body that hung in the doorway.

Prescott was standing a ways off from the crumbling soddy, the gray bandanna he wore around his neck pulled up over his nose and mouth. When McBride stepped next to him the stench hit him like a fist. Swarms of fat black flies buzzed busily around him, the usual slaughterhouse welcoming committee telling their tale.

"She's been dead for at least two days, maybe longer," Prescott said, his voice muffled by the bandanna. "Little gal died hard."

A sod brick had eroded above the heavy pine frame of the doorway, leaving just enough space for a rope. The height of the entrance was only about six feet, but the young Chinese girl who hung there had been small and her down-turned toes dangled inches above the ground.

The rope around the girl's neck had cut deep and it was hard to make out the details of her bloated features. But McBride was detective enough to determine that her neck wasn't broken — she'd been strangled to death. She was dressed in the traditional knee-length tunic and loose, black pants of the Chinese woman.

Coyotes had tried to pull her down. That was obvious from her ragged pants and the blood on her legs and lower body. They had taken what they could.

The watch in McBride's pocket was ticking, the world around them turning, but for he and Prescott time stood still as they tried to come to terms with what they were seeing.

A girl, a child really, had been brutally hanged. Why?

McBride laid his rifle on the grass at his feet. "Stay here, Luke," he told Prescott.

The man nodded. He said, "Sure thing. I ain't much inclined to get closer."

Last night's rain had washed away any prints that might have been left by the girl's killers, but above the doorway a section of the timber and sod roof was still in place.

McBride walked around to the back of the cabin and stepped inside. Half the roof had caved in and he was forced to pick his way through fallen beams and chunks of dry sod toward the door. A pack rat had made a nest in one corner and a scatter of black pellets on the dirt floor revealed where an owl had roosted.

He was behind the dead girl now, close to her body, and the smell of rotting flesh was almost unbearable. McBride put a hand over his mouth and nose and studied the soft, dry dirt behind the doorway. There was a single set of prints, the wide, low-heeled outlines of a miner's boots. The square toes were facing the girl's back.

McBride lurched away from the body and put it together when he reached the cleaner air outside.

The girl had been small and light, too light

to strangle easily in the noose. A man, probably a miner, had stood behind the girl and pulled down on her body, hastening her death. It had not been an act of mercy. He, and presumably others with him, had wanted to make certain she died.

And Prescott had been right. The little Chinese girl had died hard, slowly and with much pain and fear.

But the question remained: Why?

"We can't leave her hanging there," Prescott said when McBride rejoined him. "It isn't decent."

"No, it's not," McBride said.

"Maybe we can bury her."

"But not near deep enough."

"Then what, John?"

"There are dry timbers in the cabin. We'll burn her body." He turned and looked at Prescott. "Go into the cabin and get the fire started."

"Me?"

"Yes, you. Out here a man should know how to make a fire. He just never can tell when he'll need one."

Prescott's eyes revealed that he'd caught the irony, but he let it pass. "The smoke will be seen for miles and the men who did this could still be close."

"So? We're just a couple of travelers riding

through pass-on-by country who happened to stop to give a dead girl a decent funeral. They won't fault us for that, at least not much."

Prescott thought that through, then nodded and slipped the bandanna from his face. "I sure hope you know what you're doing, John. And after it's over, what then?"

"Like you say, the men who murdered the girl could be close. We will go find them."

"And then?"

McBride's eyes were wintry. "We'll kill them all, Luke. Everybody lives, but not everybody deserves to."

The little gunfighter grinned. "John McBride, I have the feeling you'd make a mighty bad enemy."

"Believe it," McBride said. He did not smile.

Together they cut down the girl's body, an unpleasant task that had to be done, and laid her out as gently as they could on a pile of timbers. Despite the recent rain the wood was tinder-dry. Prescott used the pack rat's nest for kindling and the old roof beams readily caught fire. When the timbers were blazing fiercely, sending up a thick column of gray smoke, they stepped back and watched the cabin burn.

"We should say some words," Prescott

said. "What god would that little Celestial gal pray to?"

"The same god we pray to, I imagine. He might have a different name in China, that's all."

"Well, I don't know any of the words anyhow," Prescott said. "The times I watched men get buried, a preacher always read from the Book. Them was a heap of words and not something a man can easily recollect."

"If we knew the words, we'd say them, Luke. I'd guess right about now the little Chinese girl knows that."

After the fire had died away to ashes, Prescott rounded up his horse and McBride reluctantly climbed onto the bony back of the mustang. As the sun dropped lower in the sky and their shadows grew long, they rode out of the meadow and again followed the wagon trail.

The trail wound upward through stands of ponderosa and aspen, curving around huge outcroppings of granite rock that grew more numerous as they climbed higher and the air thinned. After an hour the sun was a dull crimson ball low above the western horizon, adrift in a sky the color of ancient jade. A stiff breeze had picked up, whispering wild stories to the aspen that set their leaves to trembling.

They came up on the water tower of the Union Pacific just as the day was shading into night and the trail petered out to nothing. The tower stood on a siding and close to it was a piled-high pyramid of sawn logs for the furnaces of the locomotives. A small shed with a padlocked door stood a ways from the track, a wooden wheelbarrow leaning against one of its walls.

"There's nobody home," Prescott said, drawing rein on his horse, his eyes restlessly searching the shadowed, aspen-covered hills that rose on either side of the rails.

"If Trask's men take the Chinese girls and opium off the trains here, there could be another wagon trail that we're not seeing," McBride said.

"Unless they load them up and head for High Hopes right away," Prescott said.

"We didn't meet anybody on the trail," McBride said. He groaned softly and shifted uncomfortably on the mustang. "That means whoever murdered the Chinese girl is still around."

"Or she may have been dead longer than we reckoned. If that's the case, her killers could have taken the wagon trail before us."

McBride nodded. "There's still enough

light for us to scout around and see if there's another trail headed away from the siding."

Prescott found the trail a few minutes later, a narrow wagon road cut through the aspen that had been just out of sight behind the log pile. He called McBride over and pointed at the hill rising above him.

"The trail cuts across the saddleback. It's got to end up somewhere. I'm betting at a cabin or maybe a cave."

"We'll leave the horses here and go take a look," McBride said. "I don't want to be slip-sliding on the back of the mustang when the shooting starts."

Prescott glanced at McBride's gun in the shoulder holster. "You as good with that self-cocker as I heard?"

"I don't know what you heard, but I'd say I'm fair to middling."

"If there's more than two of Trask's men, you might want to try real hard to do better."

McBride smiled. "I'll try, Luke. Yes, I'll try real hard."

He watched Prescott swing out of the saddle, briefly envied the man's casual elegance, then clambered off the back of the mustang. He had not eaten since breakfast, and there hadn't been much of that, and his stomach rumbled loudly as he and Prescott took to the wagon trail and climbed toward the gap of the hollow hill.

They drew the night around them like a cloak and became one with the darkness. Very near, an owl asked its question to the heedless wind, then demanded an answer again. Prescott, a horseman unused to walking, made his awkward way along the sun-baked clay of a wagon-wheel track. His spurs were chiming, bootheels thudding on dry pine needles. McBride was glad they were not facing Apache. The dime novel he'd read said the savages heard every sound, even the faintest whisper, and would suddenly come charging out of the dark whooping and hollering, waving their murderous tomahawks.

He remembered a line from the book that had struck him: "Many a lovely lass in the first blush of maidenhood they've undone, many a stalwart frontiersman they've murdered, many a poor old mother's heart they've broken."

McBride nodded to himself. That was a haunting line, penned by a good writer. Someday he'd like to read —

"The gap is just ahead," Prescott said, interrupting his thoughts. "Keep your rifle up and ready."

They reached the crest of the gap and stopped, staring into the night. The moon was rising, but its light was dim, lying thin on the land. McBride could make out the slope of the hill falling away steeply from where he stood, and something else — the lights of a cabin hanging like lanterns in the darkness.

"Just as I thought," Prescott whispered. "They hold the girls here for a spell before taking them to High Hopes."

"How can you be sure it's Trask's men?" McBride asked. "It could be railroaders."

"I'm not sure. That's why we'll get closer and take a look around."

"Then you'd better take off your spurs, Luke. You make more racket than church bells on Sunday morning."

Prescott grinned, his teeth flashing white in the gloom. "We ain't going to no prayer meeting, that's for sure." He bent, unbuckled his spurs and set them atop a tree stump by the trail. "Ready?"

"I'm ready."

"Then let's take a stroll."

The sky was ablaze with stars and the ascending moon wore a halo as the two men made their way down the slope and onto the flat. A mist wreathed through the silver trunks of the aspen and twined like a great gray snake across the low grassland, sound-less as a ghost.

Closer now, McBride could make out the shape of the cabin, even see the smoke from the chimney, tied into bowknots by the wind. The air smelled of trees and the tang of frying bacon and his mouth watered and his stomach rumbled the more.

He followed Prescott as the man, crouch-ing low and keeping his distance, scuttled past the front of the cabin. Two windows showed to the front, rectangles of orange light in the gloom. From inside McBride heard a man laugh loud and harsh and thump a table with the flat of his hand.

To the right of the cabin was a smaller building, a windowless shed with a slanted roof. The door was locked shut by a heavy wooden bolt. Beyond the shed was a pole corral where four horses dozed, and pulled up next to it was a freight wagon. Behind the seat, a massive iron cage took up the entire bed.

Those were Trask's men in the cabin all right. McBride tightened his grip on the Winchester as he took a knee beside Pres-cott. He pointed to the cabin and whispered, "Trask's boys."

The gunfighter nodded. "Figgered that." He rose to his feet. "Let's go be sociable, just like we were visiting kinfolk."

Before McBride could protest, Prescott strode toward the cabin, his rifle hanging in his right hand. When he was twenty feet from the door he stopped and yelled, "Hello the cabin!"

As McBride joined him he heard the scrape of a chair across a wood floor and a moment later the door swung open. A huge man stood silhouetted in the doorway, what looked to be a shotgun in his hands. "What the hell do you want?"

Firing from the hip, Prescott shot him in the belly.

CHAPTER 18

The man screamed and slammed against the door-frame. His knees buckled and as he started to go down, Prescott shot him again.

Learning nothing from the death of his partner, a second man appeared in the doorway, a Colt flaming in each hand. He was shooting blindly into the darkness, but he was outlined against the greasy yellow glow of kerosene lantern light.

Prescott fired, levered his rifle and fired again.

McBride saw a sudden arc of blood and brain fan above the man's head. He staggered back out of sight, the staccato thump of his bootheels loud on the pine floor. A grinding crash of metal, then a wild yell from inside as burning logs scattered across the wood floor from the tipped stove.

McBride had been seeking a target. Now he found one. He fired at the lantern hanging just inside the cabin window. A miss. Cursing under his breath, he tossed the rifle aside and drew his Smith & Wesson. He raised the gun to eye level in both hands, aimed and fired again. The lamp exploded and instantly flames shot up behind the window.

A frantic voice came from somewhere near the smoke-filled doorway. "We're done! We're coming out."

"Put your mitts up where I can see them," Prescott yelled. "And make sure they're empty."

Two men tumbled, coughing, out through the cabin door. The one to Prescott's left was big and bearded, while the other was smaller and younger. The little gunfighter shot the bearded man and he went down shrieking, a bullet smashing into his breast-bone a few inches below where his neck met his chest. Prescott fired again, this time a careful belly shot into the younger man.

"I want that one!" Prescott hollered at McBride. "Let him be."

For his part, McBride had no intention of shooting. He was stunned by the sudden-ness of the violence and Prescott's cool skill with a gun. He'd downed four men in less than a couple of minutes. Nothing McBride had ever experienced had prepared him for that, not even growing up on the tough streets or his years in the New York police, when he'd served with many hard men.

For the first time he appreciated what it had taken for Prescott to enter the top rank of gunfighters and become a named man. Looking around him at the dead men and the youngster screaming and slowly dying, he knew he wanted no part of it. For a few minutes there, Luke Prescott had teetered on the outer rim of madness and no one could have pulled him back from the precipice. McBride never wanted to find himself there. . . . Unless . . . he suddenly thought of Shannon and realized that Prescott's bloody, insane road was one he might well have to soon travel himself.

The towheaded boy on the ground was speaking, looking up at Prescott with agonized, pleading eyes. "I'm gutshot. . . . Damn you, end it."

"I will. But first I want to ask you a question, for my own satisfaction, like."

"Then ask it and be damned to ye. My belly's on fire."

Prescott got down on one knee beside the boy, who looked to be about seventeen or so. Behind Prescott the cabin blazed, sending smoke and flames into the sky, and he was outlined in fire.

"Why did you hang the little Chinese gal?"

"I . . . I had no part in that. It was Dawson and the others who did it."

"Charlie Dawson?"

The boy bit back his pain until his lip bled. "Yeah, him an' Hank Ross an' Jess Worley."

Prescott spoke to McBride from the scarlet-streaked darkness. "A few years back Charlie Dawson rode with Sam Bass and that wild bunch down Austin way. He was the worst of them."

McBride made no answer as the boy yelped, "You've asked your question — now end it."

His voice level and matter-of-fact, Prescott said, "I'm still waiting for an answer. Why did Charlie hang the Celestial?"

Again the boy bit back a scream. "She . . . she ran away. When we caught her, Charlie hung her as an example to the others. Made . . . made them look at it."

"There are others?" McBride asked. "Where are they?"

"In the shed. Four . . . four of them."

McBride looked at the boy, then said to Prescott, "Is there anything we can do for him?"

"Sure there is." The gunfighter rose to his feet, drew his Colt and shot the boy in the head. "That's what we can do for him."

Prescott read the tightly knotted expression on McBride's face, a mix of horror and disgust. He punched out the empty shell from the Colt and reloaded from his gun belt. When he spoke his voice was flat, without emotion.

"John, we're in a hard, merciless business. You want to take down Gamble Trask and so do I. You want to save your woman and so do I. But we can't do it without killing, a lot of killing. Turning the other cheek is for preachers and them as don't know any better. Now, you either make up your mind to the killing part or we say adios right here and now and go our own ways."

"I've killed two men," McBride said, "and at the time I understood the necessity for it. But you just shot a boy."

Prescott shrugged. "War prefers its victims young. But he was man-grown enough to carry a gun and ride with wild ones. He took his chances, but the deck was stacked against him, maybe from the day and hour he was born." The gunfighter stepped closer to McBride. "We don't have much time. If there are Celestials in the shack yonder, the fire could spread from the cabin and we'll have more dead young ones on our hands." He hesitated a moment, then: "Have you made up your mind?"

"I'll go along with the killing if there's no other way."

"There is no other way. Our talking is done, John. From now until we come out on the other side, we let our guns speak for us."

"Then that will be the way of it. Now let's get those girls out of there," McBride said. "Before they burn to death."

The cabin was an inferno of smoke and flame that tinged the sky red. Inside the corral, the horses were wild-eyed, trotting in circles, snorting, tossing their heads, terrified of a predator that was worse than any other. The shack was about ten paces from the burning cabin and when McBride reached the door the heat was intense. As a torrent of sparks cascaded around him, he slammed back the wooden bolt and opened the door.

It was dark inside, but the light from the blazing cabin splashed a triangle of flickering orange on the dirt floor, revealing a pair of slippered feet. As his eyes became accustomed to the gloom, McBride made out the shadowy shapes of four women cowering against the far wall. They made no attempt to get to their feet.

Prescott stepped beside him and took in

the situation at a glance. "Out!" he yelled.

The frightened women clung closer together but did not move.

"Out!" Prescott yelled again, to no effect. "What the hell is Chinese for 'out'?" he demanded. Smoke was rapidly filling the shack and the heat was growing more intense. "Outee!" Prescott hollered.

"Drag them out, Luke," McBride said. "They won't move by themselves."

The girls were tiny, small-boned and light as birds. McBride and Prescott lifted them one by one and carried them outside, well away from the cabin. A few minutes later the shack caught fire.

Made ragged by heat, the wind gusted, fanning the flames of both cabin and shack. Prescott turned the frantic horses out of the corral, trusting that they would not run long and far. He and McBride got on each side of the wagon and pushed it well away from sparks. When they returned, the girls were still sitting where they'd left them, faces blank, black eyes reflecting the flames of the fire but nothing else.

One by one, McBride pushed up the sleeves of the girls' tunics and saw what he'd expected, the track marks of a needle, like insect bites on their smooth skin.

He turned to Prescott.

"I didn't see any drugs in the shack, did you?"

The man shook his head.

"Probably burned up in the cabin."

"You ever seen a heroin addict who can't get the drug any longer?" McBride asked.

"Can't say as I have."

"I did, a couple of times. It's nasty. In a few hours we're going to have our hands full with these women."

Luke Prescott laughed.

"Women? They're only children. What age do you make them out to be?"

McBride took a knee and cupped his hand around the chin of one of the girls, lifting her face to the dying light of the cabin fire.

"Twelve." He moved to another. "About the same age." Another. "Thirteen maybe." He looked at the last girl awhile longer. "This one is older. Fifteen, I'd say."

"Trask likes them young," Prescott said, smiling without humor.

McBride remembered Hell's Kitchen and the brothels of the Four Corners. "The men Trask sells them to like them young. It's their business — they cater to perverts." He turned bleak eyes to Prescott. "In some brothels I've known, a man can rape a girl, then beat her to death if that's his inclination, just so long as he has the money to pay for it."

"Glad I've always steered clear of big cities," Prescott said. "I didn't even know men like that existed."

McBride's laugh was bitter. "They exist all right, and the men who supply them with what they want are just as bad."

"Like Trask?"

"Just like Trask." McBride was silent for a few moments as he studied the vacant faces of the four girls. Then he said, "Now we've got them, what do we do with them?"

Prescott had been building a cigarette. Now his eyes lifted from tobacco and paper to McBride. "I've been studying on that. We can't take them back to High Hopes, but I know a man who might shelter them for a spell, if you pay him enough."

"Where is he?"

"About ten miles north of here on Cucharas Creek, a mountain stream that runs over bedrock across some pretty wild country. The man's name is Angus McKenzie. He's a trapper, sometime prospector, and he lives with a Kiowa woman in a cabin up there."

"Can we trust him?"

Prescott sealed his cigarette, placed it between his lips and thumbed a match into flame. He lit his smoke and flicked away the dead match before he answered McBride's question. "Do we have any choice?"

"No, I guess not. We can't be burdened with four young girls when we come up against Trask."

"You said that right," Prescott observed. He rose to his feet. "Now we got work to do."

He and McBride pulled the corral apart and threw the pine poles into the smoldering cabin, where they blazed immediately. Both the cabin and shack were now blackened ruins and there was little else damage to be done.

"I'd like to see Trask's face when he hears about this," Prescott said, watching the poles burn. "Four of his men dead and this place in ruins."

"He can always rebuild and hire more men," McBride said. "Unless we stop him."

"We will, John. Trust me, we will." Prescott smiled. "Unless we're dead, of course, and that possibility is just as likely as the other."

Later they ate the last of the salt pork and drank coffee. The Chinese girls refused both, huddling together, their wide almond eyes revealing nothing.

McBride and Prescott took turns guarding the girls throughout the night, fearing that they might run. But as the darkness shaded into the gray dawn, they had not moved, sitting dull and compliant, making no sound. After McBride rose and stretched, working the kinks out of his still-hurting back, the oldest girl reached out her arm and said something in Chinese he could not understand. But her meaning was clear — she needed heroin.

McBride felt a stab of pity as he shook his head. The girl dropped her arm, saying nothing. She shivered violently and moved closer to the girl beside her, cold, not from the cool morning, but from the lack of the drug.

He and Prescott rounded up the horses and hitched a pair to the wagon. Then Prescott saddled a rawboned bay for himself and a paint for McBride. "You can tie him to the back of the wagon until we get to McKenzie's place," he said.

But McBride refused. "Just throw the saddle into the wagon. I'll stick with the mustang."

Prescott laughed, but did as he was told, leaving McBride to brood about his ability to drive a horse team. The little gunfighter returned a few minutes later, a small brick of a tarry brown substance in his hand. "I threw the saddle into the wagon like you said and it sure made a hollow sound to me."

"A false bottom?"

"Yeah, and when I took out a couple of boards, I found this, and maybe another forty just like it."

"It's raw opium," McBride said. "Gamble Trask's opium. We'll burn it."

Prescott used some fallen beams to kindle a blaze in the glowing embers of the cabin. Then he and McBride began to toss the opium bricks into the flames.

Prescott turned to McBride and smiled. "Hey, John, you know we're burning money here, don't you?"

"Luke, that's all I've been thinking about for the last thirty minutes," McBride said sadly as he threw the last brick into the fire.

CHAPTER 19

When they reached the railroad siding, Prescott saddled his black and tied McBride's mustang behind the wagon. The four Chinese girls crowded together inside the cage, mewling like tormented kittens as they suffered the first pangs of heroin withdrawal. When either McBride or Prescott stepped close, the girls thrust their arms through the bars, their eyes pleading.

Prescott made a face at McBride.

"Lord almighty, what's that smell? Get near the wagon and it stinks like the Chisum ranch bunkhouse in summer."

"It's part of leaving heroin behind. Something vile oozes out through the skin. I don't know what it is, but it will get worse before it gets better."

"Glad you're driving the wagon and not me," Prescott said.

Because of the heavy wagon and McBride's inexpert driving, it took him and

Prescott two days to reach McKenzie's cabin on the Cucharas.

They'd passed through rough, broken country, a land of red canyons and majestic, aspen-covered ridges. At higher elevations they'd seen wolves move through the ponderosas like gray wraiths, trotting past towering parapets of granite rock where streaks of snow still clung.

At dusk on the first day Prescott had shot an antelope, but the girls refused to eat and took no notice of their surroundings. They clung to one another, alternately sweating and shivering, moaning softly in the grip of a merciless enemy they could neither control nor understand.

Angus McKenzie's cabin was set back from a sandy bend of the creek, shaded by an ancient cottonwood. A small barn stood behind the house and next to it a pole corral. A vegetable garden grew on one side of the cabin and nearby a well had been dug.

It was, McBride decided, a pleasant enough place, though he withheld judgment until he could determine if Prescott's description of McKenzie as an irascible, dour old Scotsman rang true.

Watching them come, the man himself stood outside his door, a rifle in one hand, the other shading his eyes. His tense watchfulness drained from him when Prescott rode close enough to be seen.

"Howdy, Luke," he said in a soft Scottish burr when the gunfighter drew rein close to him. "Still riding the American stud, I see. I recognized him fine when you were still a ways off."

"Howdy yourself, Angus," Prescott smiled. "I'll get right to it. We've come to ask a favor of you."

"Are you on the dodge, like?"

"I'm on the dodge, but I'm not asking a favor for myself." He waved a hand. "It's for them."

"In the convict wagon?"

"Yeah, four Chinese girls. They need a place to stay for a while."

McKenzie, a long string bean of a man with a gray beard that fell to the top of his canvas pants, walked over to the wagon and looked up at McBride.

"And who might you be?"

McBride gave his name.

"Would that be the Scots or Irish McBrides?"

"Irish, I believe."

"Ah weel," McKenzie said, "when all is said and done, is not one much the same as the other?"

Without waiting for an answer, he stepped

207

to the side of the wagon.

"These lassies are sick," he said. Then, alarm showing on his face: "It's not the black plague, is it?"

"It's not the plague. They'll be better in a few more days," McBride said. "All they need is rest and some good food."

McKenzie stuck an arm through the iron bars and placed his hand on the oldest girl's forehead. She looked at him dully, making no move to pull away.

"She's got a fever," he said. "They all have." He withdrew his arm and put his hand to his nose, sniffing. "They all need a bath in the creek, smells like."

"Yes," McBride said, deciding it would not be a good idea to elaborate right then.

"They look far too young to be convicts."

"They're not convicts." McBride hesitated. "It's a story long in the telling."

"I would fancy it is," McKenzie said. He looked from McBride to Prescott, who had just ridden up to the wagon. "You two look sharp-set and so do the wee lassies. Come into the hoose and my woman will feed you."

The cabin was sparsely furnished but spotlessly clean. The timber floor was swept and covered with buffalo hides, and the table and chairs were polished to an amber glow. There was a stove against one wall and an open cupboard where plates with a blue pattern were displayed. Several of Mc-Kenzie's traps hung near the door and beside them, a rack where he set his Henry rifle.

His woman was tall and slender and she wore her graying black hair loose over her shoulders in the style of the Kiowa. Humor lurked in her dark eyes and she seemed genuinely pleased to have visitors.

"Aye, she's a good woman right enough," McKenzie said after McBride had thanked her for the bowl of venison stew she'd laid in front of him. "I paid twenty dollars in gold to the Kiowa for her. That was back in the spring of fifty-six and I've never regretted it. Weel, that's not true. Sometimes I look back on the expense and feel a wee bit of regret, but what's done is done and there's an end to it."

"What's your lady's name?" McBride asked.

"Adoette. It means large tree." McKenzie smiled, revealing surprisingly good teeth. "The Kiowa only have thirty-two female names, so there's not many for a parent to choose from."

Prescott poised a forkful of stew between his bowl and mouth and jutted his chin toward the Chinese girls. "I wonder what they're called."

"They can't tell us," McKenzie said. "Unless a man knows Chinese."

The four girls were sitting on the floor and Adoette was spooning stew into their mouths. They opened up dutifully, but their eyes were still in a far place and they shivered uncontrollably.

McBride was relieved. At least they were eating. Not much, certainly, but eating.

After McBride and Prescott sighed their fullness and pushed their bowls away, McKenzie brought out a jug and three glasses. He filled each with whiskey, then said, "Luke, you asked about a favor, and I'm thinking that I ken what it might be. But I want to hear it from your own mouth."

Prescott tried his whiskey, found it good and drank more. He laid his glass back on the table and said, "Angus, you've helped me before when I was on the dodge, and I don't want to impose on our friendship and your good nature, but —"

"We want you to keep the girls for a while," McBride interrupted. "I'll pay you what you ask."

McKenzie absorbed what had just been said and bent his head, looking into his glass. He stayed silent for a long while, the

210

only sound in the room the tick of a clock on the wall and the soft cooing of Adoette as she fed and petted the girls.

Finally the old man looked directly at McBride and said, "Tell me about them."

Using as few words as possible, McBride told McKenzie how the girls had been destined for a short and violent life of prostitution until he and Prescott had freed them.

"I will not go into any more details, Mr. McKenzie," he finished. "There is no need for our enemies to become yours."

"Yet, if I give these young Celestials a home, then surely your enemies will become mine?"

McBride nodded, a man bound to honesty. "That is likely."

Again McKenzie went into a brooding silence. Adoette was whispering to the girls in a language they did not understand, and one of them answered, sounds without meaning, drifting sweet and light as birdsong through the hushed room.

It was the first time McBride had ever heard any of the girls speak, and it pleased him greatly.

Angus McKenzie lifted his head.

"Mr. McBride, you have a good name and a strong face and I'll tell you what I feel. By times, I am a harsh, unbending man, much given to ardent spirits and profanity. But I am also a God-fearing man, from an early age raised in the Presbyterian Church to know what is right and what is wrong. Yes, I will take care of your girls and when you return, you will find them happier than they were when you left."

"I'll pay you —"

"No money, Mr. McBride, not for this. I cannot take gold and silver coin for an act of Christian charity. To do so would be to spit in the eye of God."

"Angus, we're beholden to you," Prescott said.

"When will you return?"

McBride shook his head and answered for Prescott. "That I don't know. It will be when our business is done. A week, maybe two, maybe longer —"

"Maybe never," Prescott said.

"Then . . . this business of yours is revolver work?"

"It's my trade, Angus," Prescott said. "You understand that."

"Then I will ask no more questions. The less I know, the less I can tell."

McKenzie rose to his feet, sighing long, as though his new responsibilities had suddenly dawned on him. "I will have my woman sack you up some grub. Now you've been refreshed, you will be wanting to get back on the trail."

It was a polite dismissal and McBride accepted it as such.

"We'll leave the wagon if you don't mind," he said.

"Yes, leave it. I'll get rid of that damnable convict cage. It's a thing the wee lassies have no need to see anymore."

McBride stood to say his farewells. He walked over to the Chinese girls. Knowing they could not understand a word he said, he backed up his speech with an elaborate pantomime of his hands. "I am going now." He pointed to himself and made a walking motion with two fingers of his right hand, covering distance in the air. Then, a return, this time using his left. "I'll come back for you."

He was met with blank stares — then the youngest girl surprised him. She jumped to her feet and threw her arms around his waist, her cheek pressing into the hard muscle of his belly. A frantic pleading in her voice, the girl kept saying the same words over and over again, her frail arms tightening.

"She does not want you to leave," Adoette said. "It is a child's way. But you must go

213

now, make a clean break."

"John, maybe she thinks you're her pa," Prescott said, grinning.

McBride gently disentangled the girl's arms, took a knee and looked into her damp brown eyes. "I'll come back for you," he said. His eyes lifted to the Kiowa woman. "After I'm gone, try to make her understand."

"I will try. You are taking the warrior's path and will not be able to hold this child in your arms. Therefore you must hold her in your heart."

McBride rose to his feet. "I'll remember that, Adoette," he said. The girl still clung to him.

As they rode away from the cabin and a silence grew between them, Prescott turned in the saddle and said finally, "You think they'll make it, John?"

"I don't know," McBride said. "If they can get over the heroin addiction, if McKenzie treats them right . . ." He wiped sweat from the band of his plug hat, then settled it back on his head. "I just don't know."

"If you're still alive after this is done, what will you do with four Chinese girls?"

"I don't know that either."

"How would Shannon Roark take it? Having an instant family, I mean."

McBride's face showed his annoyance. "Luke, anybody ever tell you that you ask too many questions?"

"All the time," the little gunfighter said, unabashed. "I have what you might call an inquisitive nature."

They rode in silence for several minutes. Then McBride said, "I don't know how Shannon would take it."

CHAPTER 20

McBride and Prescott made camp that night in an arroyo due east of the Spanish Peaks and bedded down on a mattress of pine needles.

From out of the darkness McBride heard Prescott's voice. "John, where do we go from here?"

"I've been thinking about it, but I don't know."

"We've hurt Gamble Trask, killed a few of his men, freed the Chinese girls and burned his opium, but he'll bounce right back."

"He can rebuild his cabin and slave shack and hire more men, that's for sure."

McBride heard Prescott stir and rise up on one elbow. "We're no match for Hack Burns and the Allison brothers, not if they come at us all at once." After a few moments of silence he added, "I think I can take Burns, but the Allisons stick together. They'd be a handful."

"I'll be with you."

"It's still two against four, plus how many hard cases Trask can round up. I don't think we can buck those odds."

"I've been thinking about Shannon. I promised to protect her, but I've left her all alone in High Hopes. That can weigh on a man."

Prescott sat up and started to build a cigarette. "We can't do anything else to damage Trask out here. Hell, as it is, all we've probably done is make him mad. I reckon High Hopes is where we should be."

A match flared orange in the dark and McBride saw it reflect on the lean planes of Prescott's face. "Kill Trask and it's over," he said.

"I want to kill him bad and that would be the easy solution." Prescott lay on his back again. "It's getting to Trask without getting killed ourselves that's difficult."

McBride was silent for so long, Prescott thought he was asleep. "John?"

"I'm awake. I was just thinking that we've failed. We killed a few men, freed some girls and burned up a shipment of opium. There's nothing there that Trask can't replace. We've been a couple of hornets trying to sting an elephant."

Now Prescott fell silent. When he spoke

again there was a note of excitement in his voice. "John, you told me that Trask plans a grandstand play, something that will be his ticket out of High Hopes and into lace-curtain Washington. If we can find out what it is and head him off at the pass, it's our chance to ruin him. Once Trask is broke and alone, I'll kill him."

"His big score could be something to do with orphan trains. Have you come up with any idea of what Leggett was trying to tell me?"

"No, I haven't. Dying men say all kinds of things that don't make sense. 'Orphan trains' could be one of them."

McBride turned his head, peering into the darkness at Prescott. "Luke, I've got something to tell you. I'm a police officer, a detective sergeant. I was ordered to get out of New York after I killed the son of a man who is just like Gamble Trask, only worse."

Prescott laughed softly. "Hell, John, I knew you was some kind of law the first time I ever saw you. Wearing a star changes a man, the way he walks and talks and thinks . . . and there's something else, something in his eyes, watchful, like a hawk."

"Like a gunslinger's eyes."

"Yeah, the same, only different."

Prescott ground his cigarette butt into the dirt. "Well, as far as I know, I'm not wanted in New York, so once again, Detective Sergeant McBride, where do we go from here?"

"High Hopes," McBride said. "Only don't call me that when we're around company, polite or otherwise."

They rose at first light and fried some of the bacon and flat Indian bread Adoette had packed for them. After McBride threw the last of the coffee onto the fire he saddled the mustang and climbed on board.

"You're getting better," Prescott said, watching. "At least you don't fall headfirst over the other side any longer."

They reached Apishapa Creek by noon, then swung east toward High Hopes.

The day was hot, the hilly land standing still and silent to the sun. To the west the mountains showed as a purple haze against the denim sky and in all directions the distances shimmered, hazy curtains discreetly drawn across the wilderness that lay beyond.

Ahead of them a stand of tall cottonwoods promised shade and a chance to water the horses, and McBride, already saddlesore, was wishful of coffee and a chance to stretch his legs.

He was sitting with his back to a tree, drinking his second cup, when Prescott whispered to him urgently, "Riders."

McBride followed his eyes to the plain where three men were walking lathered horses, two of them in miners' garb, the third wearing the black, flat-brimmed hat and knee-length frock coat of the frontier gambler.

Prescott's words came out like the hiss of a hunting snake. "Well, as I live and breathe, it's Stryker Allison."

"Allison, here?"

"The wagon was overdue and I reckon Stryker and the other two were sent out to look for it. Judging by the condition of their horses, they've come far, maybe all the way from the railroad siding and the burned cabin."

McBride rose to his feet. "Have they seen us?"

"Not yet, but Stryker has caught our smoke. He's not a man to miss something like that."

Allison was squatting on his haunches, studying the creek. Then, his mind made up, he rose to his feet and swung into the saddle. The two men with him did the same and Stryker led them directly toward the spot where McBride and Prescott were standing.

"Get ready, John," Prescott whispered. "I've got a feeling this isn't going to end well, not well at all."

They watched Allison and the other two men splash across the creek, the horses throwing up brief fountains of water around their legs that caught the sunlight.

Allison led his men to within twenty feet of where McBride stood, and drew rein. The gunman touched his hat and under his sweeping mustache his mouth stretched in a grin. "Nice to see you again, Mr. Smith. It's been a spell. Have you been riding out?"

"Just that, riding out."

"Toward the Union Pacific road maybe?"

"Not particularly. Just here and there."

Allison's cold eyes moved to Prescott. "And your friend here. I don't think we're acquainted."

Prescott was standing easy, his thumbs tucked into his gun belt. But the stiffness in his shoulders and his wide-legged stance betrayed his tension. "Name's Luke Prescott. No need to give me yours, I know it already."

"Then you have me at a disadvantage. Let me see. . . . Prescott . . . Prescott . . . where have I heard that name before? Ah, now I remember. I recall some white trash who went by that handle. Brothers, I think."

It was a challenge — that sudden, that raw.

McBride stepped into it head-on. "When you ride into a man's camp uninvited, Allison, I'll remind you to keep a civil tongue in your head."

The miners had spread out, watching, eager, Allison's gun skill giving them the courage they usually borrowed from whiskey. Both wore cross-draw Colts, high up, where the draw would be shorter and faster. McBride realized there would be no backup in them unless Allison was down and then they'd fold quickly.

"No offense intended, I assure you," Allison said. The smile under his mustache was thin and sharp as a razor. "Now, will you mind your own manners, Mr. Smith, and invite a man to step down for coffee?"

McBride nodded and took a step back. His eyes moved to Prescott. The gunfighter was giving Allison all his concentration. Suddenly he looked on edge, like a man about to go into a fight he was not sure he could win.

Allison swung out of the saddle, keeping his horse between him and Prescott. He had obviously summed up the situation and judged the little man more dangerous than

McBride.

He said as much. "I recollect you now, Prescott. You have a reputation." He grinned and moved away from the horse, his body turned to the perceived danger. "You're a named man."

Prescott said, "Here. And in other places."

Allison nodded. "The day is hot." He took off his frock coat and threw it over his saddle. His gun rode high, the butt between wrist and elbow. Against the lined, mahogany skin of his face his eyes were very blue. He was a tall, elegant man who looked tough and capable.

"I am," Allison said, "a named man myself."

Prescott made no answer, using his left hand to build a smoke.

McBride handed Allison a cup of coffee. Like Prescott, he took it in his left, leaving his gun hand free.

The miners sat their saddles with the patient watchfulness of vultures. Like McBride, they knew they were witnessing a ritual as old as the West itself, two belted men of reputation choosing partners for a dance of death.

"Good coffee," Allison said, his eyes above the rim of the cup steady on Prescott.

John McBride knew it would come sooner

rather than later. He made up his mind. He would let Prescott handle Allison, and he would take the miners. It would, he decided, be no easy thing. The two men looked like they'd handled the iron before.

Now Allison pushed it.

"Some low-down bushwhackers burned private property over to the Union Pacific road and murdered four good men," he said. "Shot them in the back. I saw that myself. They also stole goods belonging to my employer. I want those goods back."

He turned his head slightly toward McBride. "Tell me where you've hidden the girls, Smith, and I'll let you live."

McBride felt like he'd been pushed and prodded enough. Now anger flared in him. "Allison, you go to hell."

Stryker Allison's only reaction was a slight smile. He said to Prescott, "Same thing goes for you. Take me to the Celestials and maybe I'll let you go on breathing."

"And I'm giving you the same answer — go to hell!"

It seemed to McBride that the air had thinned, allowing him to see everything with crystal clarity. Once again, time had stopped and the world was no longer turning.

"So be it," Allison said. He dropped his cup and it rolled, clanging away from him.

"Now let's see how fast you are."

Allison drew.

Two shots, so close they sounded like one. McBride saw Prescott stagger, take a step back. He drew the Smith & Wesson. Slow! Too slow! But the miners hadn't moved. They sat their horses, watching Allison with transfixed fascination, hands away from their guns.

Prescott fired, fired again, and his bullets crossed Allison's. Prescott was hit again, hit hard, and went to his knees, blood scarlet on his chest. Allison swayed, cursing, and leaned his left shoulder against a cottonwood trunk, but his Colt was coming up.

Prescott shot quickly. The bullet slammed into Allison's gun and ranged upward, exploding into the gunman's chin, tearing away bone and teeth. His face a horrifying mask of blood, Allison screamed his rage. He tried to trigger his Colt, but the cylinder was jammed. He lurched toward Prescott, yelling strangled words without meaning. The little gunfighter steadied his gun in both hands, took careful aim and put a bullet between Allison's eyes. The gunman's head snapped back and he recoiled a few steps before crashing onto his back. His legs jerked like a stricken insect's. Then he lay still.

Turning fast from the waist, Prescott triggered his Colt. One of the miners stood in the stirrups and toppled off his horse. Prescott tried to fire at the other man, but the hammer clicked on an empty chamber.

Stunned by the killing of his friend, the miner shot his hands into the air. His eyes were frightened and he babbled wildly that he didn't want to fight.

McBride ignored the man and crossed quickly to Prescott. The little gunfighter was lying on his back, his eyes wide open, turned to the sun. He was dead.

McBride was vaguely aware that the surviving miner had turned his horse and was splashing across the creek. The man reached the far bank and kicked his mount into a run, riding for High Hopes with the bad news.

A sense of grief and loss in him, McBride looked down at Luke Prescott, trying to make sense of his death. In the end, he'd proved himself worthy of the rank of named man . . . by being better than the worst of them. It was the terrible suddenness and finality of Luke's dying that McBride found hard to accept.

Stryker Allison was dead, his face a thing of horror. The downed miner gasped for a few minutes, tried to speak; then he too was gone.

There was no way of getting around the fact that Prescott had shot the tin pan in cold blood, while he had no weapon in his hand. But Luke shared the one quality that all men who live by the gun possess — he was a killer. That had made him the man he was.

McBride looked up at the sky, blue, cloudless, uncaring. The sun burned bright still, the deaths of three men a small matter in an infinite universe. A rising wind rippled the water in the creek and ruffled the brown prairie grass like a hand moving through the hair of a towheaded boy. In the distance a small herd of antelope walked into the shimmering heat haze, their legs strangely elongating before they slowly melted from sight.

McBride walked to the creek bank, glanced into the clear water and saw what he'd hoped to see. He slipped his suspenders off his shoulders and stripped to the waist. Then he carried Prescott's body away from the creek and laid him out on the crest of a shallow hill where pink and blue wildflowers grew. He laid his rifle and Colt beside him, the call of his ancient Celtic ancestors strong in him, reminding him that a warrior must be buried with his weapons.

It took him most of the day to carry enough rocks from the bed of the creek to the hill to cover Prescott's body completely. But when it was done, and the stones were mounded high, he considered the cairn to be a fine monument.

Luke would lie where he could be one with the land he loved.

Allison's body and that of the miner, he left where they fell. The coyotes had a right to eat.

The long day was darkening into evening when McBride unsaddled the dead men's horses, removed their bridles and sent them running into the prairie with a slap on the rump. Allison's horse and the miner's would find their way back to High Hopes. As for Luke's big American stud, he would probably find a wild-horse herd and add his blood to future generations.

Tomorrow McBride knew he would have to make decisions about his next moves. But he'd already made one decision — he had to save Shannon from Gamble Trask, and that meant riding into High Hopes and accepting its dangers.

Once the miner told his tale in town, McBride knew, he would be a marked man. The Allison brothers would not let the death of their oldest go unavenged nor would Trask ignore the destruction of his property and the killing of his men.

Now that Luke was dead, he was one man against many, yet he had to do it.

Shannon Roark needed him.

CHAPTER 21

John McBride rode east along the creek. Making a grave for Prescott had taken him a long time and the sun was falling in the sky, gifting him with his shadow, the slowly moving shape of a tall man astride a small horse.

He had taken the pot and coffee and his eyes scanned the hilly country ahead of him for a suitable campsite. He needed water and fuel for a fire, and that dictated that he stay close to the creek. High Hopes was a day's ride away, time enough to go over his plan.

If he had a plan.

Then it came to him, perfect in its simplicity.

He would ride into town, find Shannon and take her away from there, head east and ride through the sunrise, putting ground between them and Trask. He wanted to bring the man down, ruin him, but that could wait. Until? McBride had no answer for that.

And what about the Chinese girls? Could he coldly ride away with the woman he loved and leave them to their fate?

The questions had already undermined his new-found confidence. What had seemed simple had all of a sudden become complicated. McBride rode into the sullen twilight of the dying day, as many shadows angling dark through the corridors of his mind as there were on the trail ahead.

He had, he decided, come full circle, at as much of a loss as he'd been just a few minutes before.

Darkness pressed on McBride, soft as a spring rain but crowding him close. The water was no longer visible, the creek a black ribbon unwinding away from him into the night. Out on the prairie the coyotes had begun their lamentations and the first stars hung like lanterns in the sky, glittering with frosty light.

The mustang lifted its head and its ears pricked forward as it stared into the gloom. "Easy, boy, easy," McBride whispered. He lifted the Winchester from the saddle horn, levered a round into the chamber and set the brass butt plate on his right thigh.

He drew rein on the horse and raised his

nose, testing the wind. The smoke smell was a fleeting will-o'-the-wisp, but it was there.

More of Trask's men? That was possible but unlikely. Then who? Maybe punchers riding through or freight wagons coming or going from the gold mines. The road into town was close and mule skinners could be camped for the night.

Where there was a fire there would be coffee and food and McBride's stomach had been complaining for hours. In the end his hunger overcame his good judgment and he rode on, tense and ready in the saddle.

He saw a campfire winking orange in the violet darkness. He judged the fire to be on the other side of the creek and swung the sure-footed little mustang into the bank. The spring melt was long gone and the water was shallow. He splashed across and climbed the bank on the other side. The firelight was closer now, winking in the gloom like a fallen star.

McBride rode nearer. He made out the flickering shadows of men walking in front of the fire and beyond the circle of the firelight he made out the shapes of several parked wagons, pale red light reflecting on the sides of their canvas tops.

He drew rein and, remembering what Prescott had taught him, called out: "Hello the camp!"

The reply was immediate, a heavily accented voice. "Come on in!"

McBride kneed the mustang forward and rode into the camp. About a dozen men had stopped their various chores and stood watching him. They didn't look like mule skinners or miners either. Rather, they had the jaunty, weather-beaten appearance of the seafaring men McBride had seen on the New York docks.

A man of medium size stepped toward McBride, a grin on his face and a welcome in his voice. "Step down, step down, good sir. You're just in time for supper."

McBride climbed out of the saddle and the man stuck out his hand. "My name is Captain Guaspar Diaz de Lamego, a poor sailorman lately of San Francisco town. But my friends, and I hope you will soon allow me to number you among those, call me Portugee."

Wary, McBride shook hands and gave his name as John Smith. He took a few moments to study the man called Portugee. He was an inch above medium height, dressed in a crimson shirt and tight black pants stuffed into soft leather boots of the same color. He was hatless but had tied a red bandanna around his head, knotted at the back of his neck. He sported a thin mustache, waxed and curled at the ends, and a goatee. His eyes were black, glittering with good humor in the firelight, and when he smiled, which was often, his teeth were dazzling white. Gold hoops hung from both his ears and he wore a huge ruby ring on the middle finger of his left hand.

Portugee looked, McBride thought to himself, about as trustworthy as a wounded cougar, as did his scurvy crew of cutthroats. The insistent alarm bell ringing in his head told him he would have done well to avoid this camp.

"Unsaddle your" — Portugee smiled — "horse, and join us at the fire. We have but simple mariners' fare, but what we have you are welcome to share."

It was in McBride's mind to refuse and say he must be moving on. But if Portugee was planning mischief, an abrupt departure would only precipitate the action and he was still not horseman enough to risk fighting from the back of the mustang.

Annoyed at himself for getting into this situation, he climbed down from the horse and led it to where other animals were picketed. He unsaddled and returned to the campfire, his rifle in his hands. He thought he saw Portugee glance at the Winchester, then give one of his men a knowing wink, but it could have been only a trick of the light or his own overactive imagination and McBride dismissed it.

He had just made a major mistake.

Portugee cursed and cuffed one of his men away from the fire and with a polite bow bade McBride sit. When the captain saw McBride settled, he waved to a man on his right. "This is another honored guest, the great Sheik Ali al-Karim, master of a dozen fine ships that sail the wine-dark waters of the Mediterranean Sea."

Al-Karim, dressed in flowing black and white Arab robes, bowed his head and made a graceful gesture to McBride, touching his forehead and lips with the crooked index finger of his right hand.

"The sheik doesn't say much, Mr. Smith," Portugee said, "but he's known from Tangier to Baghdad as a rich and powerful man. He agreed to place himself under our protection, since he is seeking to buy a stable of fine Thoroughbred racehorses to take back to his native land. He carries much gold and was warned that brigands lurk everywhere in the West." Portugee smiled. "I have taken this timid son of the desert under my wing."

Al-Karim had a lined, dark face and there

was a hint of cruelty about his thin lips. Like a hungry hawk, he watched McBride in the firelight, his black eyes glittering, missing nothing.

A sailor with a surly expression and a cutlass scar on one cheek brought McBride a bowl of green soup and a hunk of bread.

"Parched-pea soup, Mr. Smith," Portugee said. "I learned to enjoy it while I served ten years before the mast in old Queen Vic's navy. That's why you hear the accent of Bow Bells more than that of my native Seville in my speech. Now, by all means try the soup. As I told you, it's but humble sailormen's fare, though I trust you'll like it as much as I do."

McBride tried the soup. It was surprisingly good and he said so. Portugee seemed pleased.

"A compliment on one's cooking is always appreciated. Now, where are you bound, Mr. Smith?"

"Passing through," McBride said. His eyes lifted to the circle of armed men who were standing behind their captain. He did not see a friendly face and a few were mighty unfriendly.

The soup was hot, but McBride spooned it down quickly, anxious to be gone from the camp. "And you, Captain —"

"Portugee, please," he said with a dazzling smile.

"Well then, Portugee, where are you headed?"

"Wherever the trade winds blow us," the man answered. "In the wagons we carry ivory, sandalwood and all the spices of the Orient and seek to sell them for good, hard coin. But, alas, we are but honest sailors far from the sea and there are those who would seek to cheat us, I fear."

McBride thought Portugee and his hard-bitten bunch looked more like pirates than honest sailors, but he kept his own counsel and said, "I'd head north if I were you. Follow the Union Pacific road and you'll come on Pueblo, then Denver. You'll find a market for your goods in both places."

Portugee laughed and clapped his hands. He turned his head to the men behind him and yelled, "Hear that, you scurvy knaves? Never were truer words spoke. You are gold dust, Mr. Smith, pure gold dust, and damn me for a lubber if I don't take your advice." The man slapped his thigh. "Ain't Mr. Smith gold dust, boys, and no mistake?"

"Yeah, true-blue," somebody said, his voice flat, and another man put a hand to his mouth and snickered.

Portugee's face showed sudden concern.

"The soup is not to your liking?"

"It was good," McBride said. "See —" He upturned his bowl. "I finished every drop."

"You, Jake Carter, bring more soup for Mr. Smith," Portugee yelled.

McBride shook his head. "No, thank you. I've had enough." He made to rise to his feet. "I think I'd best be moving on."

Portugee raised his arms in an attitude of surrender. "This soon, and me with so much to tell you. Why, lad, I was thinking to regale you with tales of the sea, of monsters and mermaids and tempests and other yarns that would curdle your young blood. Aye, and of blackhearted pirate rogues as well, damn their eyes."

Several men giggled and one called out, "And slave traders, Portugee. Don't forget the slave traders."

The sailors laughed derisively and Portugee hollered, "I swear, Tom Spooner, one day I'll cut out your wagging tongue. I'll be damned if I don't."

He turned his attention back to McBride. "If you must go, you must go, and there's an end to it." He stuck out his hand. "Well, here's to our budding friendship and for telling me in which direction the trade winds blow fairest."

McBride got up on one knee and took

Portugee's hand. But with surprising strength, the man suddenly yanked McBride toward him. Off-balance, McBride fell flat on his face as he heard Portugee yell, "Now, boys!"

Something hard slammed into the back of McBride's head. He caught a glimpse of al-Karim's sadistic grin. Then the ground yawned open under him and he fell into a bottomless pit where there was only pain and echoing darkness. . . .

CHAPTER 22

He was swimming for his life. The cold water filled his mouth and he could not breathe as he battled through crashing surf. Ahead of him he saw a pirate island, the great smoking cone of its volcano surrounded by a lush jungle where snakes slithered and monkeys chattered. He heard the laugh of Portugee, mocking him as he struck out for shore. But he was tiring fast and suddenly the azure sea closed over his head and he was sinking . . . down . . . down to a sandy bottom where skeletons of men with coral eyes beckoned to him, welcoming him to a watery grave. . . .

No, he was in the creek!

McBride stopped struggling and his hands found the pebbled bottom. He pushed himself up and lifted his head out of the water. But more water, stinging, lashed at him. It was rain.

McBride clambered to his feet, the creek

rushing past the middle of his thighs. His head ached and the hard morning light spiked at his eyes. He waded out of the water and collapsed on the bank.

Darkness took him again.

He woke to rain battering on his face and heard the sound of distant thunder. His head aching, he struggled to a sitting position and looked around him. Judging by the light, the day was far along. The sky above him looked like a vast sheet of curled lead from horizon to horizon. There was no sign of Portugee and his wagons, only the empty, far-flung distances of the plains and the kettledrum rattle of the raking rain.

McBride looked at his feet. He wiggled his toes, puzzled. Then it dawned on him through the red haze of his headache — they had taken his shoes. He made a quick inventory. His shoulder holster was gone and with it his gun. His watch was missing and his hat. So too was the money belt he'd worn under his shirt. It had held more than seven hundred dollars, the remainder of the money he'd gotten from Inspector Byrnes. All he had left was the soaked clothes he stood up in.

Piece by piece, McBride tried to put it together. He remembered talking to the man named Portugee . . . shaking his hand . . . and then . . .

Somebody had hit him over the head with some kind of club. Then they'd taken everything he'd owned and thrown him in the creek. He must have washed downstream with the current and then fetched up to a sandbank. He'd later rolled into the water again and had experienced the terrible dream about a pirate island and drowning. And he had been drowning, facedown in the creek, but had woken up in time.

Wearily, McBride climbed to his feet. He staggered, looking around him, trying to take his bearings. He had no idea where he was, except that the creek was close. He could follow it east until he reached High Hopes. And then? He had no idea.

Staggering, falling time after time, getting up again dizzy and sore, McBride lurched along the creek bank. The rain was his enemy, hammering at him, giving him no peace. The downpour pockmarked the surface of the creek with startled Vs of water and hissed at him, mocking his puny efforts to cover the wet, slippery ground. Lightning forked from the black sky, bony white fingers pointing at him, threatening to strike.

McBride stumbled and fell, this time landing heavily on his face. On the creek bank thick underbrush surrounded the slender trunks of a pair of willows. On his hands and knees he crawled between them and worked his way into the brush. He sat up and wrapped his arms around him, shivering uncontrollably, thorns snagging sharp and wicked at his shirt and pants. Rain filtered cold through the brush and above him the thunder roared, the sky flickering between blackness and flashing, searing light. Despite it all, McBride closed his eyes and slept. He was still asleep when the storm clouds parted and the tranquil night lay soft on the land.

Through most of the long day McBride alternated between sleep and blurry wakefulness. Once he crawled out of the brush and drank at the creek, then crept back into his thorny haven and slept again.

The sun had just kept its appointment with the peaks of the Sangre de Cristo when McBride woke to twilight. He backed out of the brush and stood, testing his battered body. For a few minutes the land around him rocked and spun, but gradually the world righted itself and he found he could take a few steps without staggering. But his skull clanged in pain, like a hammer beating on an anvil, and he felt sick to his stomach. His fingers went to the back of his head and touched dry, crusted blood. It was a bad wound and he was sore in need of medical attention. But there was little chance of finding a doctor in all that wilderness.

McBride tried to think. What were his wants? A horse, but he had no horse. Food? That could wait. Water? There was plenty in the creek. A gun? Where to get a gun? He forced himself to work it out, his aching brain protesting. Then he remembered. Stryker Allison and the dead miner probably still lay where they'd dropped and both had been armed. The bodies were back along the creek to the west, where blood was staining the sky red as the sun died.

He would retrace his steps and recover Allison's guns.

The night drew tight and dark around McBride as he walked. Above him stars were dusted like diamonds across black velvet. A rising prairie wind tugged at him and far away to the northwest, over the Wet Mountains, distant thunder grumbled and arcs of blue fire shimmered above the horizon.

After two hours the rock cairn McBride had built over Luke Prescott's body came into sight, the white rocks gleaming like a ghost in the darkness. McBride was exhausted, his body battered and bruised from the constant falls he'd taken during the walk to get there.

He found the miner's body first. The man was sprawled on the grass like a rag doll, his clothes ripped where the coyotes had pulled at him. McBride cast about, searching around the body, but could not find the miner's gun.

A few steps away, Stryker Allison lay on his back, one white, clawed hand raised to the night, a talon attempting to tear the living stars from the sky. McBride found the man's Colt close to his body. Although he had never shot such a weapon, he was familiar with its operation, Inspector Byrnes and other detectives often carrying a short-barreled model. He swung open the loading gate and let the spent shells drop from the cylinder. Then he took a knee beside Allison and unbuckled his gun belt. The gunman's filmy eyes were open, accusing, as McBride dragged the belt out from under him. Allison's body jerked and the smell of death was already on him. Soon the coyotes would come for him.

McBride buckled the gun belt around his waist and slipped the Colt into the holster. But he was uncomfortable with the heavy, lopsided hang of it, and immediately took the belt off again. He filled his pocket with shells from the cartridge loops, tossed the gun belt away and loaded the big revolver. He stuck the gun in the waistband of his pants and its cold bulk returned a measure of confidence to him.

He started walking again, east in the direction of High Hopes, under a sky where the stars were going out one by one. Thunder banged close and the blue fire was all around him. Head down against wind and slanting rain, he trudged on, the flat echo of thunderclaps crashing over him like the waves of a turbulent sea.

McBride had wandered from the creek and the sheltering cottonwoods. His thinking muddled as it was, he did not realize that he was now the tallest thing on the prairie. He would very soon pay for his mistake.

The storm had brought an inky blackness to the land around him, now and then lightning flashes bathing the flat in brief, blinding light. During those moments McBride saw that he'd strayed far from the creek and he changed direction, heading north again. He was just yards from the cottonwoods when thunder bellowed right overhead. McBride felt the hair lift on his head and the air around him crackled with electricity. Thunder roared again. Immediately McBride found himself in the middle of a searing silver shaft of light that rent apart the fabric of the darkness. He was hurled backward, stunned, as the world exploded around him. He felt no pain, only a numbing shock that paralyzed his entire body.

He heard the thunder hammer again. Then he became one with the shattered night, fragmenting into a million crystalline pieces that fell scarlet and hissing hot to the wet earth that returned them to blackness.

CHAPTER 23

Shannon, more beautiful than he remembered, gracefully walked toward him, a welcoming smile on her lips, her arms outstretched for the embrace of love. Her silk gown slipped from her shoulders, and then from her milk-white breasts, tipped with pink coral. As he reached for her he heard her gown swish to the floor. . . .

He woke, the swishing sound still in his ears. The *swish* repeated, repeated again, coming closer.

McBride opened his eyes as the beautiful image of Shannon faded like a fairy gift from his memory. The *swish, swish, swish* was even closer now.

He turned his head and saw the little mustang nosing through the long grass, pushing aside the tough blades as it searched for more succulent shoots.

It seemed that even Portugee and his scoundrels had no use for the bony little hammerhead.

Glad as he was to see the horse, McBride stayed where he was, looking up at a blue sky with not a cloud in sight. Piece by piece, like a man waking after a three-day bender, he put together the events of the night. He had been struck by lightning — that, he recalled — but for some reason it had not killed him. He struggled to a sitting position and looked around him. Nearby a cottonwood was down. The tree's blackened trunk had snapped about halfway up its height and fragments of scorched branches lay scattered everywhere.

Now McBride knew why he was still breathing. Lightning had struck the cottonwood, not him, but he'd been close enough to suffer the effects of some of the blast. He'd been lucky — if you could call it that. Still, the mustang had sought him out, so maybe the shadow of the dark star that had been dogging him had moved on. He sure hoped so.

McBride struggled to his feet. He'd already been groggy from the whack to his head and the lightning strike had made it worse. He felt punch-drunk, like he'd gone ten rounds with John L. Sullivan and had come out on the losing end.

The mustang lifted its head and eyed

McBride suspiciously as he lurched close. When the man got within three feet, the little horse sidestepped away from him, leaving McBride to curse a blue streak.

But then, its contrary point made, the animal stood, making no fuss when McBride clambered onto its back. He turned the mustang until its nose pointed east, then lay across its neck and let the threatening darkness take him again.

The mustang plodded east through the heat of the afternoon, keeping to the low ground between the hills. Once, toward late afternoon, he stopped in a glade shaded by piñon and juniper and grazed for an hour. The unconscious man on his back groaned softly a few times but did not wake.

As the day shaded into night, the call of the barn grew strong in the ungainly little horse, and it was for that scant haven he headed as the moon rose and the coyotes talked around him. The mustang was five years old and had run free on the plains until he was three. Gelded, then broken as a cow pony with whip and spur, for almost two years he'd known little of kindness but much of abuse. He'd later been sold for fifteen dollars to the City Transfer and Hack Line as a carriage horse, but his wretched lot had improved little since then. Eventually he'd be butchered to supply meat for one of the Indian reservations.

But for now the barn in High Hopes was home, a place where there was hay and protection from predators. The mustang journeyed on, walking through the dusky night as the moon, cool, aloof and disinterested, looked down on him.

"He's comin' round, Doc. Ain't dead like I figgered."

McBride opened his eyes and looked up at the hairy face of Ebenezer Keble.

"Hoss brung you back, young feller," the old man said. "You was lucky you wasn't seen, on account of how the whole town is gunning for you." He smiled. "You sure have a way o' gettin' on the wrong side of folks."

"Where am I?" McBride asked. His voice sounded like a rusty gate hinge.

"At the T. J. barn, of course, and in the hayloft to be exac'. Doc Cox tol' me to hide you up here from Gamble Trask an' them Allison boys. Ol' Gamble, now, he's so mad at you he's spittin' nails, and the Allisons, well, don't count on them to make any friendly noises in your direction."

Ebenezer's face was replaced by one

younger, the concerned features of a handsome, clean-shaven man who looked to be in his early thirties. "How are you feeling?" he asked. "I'm Dr. Alan Cox."

McBride had been struggling to rise. Now he lay back on the straw and his fingers went to the fat bandage around his head. "Headache, Doc, as you might expect."

Cox nodded. "You took quite a blow. A rifle butt, I suspect. I had to stitch you up to stop the wound opening again." The physician rooted around in his medical bag and found a small mirror. He held it so McBride could look into it. "See anything strange?" he asked.

McBride glanced at the mirror and was appalled. He hadn't shaved in days and his face was scraped and torn by thorns. His eye was no longer as swollen, but it was surrounded by yellow and purple bruises. But what really caught his attention was his color — his skin was bright red, peeling in places, as though from a bad sunburn.

"The backs of your hands and the tops of your feet are the same color," Cox said, reading McBride's expression. "Have you been exposed to anything?"

"Lightning. It damned near killed me."

Understanding dawned on Cox and he smiled. "Ah, that would explain it. You must

252

have been close to the strike to get scorched like that."

"Sure I was. It was almost right on top of me."

"You're lucky to be alive."

McBride's smile was grudging. "If what Ebenezer told me is correct, I may not be alive much longer."

Cox's face showed his concern. "It's true, every word of it. Gamble Trask wants you dead, and that means Hack Burns does too. As for the Allisons, you killed their brother and they're not ones to let a thing like that go unavenged."

"I didn't kill Stryker — a man called Prescott did."

"Luke Prescott, the gunfighter?"

McBride nodded. "Was. Stryker killed him."

"They killed each other?"

"Both were real good with a gun."

"I'm told that gunmen of reputation usually try to avoid confrontations like that. When named men meet in a fight, the margin for error is small."

"Maybe so, but Stryker was on the prod and he was confident," McBride said. "He pushed it." He hesitated a heartbeat. "He died hard."

"Here, sonny, is that ol' Stryker's fancy

253

pistol in your pants?" Ebenezer's face swam into view.

"You mean, I didn't lose it on the way here?"

"Hell no, boy, it's layin' right beside you there. I figgered you mought need it in a hurry." He shook his head. "Well, well, well, ol' Stryker dead an' another ranny carryin' his iron. Who woulda thunk it?"

"He sure didn't," McBride said. He struggled to a sitting position — and his eyes met Shannon's.

Reading the signs, Cox grinned. "She insisted on coming, even though I told her it could be dangerous."

A tangle of emotion showed on McBride's face. "But how, I mean —"

Shannon crossed the floor and threw herself into McBride's arms. They kissed with a passion born of separation. When their lips finally parted, Shannon said, "Dr. Cox and I confide in each other, John. We share common enemies in Gamble Trask and the Allison brothers."

"I freely confess all." Cox smiled. "After Ebenezer told me you were back in town, I went to Shannon right away with the good news."

"And it is good news," Shannon said. She kissed McBride again, this time with more affection than passion. "I'm so glad you're back in High Hopes." She hesitated, fear a fleeting wraith in her eyes. "I'm scared, John, really scared. Since you burned his cabin and freed the Chinese girls he's out of his mind with rage. He says he's going to kill you and tack your hide to a wall of the saloon. I think — no, I don't *think* — I *know* he suspects me of helping you. He told me once we're married he'll teach me about faithfulness with a dog whip."

"He won't hurt you while I'm around," McBride said, a boast that rang hollow as a bronze gong even to his own ears. He was one man, a good man, he believed, but just one against many.

"I have an armed guard posted near the door to the stable," Cox said. "In four hours he will be relieved by another. I don't think Trask knows you're in town, but it pays to be careful." The doctor moved away, then returned with a bundle of clothing. "Ebenezer told me you were in rags." He smiled. "He was right." Cox dropped the items one by one next to McBride. "Pants, shirt, shoes, socks, that's it. By the way, you owe Andrew McAllen's General Store ten dollars for this stuff."

McBride grinned. "He'll have to wait for his money. After I was hit over the head I was robbed."

"I'll take care of it, John," Shannon said.

"Shannon, I don't want you —"

"Let her pay for it," Cox said. "When you two are married you'll have a joint bank account anyway."

"And let's hope that's soon," Shannon said.

McBride was pleasantly surprised. "Do you mean that, Shannon? Will you marry me?"

"Of course I will, but we won't talk about it now. After all this is over, we'll have a lifetime to talk."

McBride was like a runner who'd just gotten his second wind. His eyes lifted to Cox. "How many men can I count on, Doc?"

"I'd say maybe a dozen don't like what Trask is doing to the town. As to how many you can count on, the answer is, I don't know. When lead starts flying, men have a way of suddenly remembering that they're married."

"And you, can I count on you?"

Cox nodded. "Yes, you can. But then, I don't know one end of a rifle from another."

"Count me out too, young feller," Ebenezer said. "I'm too old and slow to be getting myself into shooting scrapes."

Then the only man he could count on was

himself. McBride accepted that. He didn't like it, but he accepted it. The question was, where to go from here? Inspector Byrnes had told him one time that heaven never helps a man who will not act. He had it to do.

Shannon rose to her feet and brushed straw from her dress. "John, I have to get back to the hotel. I may be missed."

"Will I see you later?"

"I'll try. I don't want anybody following me here."

"I have to be going too," Cox said. He moved to help Shannon to the ladder, then stopped. "I almost forgot. There was a letter for you at the post office and I picked it up for you yesterday. The clerk is a man I trust and he has no love for Gamble Trask. He gave it to me because he figured you'd be unable to get it yourself."

"Without getting shot, he meant," McBride said.

"Exactly." Cox handed over the envelope and smiled. "It pays to have friends in both high and low places."

After Shannon and Cox left and Ebenezer went about his business, McBride dressed hurriedly in his new clothes, then opened the letter. It was short and to the point and McBride smiled at its opening formality, but the smile faded as he read on:

To Detective Sergeant McBride, NYPD:
Bad news. A clerk with this department intercepted your letter to me. The envelope was steamed open, the contents read and communicated to those who would do you harm. The miscreant has since been severely dealt with.

John, your cover is blown and you are in the greatest danger. Now that there is mischief afoot, I wish you to remain in High Hopes and lie low. I am on my way.

I am, your obedient servant,

Thos. Byrnes, Inspector

P.S. I have reason to believe Sean Donovan has criminal contacts in Colorado. Be on your guard.

Byrnes was on his way to High Hopes. McBride shook his head and stuck the letter and envelope in his pocket. The inspector was a good police officer, and an excellent detective with amazing deductive powers, but he was not a gunfighter.

The task that lay ahead of McBride required men who were good with guns. In a revolver fight, Byrnes would be as much a liability as Alan Cox and the rest of them.

The man's letter had not brought Mc-

Bride any comfort. It had only added to his problems.

McBride crossed to the opening of the hayloft and looked down into the stable. A tall, round shouldered man with hangdog eyes stuck the stock of a shotgun under his left arm and waved with his right.

"All quiet," he said, his prominent Adam's apple bobbing.

McBride nodded. "Thanks for the help."

"No problem. Glad I can be of assistance."

McBride sat back on the straw and calculated that his guard would last about two seconds against Hack Burns or the Allison brothers. And he looked like a married man.

A couple of hours later, McBride heard muted conversation as his guard changed. This man was smaller, stockier, with muscular shoulders and arms   probably Ned Barlow, the blacksmith. The man was apparently not much given to conversation, giving McBride only a perfunctory nod when he appeared at the hayloft trapdoor.

Night fell and High Hopes started to come alive. A piano was playing in one of the saloons and McBride was aware of a stealthy shuffle of feet as his guard faded into the darkness while a man stabled his horse, talking to himself or the animal, he could not decide which.

Quiet again filled the barn to its shadowed corners. A horse stamped and blew through its nose, and McBride heard Barlow hawk and spit soot from his lungs.

He'd had enough. He could no longer allow himself to remain in the barn like a trapped rat in the darkness, waiting for Trask and his toughs to come at him. There was a tight feeling in his throat and a green serpent writhed in his belly. It had a name, that reptile — it was called Fear.

McBride rose to his feet, then stepped back in alarm as something swooped past his face. It was a bat! It fluttered away from him on silent wings, leaving a faint odor of guano behind it. His heart hammering, McBride listened into the night. He heard nothing. Slowly, measuring each step, every creak of the floorboards sticking a knife into his gut, he made his way toward the trap-door.

What was that?

He heard it again, a frantic shuffling of feet, like a hanged man kicking at the end of a rope. Then a long, drawn-out sigh that bubbled liquid and thick.

McBride took a step back and then another. He drew the Colt from his waistband and thumbed back the hammer. In the breathless hush the triple click was as loud as iron bolts hitting the bottom of a tin pail.

A man's voice whispered low, fragmented sound reaching McBride's ears. "Where . . . hell . . . he . . . there . . ."

A second of silence dragged past, then another. McBride was sure someone was pointing up to where he was hidden. He switched the Colt to his left hand, wiped the sweaty palm of his right on his pants, then switched back. All he could do now was wait for what was to happen. He swallowed hard, swallowed again. It was like trying to gulp down a rock.

The ladder to the trapdoor thudded softly against the pine frame. Thudded again. And again. Somebody was slowly climbing toward him. A blue darkness filled the barn, slanted with deeper shadow. McBride heard the saloon piano, a cheerful chiming made tinny and thin by distance.

The thud of the ladder became no louder but more rapid. The dome of a hat rose through the opening, then the pale blur of a face. The man's head swiveled as he looked around. He made out the faint image of McBride's body and recoiled, his back slamming against the trapdoor frame, cursing as his gun came up.

McBride fired. Too quick. A miss. Straw

and wood splinters erupted near the man's head.

The man's gun flared, flashing orange in the gloom. But McBride had moved. He was already diving for the floor and the bullet cut through the air inches above him. He landed with a crash, flat on his belly, the air bursting from his lungs. He was much closer to the unknown gunman, separated by only a few feet. He stuck the Colt out in front of him and fired.

A shattering scream and the man disappeared from sight. McBride heard the body crash heavily to the floor below. His breath coming in labored shudders that racked his chest, he scrambled down the ladder and his feet hit bottom. A scattergun roared and the ladder jerked under the impact. McBride threw himself onto his left side and immediately a second blast kicked up dirt and manure near his face, stinging into his eyes. A click as the shotgun was hastily opened. He fired in the direction of the sound and heard an agonized gasp as a man was hit hard. A body slumped to the floor and McBride rose to his feet, his gun up and ready.

"Don't shoot no more. I'm done."

It was Ebenezer's voice.

Warily, McBride stepped to the old man

and looked down at him. His voice tight, he asked, "Why?"

"Every man has his price, young feller. Gamble Trask paid me mine."

"Fool's gold," McBride said. Anger and compassion were fighting a battle inside him.

"Best you saddle up the mustang and get out of here," Ebenezer said, his voice unraveling into thin threads as his dying hastened closer. "They will be coming for you soon."

McBride's head moved, nodding to the dead man at the foot of the ladder. "Him?"

"His name is Harland. He's the youngest of the Allison brothers. He told them he could take you by hisself, wanted to prove something, I guess." The old man coughed blood into his beard and cackled. "He . . . he was wrong. . . ."

Then he groaned deep in his chest as death took him by the ear.

McBride had not been long in the West, but he had come to know much of gunfighter arrogance. Trask and the Allison brothers would have heard the shots and think him dead. They would not come for a while, but he had no time to lose.

He saddled and bridled the mustang in the dark, fumbling with straps and buckles in his haste, then spared a few moments to look for Ned Barlow.

The man was lying on his back in an empty stall and his throat had been expertly cut. Whether Harland Allison or Ebenezer had killed him, McBride did not know, nor did he care. The end result was the same. He climbed awkwardly into the saddle and swung the mustang out of the stable.

For the most part McBride had walked the little animal, uncertain of his horsemanship, but he ran him now. The mustang hammered at a fast, choppy gallop into the night and McBride, hanging on grimly to the saddle horn, was nonetheless glad to let the darkness of the plain swallow him.

CHAPTER 24

After fifteen wild minutes, the mustang slowed to walk, blowing hard, and McBride drew rein. He turned and looked behind him into the night but neither saw nor heard anything.

He swung to the west, then looped to the south until he met the Santa Fe tracks. He followed the tracks back toward High Hopes, riding under stars and a still, dreaming moon. The wind tugged at him, eager to tell its tale, and out on the flat grass the coyotes were silent, listening.

McBride followed the tracks for miles until the station came in sight. The platform was in shadow, but a lamp still glowed in the ticket office. Beyond the station High Hopes was a random scatter of lights, the buildings lost in the gloom. McBride listened and thought he heard men shouting his name, but the wind shredded their words so he was not sure.

He drew rein on the mustang and sat the saddle, deep in brooding thought. He had to be near Shannon, and that meant he needed a place to hole up that was close to her. He thought of trying to reach Doc Cox's house, but dismissed the idea. Why put the man in danger? Besides, he didn't even know where he lived.

He could try to find an empty shack or some other building, but that was an uncertain undertaking. He could be seen as he bumbled around in the dark like a fool, trying doors.

It came to him then. . . .

There was one man in town who might welcome him and hide him out, a fellow lawman — Marshal Lute Clark. The more he thought about, the more McBride decided it was his only option.

He remembered that there was a small barn behind Clark's house. He could stable the mustang there, where it would be seen by no one. A dying tin-star marshal of a two-bit town has few visitors.

Still, it was with some reluctance that McBride swung away from the station and made his way to the edge of town. He knew danger rode with him and he was bringing that unwelcome guest right to Clark's doorstep. But he was desperate. Shannon was depending on him and he had to be close.

McBride ground tied his horse behind the Clark home, then walked around to the front and tapped on the door. It opened a few moments later.

"Oh, it's you," Dolly said without evident surprise. She looked tired, worn. "Come to see Lute again?"

"How is he?" McBride asked.

"He's dying a little quicker today. That pleases him."

"I need to talk with him."

"I'll tell him. He'll say yes or no." She looked McBride up and down. "You look like hell. Come in."

Dolly opened the door wider and McBride stepped into the dark hallway. She closed the door behind him. "I'll tell him you're here." The woman hesitated a moment, then said, "Talking about looking like hell, I was pretty once myself, can you believe that?"

"I can believe it. You're still pretty."

"No, I'm not. One time I was so pretty that Lute killed two men over me. How many women can say that?"

"Very few, Dolly. Maybe none at all."

"I just wanted to tell you that, about the two men, I mean, not that it matters a hill of beans anymore."

"I'm glad you did, because Lute told me the same thing."

"I was a good woman to him, to Lute," Dolly said.

"You still are."

"Not any longer. I'm leaving him, tomorrow, the day after, the day after that. I won't stay around and watch him die."

McBride shook his head. "Dolly, I don't know what to say. I don't have the words."

"It's not about words, McBride. It's about feelings."

"He told you my real name."

"Lute tells me only what he wants to tell me." She turned away. "I'll speak to him."

Dolly returned a few minutes later.

"Lute will talk to you." Her tired eyes lifted to McBride's in the gloom. "You may be bringing death to this house, John McBride. I know it and so does Lute. That's why he will welcome you. Just don't expect me to do the same."

"I'll do my best to see that neither of you gets hurt."

Dolly's mouth stretched in a wan smile. "Then you'll disappoint Lute and please me." She waved a hand to the door at the end of the hallway, a small, lost gesture. "Go, have your talk. Afterward I'll have hot coffee waiting. You look all used up, or did I already tell you that?"

"Yes, you did. More or less."

"Well, it's true enough."

The woman left him then. McBride walked to Clark's door, knocked once and stepped inside. A single lamp beside the marshal's bed lit the room and he was propped up with pillows. His gray face, etched with shadow, was the face of a cadaver.

"I warned you not to, but I figured you'd be back," Clark said. "Dolly told me what's been happening in town. Bucking a stacked deck, ain't you? I mean taking on Trask and the Allison boys."

"I killed Harland Allison earlier tonight," McBride said. "He didn't give me any choice."

"That boy needed killing. So do the other two, Julius and Clint." The cadaver head moved on the pillow. "They won't be so easy."

McBride smiled grimly. "It wasn't easy. It was damned hard. Harland came close." He thought about telling Clark about the deaths of Ebenezer and the blacksmith, but decided to let it go. Besides, the marshal was talking again.

"Why are you here, McBride? It's hardly to ask the help of a dead man."

"I need a place to hide out," McBride said. "I need to be close to Shannon Roark."

"Still planning on taking down Gamble Trask, huh?"

"No. Right now my only plan is to get the woman I love out of High Hopes."

"That's good thinking on your part. You can hurt a man like Trask, burn a cabin or free a few Celestials, but you can't take him down. Not alone, you can't."

"But, how did —"

"Dolly told me. No big surprise, everybody in town is talking about your little foray into the badlands, you and Luke Prescott. A miner rode in on a lathered horse and told everybody that Stryker Allison had been killed."

"Luke is dead too. Allison killed him. Did Dolly tell you that?"

"The word around town is that you shot Allison."

"It's wrong. If I'd taken on Stryker in a revolver fight, I'd be dead right now."

Clark absorbed that in silence. The flesh had melted from his face and his temples and cheeks were sunken. It looked to Mc-Bride that the man was starving himself to hasten his death.

Finally he waved McBride close and said, "Suppose I let you stay here. What do you hope to accomplish?"

"Watch, wait for my chance and when the time is right get Shannon out of town."

"Watch?" Clark's laugh was like ancient parchments being rubbed together. "Watch from where, McBride? My front porch? You have to be able to get around town, man."

"I can hardly do that, Marshal. My face is too well-known."

"You told me you were a detective, Mc-Bride. What the hell kind of shadow do they raise in the big cities?"

McBride did not want to rankle the man, and his reply was mild. "Good ones, I'd hope."

Clark mimicked him. "Good ones, I'd hope." He laughed again, a dry, unpleasant sound. "You claim to be a good detective yet you've never heard of a disguise?"

It was McBride's turn to laugh. "Disguise myself as what?"

The marshal made no answer. He tilted his head back and bellowed, "Dolly!"

Almost immediately, as though she'd been listening outside, the door opened and the woman stepped into the room. "Do you recollect them four Texas cowboys that tried to rob the Mercantile Bank a few years back?" Clark asked her.

"I remember you killed two of them,"

Dolly said. "I recollect that."

"They'd been notified," the marshal said. "Anyways, they were wearing false theatrical beards and wigs and —"

"You stashed that stuff in the closet in the spare room," Dolly said.

"Yeah, that's right. I kept the disguises as trial evidence, except they never got a chance to go before the judge."

"What happened to them?" McBride asked.

Dolly answered for the marshal.

"Vigilantes did for them. A bank clerk was killed during the robbery, a man with a wife and three kids. Dr. Alan Cox, Theo Leggett, Ned Barlow, the blacksmith, and a bunch of others told Lute to go fishing for a couple of days. Then they dragged those two poor cowboys out of the jail and strung them up. I don't think either one of them had seen his seventeenth birthday."

"They were plenty old enough to hold up a bank," Clark said. His eyes glittered as they moved in their shadowed sockets. "Dolly, bring them disguises here. Oh, and that old black hat I used to wear for gardening."

The woman did as she was told, leaving McBride with a sick, hollow feeling in the pit of his stomach. Cox . . . Leggett . . . Barlow . . . men he'd trusted were vigilantes, in their own way just as ruthless and cold-blooded as Gamble Trask.

Back at the train station when he'd first arrived in High Hopes, the ticket clerk told him nothing in the town was as it seemed. Now McBride was beginning to understand what he'd meant. The question now was, apart from Shannon, whom else could he trust in High Hopes? Even Ebenezer, who had seemed to be a harmless old man, had sold him down the river for thirty pieces of silver. Could he depend on Marshal Clark to keep silent? And what about Dolly? She'd need traveling money and Gamble Trask was a ready and eager source.

McBride had plenty of questions and no answers and he felt like the walls of Clark's room were closing in on him.

Dolly returned with the disguises and handed them to McBride.

"The gray beard and wig, try those," Clark said.

Feeling foolish, McBride hooked the beard onto his ears. It fell away from him in a frizzy mat, covering most of his chest.

"Now the wig," the marshal said. "The beard is a big improvement, McBride. Makes you almost look handsome."

McBride was irritated, but said nothing.

He placed the wig over his head and its ragged gray locks hung to his shoulders, covering the beard's ear loops.

"Now let's see you walk," Clark said.

McBride took a few steps up and down the room.

"Hell, man, you're not in New York! You stand like a copper and walk like one," the marshal said. "Hunch those shoulders and shuffle. Remember, you're supposed to be an old codger." He watched McBride for a few moments and said, "That's better, but drag your feet a bit more. Now, put on the hat."

McBride did as he was told, settling the battered, shapeless old Stetson on his head.

"You look just fine," Clark said. "Even your own mother wouldn't recognize you." His eyes moved to Dolly. "What do you think?"

"He'll pass for an old, broken-down prospector at a distance."

"What did you say you were, McBride? A detective sergeant?"

"Yes, that's my rank."

"Then I shouldn't have had to give a big-city detective sergeant like you a lesson in police work."

McBride bit back a sharp reply and said merely, "I'm obliged to you, Marshal."

"Dolly, he's staying with us for a spell," Clark said.

"I thought as much." She turned to Mc-Bride. "You can sleep in the barn. Nobody will trouble you there. I'll bring a pillow and blankets, and there's a stall for your horse. Lute sold his dun a while back."

"No need for it now," the marshal said. He looked up at McBride. "Have you any money?"

"No, I was robbed of my money belt. I ran into a band of thieves headed by a man called Portugee."

Clark was surprised and it showed. "Portugee Lamego? Where did you run into that damned pirate?"

"West of here, at Apishapa Creek. Do you know him?"

"I know of him. He's pretty much a legend in the Barbary Coast district of San Francisco. Years ago he killed a man in New Orleans and got out of town just ahead of the law. Then he showed up in 'Frisco, calling himself a sea captain. He was hired on by a tea importer as first mate, led a mutiny and took over the company schooner. He hanged the captain from his own yardarm. Since then he's been running slaves, opium, rum, whatever will turn a profit. But to my knowledge Portugee has never operated east of the Divide. What's he doing in Colorado?"

"Busily robbing me," McBride said. "That's all I know."

"Over on the dresser, McBride, a tin box. Bring it here."

McBride found the box and brought it to the bed. "Open it," the marshal said.

"There's money in here," McBride said.

"How much?"

McBride counted out silver coins onto the bed quilt. "Twenty-eight dollars and eighteen cents in change."

"That's what I had in my pocket the day Hack Burns shot me," Clark said. "Take it. You can't survive in High Hopes without money."

"Marshal, I can't —"

"Take it, McBride. This is no time for getting proud on me."

McBride saw the logic in what the man was saying and he dropped the coins into his pocket. "I'll pay you back," he said.

Clark's head moved in a nod. "You surely will, McBride. You surely will." His eyes moved to Dolly. "Get out of here, woman," he said. "Men need to talk."

Clark waited until Dolly closed the door behind her, then said, "She's leaving me, you know. She told me so this morning. She says she's hired a widow woman to do for me, whatever that means."

"I'm sorry, Marshal, I truly am."

"No need to be sorry, McBride, I don't plan on living much longer. I can't get up out of this bed and Dolly took my guns away. That's why I'm asking you to repay whatever favors you think I've done you."

"Anything. Anything at all. Just name it."

"If I'm still alive when you finally leave town, shoot me. Make it quick, right between the eyes." The marshal's voice took on a pleading tone. "You'll do that for me, one lawman to another?"

McBride could have argued, told the man any kind of life was better than death, but he didn't. Clark wouldn't have listened anyway.

"Sure, Marshal," he said. "When the time comes I'll be glad to."

He didn't mean a word of it.

There were two stalls in the barn and Dolly had set up a bed for him in the corner of one of them. McBride walked the mustang into the other and stripped the saddle and bridle. He forked hay to the little horse, then discovered a sack of oats standing in a corner. He scooped a generous amount for the mustang and affectionately slapped its rump as he was leaving. The horse continued to eat and paid him no mind.

The hour was late, but High Hopes was still wide-awake and roaring drunk. The saloons were blazing beacons of welcoming light, the Golden Garter brightest of all. Miners in mule-eared boots stomped along the boardwalks, laughing, talking, arguing about everything and anything. Here and there cowboys, wide sombreros tipped back on their heads, burst in and out of batwing doors, all jingle and shine, confident and belligerent youngsters who were worthy heirs to the traditional arrogance of the horseman.

As McBride took to the boardwalk, shuffling like an old, bent man, tin-panny pianos tumbled tangled notes into the street, where they floated like snowflakes before melting into nothingness. A saloon girl in a vivid scarlet dress stepped out of the Golden Garter, took a few quick gulps of fresh air, then pinned on her smile again before going inside.

McBride's disguise was tested a few moments later.

A sallow gambler in a black frock coat and frilled shirt emerged from the shadows, a long, thin cheroot extended in his right hand. "Got a light, old-timer?"

McBride shook his head, then tightened his throat, attempting the peevish voice of an old man. "I don't smoke and neither should you, sonny. Stunt your growth."

The gambler laughed briefly and faded back into the shadows. So far, McBride decided, so good.

But his biggest test was yet to come. He had to walk into the Golden Garter and find a way to talk to Shannon. He wanted her to leave with him that night. The train was out of the question, but if she had a horse, they could put distance between themselves and Trask by daybreak.

It was a dangerous plan, but McBride convinced himself he had no other choice. He had to get the woman he intended to marry out of High Hopes and time was not on their side.

For a few moments McBride stood at the door of the Golden Garter and looked inside. The saloon was crowded and couples were waltzing around the dance floor. It was unlikely a broken-down old graybeard would even be noticed.

McBride stepped inside, found a place at the bar and ordered a beer. He slid a nickel across the counter, and the harried bartender scooped it up without comment. Holding the glass up close to his face, he glanced around him.

Because of the packed patrons he could not see Shannon, but as though nobody cared to get too close, the way was clear to Gamble Trask's table in the corner.

The man sat with his back to the wall. On his right was the cold-eyed gunman Hack Burns, beside him the two surviving Allison brothers. Then McBride got a double jolt of surprise. The man sitting with his back to him turned to say something to Trask. The expensive clothes, flashing diamonds and handsome, brutal features were unmistakable — it was Sean Donovan, late of Hell's Kitchen, New York City. Next to Donovan, McBride saw his battered plug hat, and the man sitting under it was Portugee Lamego.

For some reason all the rogues had gathered in one place, and for John McBride that could only mean more trouble was about to be added to the mess of trouble he already had.

CHAPTER 25

Wary of being recognized, McBride stood at the bar, the untasted beer in his hand. Now and then he sneaked a glance at Trask and the rest of them. The men were deep in conversation, ignoring him and everyone else. Portugee was very animated, grinning widely, waving his hands around. Then he turned and slapped Trask on the back as though something the man had said had greatly pleased him.

At that moment McBride wanted his hat back. And he wanted to kill Portugee Lamego for wearing it.

After a few minutes Trask's business with the others seemed to have concluded amicably and champagne made its appearance. A small, dapper man stepped into the saloon, bent over and whispered something into Donovan's ear. The gang leader nodded, smiled and said something in return that made the others laugh. The small man straightened and took his place beside Donovan's chair. Hack Burns looked up at the man, his gunman's eyes wary and calculating. And so he should be wary, McBride thought.

The little man was Gypsy Jim O'Hara, an icy killer without a shred of conscience or human decency.

McBride had seen enough. Now his need to talk to Shannon was more urgent than ever. But how to get close to her without arousing suspicion?

His eyes slanted to Trask's table. O'Hara's cold gaze swept the room, lingered on him for a moment, then dismissed him. O'Hara was paying no mind to a useless old man.

Reassured, McBride moved closer to a black-haired girl standing at the bar, her foot tapping to the piano music. He set his beer on the bar, grabbed the woman around the waist and yelled, "Let's cut a rug, girlie!"

McBride dragged the protesting girl onto the dance floor and spun her around in what he hoped was a reasonable imitation of a waltz. But his partner was having none of it.

"Hey, watch your big feet, Gramps," she hollered. She twisted out of his arms and stepped away from him, her eyes blazing.

"Go on home to Grandma, you crazy old coot!"

Around him people laughed and jeered and out of the corner of his eye McBride saw several heads at Trask's table turned to him. But Donovan grinned and said something that made the others laugh and they went back to their champagne and cigars.

The saloon girl had called him a crazy old coot and now McBride played that role to the hilt. He staggered toward where Shannon usually sat, elbowing men out of his way. One miner, a big man with a broken nose and the spiderwebbed eye scars of a skull and knuckle fighter, took exception to being bumped and stepped close to McBride. The man's face just inches away from his own, McBride could smell the rank stink of whiskey on his breath.

"Hey, you, scat!" the miner said, tight and hard. "If you don't, old man or no, I'll break your damned jaw."

People were crowded close around the two of them and McBride brought up his right knee, very fast, into the man's crotch. The miner gasped and his face instantly changed color from angry red to ashy gray. He bent over and went down slowly, groaning, his hands clutching at his tormented nether regions. McBride took a step back and let the man fall. Beside him a girl and her dance partner looked down with mild curiosity at the writhing miner.

"Heh, heh," McBride cackled. "I'd say that young feller's had too much to drink."

He stepped over the miner's recumbent form and made his way to Shannon's table. He stood behind one of the poker players, looking down at her, willing her to look at him. She did. Shannon's beautiful eyes lifted to his face, but as O'Hara had done, she dismissed him without interest.

But then she looked back with a spike of startled recognition.

McBride smiled under his false beard and slowly pointed over his shoulder with his thumb. Shannon caught his drift immediately and nodded. She bowed her head to her cards and McBride again faded into the crowd.

The stricken miner was being dragged backward, his booted feet trailing, toward a chair by a couple of his friends. The man's head was lolling on his shoulders and a thin line of drool ran from the corner of his mouth. As McBride walked past, somebody called out for ice and he grinned. The miner was obviously in a world of hurt.

Served him right for picking on a poor old man.

McBride left the saloon and no one at Trask's uproarious table saw him go. Girls had arrived shortly after the champagne and Trask and the others were distracted, carousing in a haze of blue cigar smoke and cheap perfume.

That was all to the good and McBride hoped they all got blind drunk. It would give him and Shannon more time to put trail between themselves and Trask.

The moon, as carefree as ever, was sliding lower in the sky as McBride stepped into the alley beside the saloon. There, in slanted, sulking shadow, he waited for Shannon to appear.

McBride's fingers moved to the grip of the Colt in his waistband. He took comfort in its cool steel for a moment, then moved his hand again, this time to scratch under his chin where the false beard itched.

Marshal Clark's tiny calico cat, on the prowl, emerged from the darkness and rubbed against his ankles in a friendly greeting. McBride leaned over, stroked the cat's soft fur and whispered, "You go on home now."

The calico arched its back, made a faint mewing noise and faded again into the night. McBride straightened, his eyes slanting to the door of the Golden Garter.

Slow minutes dragged past, men came and went, the moon dropped lower and the shadows around him darkened. A half-hearted wind wheezed through the alley, teased McBride for a moment, then gave up the effort and died into stillness.

The moon glided lower in the sky. Time moved on — thirty minutes went past, then ten more.

McBride grew worried.

Then Shannon stepped through the door. Against the ashy gray of the saloon's planking and the dull orange circles cast by the oil lamps, the woman stood as a slender, vivid column of light. Diamonds sparkled in her ears and she wore a satin dress of lustrous yellow, ribbons of the same color in her hair. Her naked shoulders were beautiful, shapely as those of a Greek goddess, and a thin band of black silk encircled her throat.

McBride could only look at her in stunned wonder from the shadows, the breath catching in his chest, his heart pounding.

Shannon stepped to the edge of the boardwalk and looked around her. She pushed a stray lock of hair from her forehead, then turned to her right, walking away from McBride.

"Psst . . . over here."

Shannon's back stiffened and she stood still. She glanced over her shoulder, then slowly walked back in McBride's direction.

When she was close, McBride whispered again: "Stay there, don't look at me."

The woman nodded and looked straight ahead into the darkness.

"We're leaving tonight," McBride said. "When can you get away without being noticed?"

He thought he saw a fleeting expression on Shannon's face that could have been fear or apprehension. But the woman nodded a second time.

"Do you have a horse?" McBride asked.

Another nod. Then, without turning her head: "John, be at the City Transfer livery in an hour. My horse is there."

"I'll be there."

"I have to go," Shannon whispered. "I'll be missed."

Before McBride could say anything further, Shannon turned on her heel and walked into the saloon. The night closed around the place where she'd stood and suddenly all the light was gone.

McBride stepped out of the alley and took to the boardwalk. He had little time. He would saddle the mustang and be ready. One short hour. The thought of leaving with

Shannon made his heart beat faster.

Just sixty fleeting minutes from now she'd be his . . . at the beginning of forever.

CHAPTER 26

McBride was tightening the cinch on the mustang's saddle when a shuffle of feet made him turn fast, drawing from his waistband.

"Take it easy, gunfighter. It's only me."

Dolly's voice. She stepped out of the shadows and stopped a few feet from McBride. "You're pulling your freight?"

He shoved the gun back in place. "Looks like." The woman was silent and he was forced to add, "I've had enough of High Hopes to last me a lifetime."

"Did Shannon Roark say she'll leave with you?"

"You know about Shannon and I?"

"Lute told me."

"Yes, she's leaving with me. I'll meet her at the livery an hour from now, a bit less."

McBride saw Dolly's smile flash in the gloom of the barn. "Don't count on it, McBride."

He was startled. "What do you mean, don't count on it?"

Dolly took a step toward him. "Miss Roark has become accustomed to the good life. I haven't seen her tonight, but I bet the dress she's wearing cost more than a city policeman makes in three months."

"We'll get by," McBride said defensively, but all at once a strange twinge of unease began tugging at his belly.

"What was she wearing in her ears tonight?"

"I don't know."

"Yes, you do, McBride. What were her earrings like?"

He hesitated, like a man standing at the edge of a precipice, afraid to take a step into the unknown. "Diamonds," he said finally. "She wore diamond earrings."

Dolly's laugh was scornful, without humor. "And when you get to New York or Boston or wherever you're going, you'll buy her diamonds?"

McBride slapped the mustang's neck. "Like I said, we'll get by."

"Not without jewels, fine clothes, a big house and a carriage and four horses, you won't."

"Dolly, you're forgetting one thing — Shannon loves me."

"Does she, now?"

"Yes, she does."

"McBride, Shannon Roark loves only herself. That's something you'll learn, maybe sooner, maybe later."

McBride smiled, thin and bitter. "Dolly, what do you know about love? You're running out on a man who needs you."

The woman's shadowed face revealed no offense. "That's where you're wrong, McBride. I love Lute, I love him dearly — that's why I won't stick around and watch him die one day at a time. I owe him that much, I owe myself that much. Years from now, when I'm old, I'll remember him, but I'll remember how he was. I'll remember the good times we had together when we were young and the sun shone brighter."

Unbidden, McBride felt a surge of compassion for Dolly that she noticed and laid aside. "Don't feel sorry for me, McBride," she said. "Feel sorry for yourself."

She turned to go but stopped, as though she'd suddenly remembered something. "The first time you came to Lute's house, you asked him if he knew about orphan trains. Are you still interested?"

"You were listening?"

"No, Lute told me. You intrigued him, McBride, and he wanted to talk. It was one of his better days."

"I was interested then, hardly at all now. But I guess I'd still like to hear what they are."

Dolly leaned and rested her arm on a stall partition. "The trains seldom get as far west as Colorado, but a few have pulled into Denver in past years. They leave from Chicago, New York, Boston, St. Louis, Cleveland and Cincinnati and they're packed with children removed from city orphanages. Most of the kids are under fifteen, and they're chosen for their health and good looks.

"Handbills, flyers and newspaper articles alert people along the rail route when the trains will be stopping. When an orphan train pulls into a town, the children are displayed for, as it's called, adoption."

McBride was interested despite himself. "It's a good way for orphans to find a home."

"For some it is. But others are beaten and worked to death and God knows how many fall into the hands of perverts who abuse them horribly. There's no oversight to the orphan trains, no follow-up, and if a child is beaten or worked until he drops, nobody cares. In some places there are so many orphaned teenaged girls, they're worth only twenty cents more than a Missouri mule.

"Of course, saloon owners and pimps like Gamble Trask are eager participants in the adoption process. They know that many girls, and boys, prefer being forced into the worst kind of sexual slavery than starving to death or dying of disease in an orphanage."

Dolly's teeth gleamed. "You're from the big city, McBride. Ever visit an orphanage?"

McBride said he had not, an admission that gave him a twinge of conscience.

"They're prisons, cold, dark prisons, overcrowded, disease-ridden, hellholes of starvation and abuse."

"How do you know so much about orphan trains?" McBride asked. He anticipated what the woman's answer would be and she did not prove him wrong.

"I was a child of an orphan train. I was sixteen then and quite pretty. A man just like Gamble Trask bought me and forced me to service any cowboy who got drunk and felt the need for a woman. I was working the line when Lute found me. He killed the man that owned me and then a lawman who tried to stop us leaving town. I owe him for that, but I figure my debt is paid."

McBride told himself that none of this was his concern, but the policeman's curiosity remained strong in him. "Why did Theo

Leggett hang on to life long enough to mention orphan trains? Is one stopping here?"

"Yes, day after tomorrow. It's a special train out of New York, put together by a man named Sean Donovan for Gamble Trask. All of it done with the blessing of the city's charitable organizations, I should add."

"Special, how?"

"All beautiful, blue-eyed, blond girls between the ages of twelve and sixteen. An even hundred of them. The train will make no other stops. It will arrive in High Hopes directly from New York."

"How do you know all this?"

"Silas Knowles, the ticket agent, told me. He is aware of everything that happens on the Santa Fe railroad, has a lot of friends down the line."

"I remember him as a free-talking man," McBride said.

"He is at that. But he told me because at a later date I promised to give him something he wants. But he may not need it anymore. Silas has two hundred dollars saved and he plans on asking Donovan and Trask if he can use it to adopt the prettiest twelve-year-old he can find on the train. He says even a man his age has his needs."

McBride was thinking. The orphan train

could explain why Donovan was in town. He was looking out for his merchandise. But what was Gamble Trask going to do with a hundred young girls? Then he remembered Portugee. The man was a slave trader. He could buy the girls from Trask and later sell them at a profit . . . but where? San Francisco? Or somewhere else?

A hundred girls was a lot of females to ship, but Portugee had a silver, persuasive tongue. He could tell them he was taking them to a wonderful new life in California, load them on a train and scuttle back across the Divide. If any of the girls guessed what was going on and balked, he had a dozen men to ensure that they stayed in line during the trip.

There could be another, perhaps even more pressing reason why Donovan was in High Hopes. Someone at police headquarters in New York had opened the letter McBride had sent to Inspector Byrnes and had told him the man who killed his son was holed up in High Hopes. Donovan was ever a man who liked to mix business with pleasure and he'd be eagerly anticipating putting a bullet into John McBride. Or a death much worse and a whole lot slower.

Dolly's light laugh lilted from out of the darkness. "McBride, no matter what you think, you're still a peace officer. I can see your brain working."

McBride shook his head, clearing his thoughts with the clean sweep of self-interest. "Dolly, the orphans are not my problem. I'm getting out of town with Shannon."

"You'll turn tail and run and leave a hundred young girls to their fate?"

"Yes, that's exactly what I'm going to do."

"Then you're very much less of a man than I thought you were. No wonder you feel the need to hide your face behind a false beard."

McBride was exasperated and it honed a hard edge on his voice. "Look at me, Dolly. What do you see? I'm one man. There's only me. What the hell do you expect me to do?"

"Be the sworn law officer you claim to be. Don't allow those girls to be bought and sold like cattle. Five years from now not one of them will still be alive."

"That's no business of mine."

"At one time you thought all the terrible things that were happening in High Hopes were your business."

"That was then, this is now. To reach where I am this very moment I've had to step over the bodies of dead men. Well, I've had my fill of death and killing. I want out of it, and so does Shannon."

Dolly's head nodded in the darkness. The mustang chomped on his bit and in the distance the mournful coyote chorus was in full voice.

"Then God help you, John McBride," Dolly said. "From this night until the end of your life you will never again be able to hold up your head in the company of men."

The woman's words hit McBride like blows. He watched in silence as Dolly turned her back on him and walked out of the barn. A sick, empty feeling in his gut, he knew that a piece of him had gone with her . . . and it would never return.

McBride gathered up the reins of the mustang. He would take the long way around to the livery, holding to the darkness. Where he belonged.

Two shots, close together, hammered apart the glassy fabric of the night.

"Oh God, Shannon!" McBride whispered, his face wild with fright.

Then he was running . . . running toward the sound.

CHAPTER 27

A crowd of men was gathered at the entrance to the alley beside the Golden Garter — Sean Donovan, the Allison brothers and Gypsy Jim O'Hara among them.

He slowed to a walk when he got closer, and tapped a miner on the shoulder. "What happened?" McBride waited for an answer, fearing what it might be.

"Gamble Trask," the man said. "Shot twice in the back." The miner grinned. "I wouldn't get any closer, old-timer. The killer is still around and maybe he'll decide to take a potshot at you."

McBride had forgotten that he was wearing the false beard and wig. Now, as relief flooded through him, he was grateful for both.

Hack Burns, wearing his marshal's star, strolled out of the saloon and roughly pushed men from his path. He had a hurried conference with Donovan, then disappeared from view as he bent to examine the body.

Confident of his disguise, McBride elbowed his way though the excited, chattering crowd. He drew a few annoyed looks, but no one moved to stop him.

Gamble Trask lay on his back, his eyes wide open, staring at nothing. A look of horror and surprise was frozen on his face, as though he'd been unable to understand the manner and reason for his dying. McBride's practiced eye pieced it together. Hit twice in the back, Trask had tried to turn to face his assailant, drawing from a shoulder holster. His gun was in his hand, but he'd never gotten the chance to use it. He'd collapsed, dead when he hit the ground.

Someone had lured Trask to the alley and then murdered him. Sean Donovan killed like that. He had set up the orphan-train deal and it could be he figured the profits were too thin to be shared. The killing of Trask had Donovan's slimy paw prints all over it.

But the man's death had removed his claim to Shannon. A major obstacle had been removed and now McBride's path out of High Hopes with his future wife was clear. In a few minutes they would be on their way to a new life in a new place well away from the sullen drift of gun smoke.

It had cost just two cents, the price of a couple of cartridges, to end Gamble Trask's dream of political power forever. The big deal he'd talked about, the sale into sexual slavery of one hundred young girls, had cost him his life and all his ambitions.

McBride considered that dying in a stinking, muddy alley had been a fitting finish for a man who had deserved no better.

"And what kind of finish do you deserve, Detective Sergeant McBride?"

It was Dolly's voice in his head, haunting him, taunting him, giving him no peace.

McBride made a tremendous effort of will and pushed the thought away from him. What did Dolly know about anything? He was the best judge of what was best for him, for the woman he loved, not her.

He looked over at Donovan, who was talking with Hack Burns. Then his eyes fell on O'Hara. The man was watching him intently, a fixed, puzzled expression on his dark face, as though he was trying hard to remember something.

Quickly, McBride looked away. He turned and hurriedly retraced his steps along the boardwalk. It was time to pick up his horse and go meet Shannon.

■ ■ ■ ■

Marshal Clark's house was in darkness as McBride stepped into the barn and led the mustang outside. The moon was much lower in the sky and a streak of pale blue light showed above the horizon to the east, where the dawn was preparing to boost the sun above the low hills. The plains were still shrouded in darkness and a few sentinel stars remained awake as McBride swung into the saddle and rode out into the gloom.

He shed his beard and wig, then made a wide arc around town and came up on the livery from the west. A tin rooster stirred in a gusty breeze at the peak of the roof above the door, screeching as it swung this way and that, frantically trying to point out the direction of the capricious wind. Darkness clung close to the stable and the open door was a mysterious rectangle of black.

Where was Shannon?

McBride stepped out of the saddle and walked toward the door. He stopped when he was a few steps away and whispered, "Shannon?"

There was no sound but the constant *shriek . . . shriek . . . shriek* of the tin rooster on the roof and the sighing of the wind. A dust devil spun like a dervish a few yards from McBride and collapsed at his feet, sifting mustard-colored sand over the toes of his shoes.

"Shannon?" he called again, louder this time.

A man emerged from the door of the stable, small, dapper, grinning. "She's not here, McBride. But I am."

McBride was stunned. "O'Hara! How did you —"

"Know you were coming here? Let's just say a little bird told me, a pretty little female bird at that."

Dolly! He'd said he was meeting Shannon here. This was how she'd gotten back at him for leaving High Hopes — by betraying him to Gypsy Jim.

"You made a big mistake, McBride," O'Hara said. The little assassin was poised, ready, a deadly scorpion about to strike. "A man can wear a disguise, but he can't change the color of his eyes. That got me to wondering when I saw you in the saloon, and later when you came to pay your last respects to poor Mr. Trask. See, an old man has faded, milky eyes, but yours are bright blue. Young eyes in a graybeard's face? It just didn't ring true. The more I thought about it, the more I became convinced I was looking at Detective Sergeant McBride as ever was." O'Hara shook his head. "A smart shadow like you should have known that."

"Donovan send you here?" McBride asked.

"No, I came on my own." O'Hara threw a burlap sack at McBride's feet. "But I'll give him your head in that after I kill you." The little man was reaching down to the right pocket of his coat. "I never liked you, McBride, the stiff-necked copper who couldn't be bribed. It's going to be a real pleasure to put a bullet into you."

"Where's Shannon?"

Was she in the barn, bound and gagged and unable to cry out?

"Like I said, she's not here, McBride. It's only me . . . and you."

O'Hara had made his intention to kill him clear. The time for talking was over.

If McBride had learned anything in the West, it was not to underestimate the sudden effectiveness of the gunfighter's fast draw.

"Listen, O'Hara, let's talk —"

He drew, very fast from the waistband. O'Hara, smirking, overconfident of his gun skills, was taken completely by surprise. He was still groping for the gun in his coat pocket when McBride's first bullet hit him.

The man spun halfway to his left. But now he had a gun in his hand. He was bringing it up for an aimed shot when McBride fired again. The bullet hit O'Hara's collar stud and drove it through the back of his neck, smashing the spine. The man let out a scream and dropped to his knees. He looked at McBride for a few moments, his eyes unbelieving, then fell flat on his face.

The rooster on the roof screeched its frustration with the wind as McBride stepped to O'Hara and turned him over with his foot. The man was dead.

Without conscious thought, McBride punched the two empty shells from his Colt and reloaded from the rounds in his pocket. He stuck the gun back in his waistband. It was likely that others would come to investigate the shooting at this hour of the morning, but he took time to search the barn. Shannon was not there.

McBride swung into the saddle and rode into the plain, where the light was shading from black to cobalt blue. A time to think, then he'd look for Shannon.

He was sure she was in the hands of Sean Donovan, and he knew how badly the man treated women.

He had to free her — even if it cost him his own life.

CHAPTER 28

John McBride rode due north into the brightening morning.

Miles ahead of him lay the great rampart of the Kaibab Plateau, where deer and antelope fed among vast forests of fir and ponderosa pine. But McBride had no intention of riding that far. He was looking for a place where he could sleep through the day and then return to High Hopes under the cover of darkness.

He found it just as the sun was lifting over the horizon to the east, a shallow valley between two low hills, shaded by a grove of wild oak, cottonwood and juniper. A stream cut through the trees and bubbled around the eroded bulk of a great sandstone boulder, thrown there during some ancient volcanic eruption.

McBride unsaddled the mustang, then found a place among the juniper where he could stretch out. He was both hungry and tired, but could satisfy only one urge. He tipped his battered hat over his eyes and willed sleep to come to him.

The sun rose higher and clothed McBride in dappled light. Jays quarreled in the tree branches, raining leaves and pieces of bark on him, but he slumbered on.

By late afternoon deer came to drink at the stream and McBride woke. He rose and stretched, scattering the whitetails, then saddled the mustang again.

Darkness was falling as McBride swung wide of town and rode up to Marshal Clark's barn. Dolly had betrayed him, but in a town filled with betrayal, this was as safe a place as any other.

He forked hay to the mustang, then, pulling his hat over his eyes, made his way into the street, walking toward the Golden Garter. Hack Burns and Sean Donovan were men to be avoided. And so was Portugee. The two Allison brothers had never seen him and might not recognize him in his different clothes and hat.

No matter, that was a chance he'd have to take.

The saloon was already crowded, but Shannon was not at her usual table. There was no sign of Donovan and the others.

Afraid of being seen, McBride left immediately and walked along the boardwalk to the Killeen Hotel.

A bored clerk sat behind the desk, his feet up, contemplating his twiddling thumbs. McBride waited, looking down at the man, then palmed the bell on the desk, loudly, several times.

A surly look on his face, the man rose to his feet. "No need for that. I knew you were there."

"Then look up the next time," McBride said. He nodded toward the stairs. "Is Miss Roark in her room?"

"Who wants to know?" the clerk said, his thin mouth twisting into an insolent grin.

McBride was in no mood to put up with an uppity hotel clerk. His gun was suddenly in his hand, the muzzle shoved hard against the man's forehead.

"I think I'm going to have trouble with you, but I'll ask you just once again — is Miss Roark in her room?"

Terror showed in the clerk's eyes and his throat bobbed a time or two. "No . . . no, she's not. She left a couple of hours ago."

"Was anybody with her?"

"Yeah . . . yeah . . . a big man, near as big as you."

So Donovan did have Shannon in his

clutches. But why? Did he believe she knew about Trask's business dealings and thought he could profit by that knowledge? Would he torture Shannon to get at the truth?

"Did Shannon — did Miss Roark — say where she was going?"

The clerk's throat bobbed again. "No, she said nothing. She just walked out with the big feller."

McBride thumbed down the hammer of the Colt and shoved the gun back into his waistband. He ignored the frightened clerk and stood at the desk deep in thought. Where had Donovan taken her? He didn't know this country and would be reluctant to stray far from town. Shannon must still be in High Hopes. All McBride had to do was find her.

He walked out of the hotel and stood on the boardwalk, his eyes searching up and down the street. He was at a loss at what to do next.

Men were stomping back and forth, heading into one saloon or another, but the Golden Garter was busiest of all. It seemed that the death of its proprietor had not put a dent in business. Had Sean Donovan already taken over, bought drinks for the house and made it clear he was the new big man in town?

Once he forced Shannon to tell him about Trask's other operations, he would also take over the drug trade and the trafficking of Chinese girls. Donovan was not a man to pass on making easy money, and he likely planned to spend some time in High Hopes to clean up before returning to New York.

McBride had no illusions. Sean Donovan was a ruthless man, a conscienceless killer when he had to be, and Shannon was in deadly danger.

Damn it, where was she?

The question again clanged through McBride's mind like a fire alarm. He was standing uselessly in the street while his future wife faced Donovan alone. By now she must be terrified, confronted by the man's devouring ambition and raw power. Donovan was not gentle with women, and those he couldn't have he took by brute force. For Shannon, that would be a fate worse than death itself.

There was only one way. McBride knew he had to find Sean Donovan and kill him. And he was prepared to walk over the bodies of Hack Burns and the Allison brothers to do it.

Back at the barn, Dolly had casually referred to him as "gunfighter," and maybe that's what he'd become. If he had, now was the time to live up to the name.

Sooner or later Donovan would return to the saloon. And McBride would be there . . . waiting for him.

He stepped to the edge of the boards, then stopped. Two men had walked out of the saloon and stood together, lighting cigars. Both wore black frock coats and low-crowned, flat-brimmed hats, and the buckles of their gun belts gleamed in the lamplight.

They could only be Julius and Clint Allison.

One of the brothers glanced across the street and started to look away. Then his head swung sharply back. McBride felt the man's eyes, shadowed by his hat brim, crawl over him.

McBride's height and massive chest and shoulders were enough to draw any fighting man's interest, and whatever Allison brother that was, the man was interested now.

There were enough men in town, including Donovan, who could have given the Allisons a description of McBride that his shabby clothes could not hide. The man across the way was suspicious, and it showed. He whispered to his brother and the second man looked across at McBride, his eyes lingering long. Then he abruptly turned and walked quickly into the saloon.

The other brother strolled to the edge of the boardwalk and brushed his coat away from his gun. His cigar glowed red in his teeth and his lips were shaped into a grin.

He knew! And he was ready.

McBride had it to do. He stepped down into the street but stopped when the doors of the Golden Garter swung open — and Sean Donovan walked onto the boardwalk, Hack Burns and the Allison brother at his side.

It took only a moment for Donovan to recognize McBride.

"You!" he screamed. His hand flew for the gun under his coat. The Allisons were also drawing, very fast and smooth.

A crowd of miners saved McBride's life. Drunk and unaware, they stumbled, singing, their arms around one another's shoulders, in front of Donovan and the two gunmen.

McBride heard Donovan curse, saw him roughly push a young, redheaded miner aside. Too drunk to realize what was happening, the man angrily yelled something and pushed back. Donovan cursed again, rammed his gun into the man's belly and fired. The miner staggered a few steps, looking down with shocked, unbelieving eyes at the blossoming scarlet flower that would soon kill him.

Suddenly McBride was running.

A bullet kicked up dust at his feet and a second split the air above his head. He dived into an alley and ran into the darkness. Behind him he heard Donovan's angry yell. Then feet were pounding after him.

McBride cleared the far end of the alley at a jolting, flat-footed sprint. He did not try to hide because there was nowhere to hide. Ahead of him lay the inky wall of the prairie, deep shadows streaked by moonlight, and he ran on and let the night embrace him.

He knew the Allisons and Donovan were close behind him, but they would not charge blindly into darkness and his waiting gun. The gloom would slow them, make them careful, and that's exactly what he wanted.

At a walk, McBride headed for the train station. The soft rustle of grass under his feet was lost in the whisper of the wind and the talk of the coyotes out on the plain. If he could lure Donovan and the others to the station, he could make a fight of it there. The station would provide cover and the fast draws of the Allison brothers would not be a factor.

McBride climbed the freight ramp to the platform, keeping to the shadows. A light burned in the ticket office and he opened the door and stepped inside. Silas Knowles, wearing a green eyeshade, was sitting at a desk, a sputtering pen in his hand. The man set the pen down when McBride entered, and looked up, a sour look on his face.

"Hell, are you still alive?" he asked. "I hear you and that gunfighter Luke Prescott played hob."

"I may not be alive much longer," McBride said pleasantly. A shrewder man than Knowles would have noticed that his eyes did not match his tone. "There are men after me."

"Then get the hell out of my office. You ain't dying in here."

"Sure, Silas, sure."

McBride moved as though to turn away, but he swung back fast and his big right hand grabbed the front of Knowles' shirt. He dragged the man across the desk. The toes of Knowles' shoes scraped across the desktop, scattering papers, and the inkwell tipped, spreading like a pool of black blood.

Knowles tried to wrench himself free. McBride held him at arm's length and backhanded him hard across the face. Knowles yelped in pain, then took refuge in a whimper, his mouth dripping scarlet saliva.

McBride hauled the clerk to the door. He stuck his head outside and looked into the darkness, but there was no movement or sound. He dragged Knowles along the platform to a shadowed recess where a bench stood, and slammed the man's back against the wall. He smiled. "So, Silas, how are you?"

"Damn you, what do you want from me?"

"Information. And I don't have much time, so I want it real fast."

"I can give you train times. That's the only information I have."

McBride slapped the man again. Knowles shrieked and his head rolled on his shoulders. McBride lifted the man's chin with a crooked forefinger. "Silas," he said, "I'm not very happy with you. That scream could have been heard clear to town. I also don't like grown men who want to prey on little girls. Now, you either tell me what I want to know or I'll make sure you're never able to molest a child again. You know where my bullet will go, don't you, Silas?"

McBride drew his gun and pushed the muzzle into the man's groin. He thumbed back the hammer.

"No, oh please don't," Knowles wailed. "What do you want to know? I'll tell ya, swear to God, I will."

McBride nodded. "That's better. Now, it's amazing how clearly a man thinks when he's running through the dark being shot at. I had this moment of wonderful clarity when I realized that the only way I can safely leave High Hopes with my future bride is to bring your whole rotten town to its knees. I thought, What good is it to have a beautiful wife at your side, John, if you can never again raise your head in the company of men? It took some time, but I also remembered that I'm a police officer, sworn to uphold the law. A woman told me to remember that, but at the time I didn't heed her. Thinking back now, I should have."

McBride smiled. "Do you understand all that, Silas, or am I talking too fast for you? If I am, I'm sorry, but my time is short."

"I understand, I understand," Knowles stammered. There were tears in his eyes. "What do you want from me, lawman?"

"Tell me about the orphan train that's due here tomorrow."

"I don't know anything about that."

McBride pushed the gun harder into the man's groin.

"It will be here at noon. Big train. Maybe three, four passenger coaches. It's a cannonball, straight through from New York City."

"How many girls?"

"A hundred, maybe more. I don't know."

"Who is Sean Donovan paying?"

"The engineer, fireman, conductor, a few more."

"You, Silas, is he paying you?"

"Yes . . . to keep my trap shut if any Santa Fe big shots ever get curious."

"But you're talking to me."

"I know and if Donovan finds out, he'll kill me."

"How did you meet Mr. Donovan?"

"I didn't. The money was all paid through Gamble Trask. I got two hundred dollars."

"And you wanted to use it to buy a little girl, right?"

Knowles' eyes grew sly and guarded and he made no answer.

McBride asked, "Trask planned on selling the girls to Portugee Lamego?"

"Yes, him and another man, a foreigner."

"An Arab trader? Goes by the name Ali al-Karim?"

"I don't know."

"How much was Portugee paying Trask?"

"I don't know. A thousand a girl, less Donovan's cut. I heard that, but I don't know."

"Steep price. I heard in some parts you can buy a young girl for the cost of a Missouri mule."

"Them Arabs you're talking about, they'll pay ten times what Trask was getting at the slave markets in Tangier. They like blue-eyed girls with yeller hair for their harems, and the prettier, the better."

"How do you know about slave markets and harems, Silas? You're a railroad ticket clerk at the nub end of nowhere."

"Hack Burns told me. He'd spoken to Gamble Trask a heap of times and from what Trask had let drop, Hack had it all figured out."

McBride thought for a few moments.

Even after paying off Donovan, Trask would have had enough money from Portugee and his trade in opium and Chinese girls to head for his new political life in Washington. A hundred thousand dollars and more could buy a lot of friends with influence. Portugee was the middleman, but it would be up to al-Karim to use his dozen ships to get the girls to slave markets at Tangier. The girls could be taken from a train, herded onto some remote beach on the California coast and picked up from there with no one the wiser.

It was a neat setup where everybody involved, even minnows like Silas Knowles, came out ahead. Only now Trask was dead, and it was Sean Donovan who stood to profit.

McBride dropped the hammer of the Colt and shoved the gun into his waistband. He took a step back and said, "Get the hell away from me, Silas."

Knowles threw McBride one last, scared glance, then scampered along the platform to his office, looking over his shoulder all the way.

It had been in McBride's mind to fight Donovan and the Allisons at the station. Now he decided against it. He'd only be throwing his life away and that would hardly be of any help to Shannon, or the hundred young girls coming in on the next day's train.

McBride walked from the station and faded into the darkness. When he was hidden by the night he lay on his back in a clump of tall Indian grass and stared at the spangled stars. He needed time to think.

Less than ten minutes later he heard the flat statement of two shots from the station.

McBride smiled. Apparently Sean Donovan had been most displeased with the talkative Mr. Knowles.

CHAPTER 29

John McBride spent an hour listening to the night. Finally, when he heard no further sounds of pursuit he climbed to his feet. For a moment his wide-shouldered silhouette stood against the sky and blotted out a thousand stars, but the rest drew closer around him, outlining him in a blaze of icy fire.

Tired of the smiling, silent moon, the prairie wind sought out McBride, eager to tell its tales, tugging at him to get his attention. Unheeding, he walked into the darkness toward the lights of town.

It was time to take the fight to Sean Donovan. There was now no other way to free Shannon and leave behind High Hopes forever.

Wary of the prowling Allisons, McBride kept to the alleys, lost in their secretive shadows. Nothing about him shone or glittered and he became one with the darkness, a tired, hungry, grim-faced man about to battle odds that would make lesser men shudder and choose a different path.

McBride wondered at that. Had the West changed him so much? Only recently, as early as tonight, had he at last come to accept its values. He realized that there were some injustices a man could not turn his back on, no matter how much he told himself that they were no concern of his. To take Shannon and run away from what was happening in High Hopes would be to undo all that he'd once held sacred — honor, courage, integrity. Blinded by his love for a woman and bound to protect her, he'd lost his way. Now he had found it again.

No matter what might happen in the next few hours, he would not run away and piss on his life.

McBride crossed the crowded, jostling street, unnoticed among so many, and took to the alley alongside the Golden Garter. He had seen no sign of Donovan and the Allisons, and the young miner's body had long since been removed from the boardwalk.

Gamble Trask's office had been at the back of the saloon, walled off from the rest of the building. On cat feet, McBride stepped through the alley to the rear of the

Golden Garter. If Donovan was in the office, he'd find a way to get at the man. A curtained window spilled subdued light onto the ground and gleamed on the blackened, upright beams of the fortune-teller's shack McBride had destroyed.

He stepped closer to the window.

The curtains were drawn, but one had snagged on a splinter of wood sticking up from the sill, leaving a small, triangular opening at the bottom. McBride got down on a knee at the window and peered inside.

He watched for a couple of minutes, then rose to his feet. A retching pain clutching at his gut. He reeled away from the window and stumbled into the darkness.

There was only one safe place he knew, a place where he could ride out the pain that racked him and bring order to his whirling brain. He would go to Marshal Clark's barn.

McBride staggered through the cartwheeling night, bent over, his fevered gaze on the ground ahead of him. Finally — he would never know how — he reached the barn and threw himself into a stall. The mustang turned its head, saw him and whinnied softly. Too sick to notice, McBride rolled on his back, his eyes open but staring into nothingness.

The pain had faded, to be replaced by a

green sickness that twisted and turned in his belly. He closed his eyes, trying to blot out what he'd seen in Donovan's office, but the vision stayed with him, stark and painful as sunlight reflecting on ice.

Try as he might, the scene replayed itself in his head, over and over again, a torment reserved for the worst of the damned.

He again saw Shannon in Donovan's arms, their hungry, open mouths together. He watched Donovan reach with thick, fumbling fingers for the hooks at the back of Shannon's dress. He saw her throw back her head and laugh, then lightly slap Donovan's hands away and, one by one, start to undo the hooks herself. Donovan, his eyes hot, nuzzled her neck and finally the top of the dress dropped around Shannon's hips. Her naked breasts thrust against his chest. . . .

Unable to watch anymore, McBride had turned away and fled blindly into the mocking night.

He rolled on his side and pressed his face into the harsh straw under him. He felt dirty, a lousy, crawling kind of uncleanliness, both from watching what had happened and from the certain knowledge that he'd been used, played for a fool.

Dolly had been right, McBride realized.

Shannon Roark loved only herself, and it hadn't taken her long to figure out that Sean Donovan could do more for her than he ever could.

A big house, servants, expensive jewels, a carriage and four — all those things Donovan could provide and more. She had made her choice.

Sick at heart, McBride pushed his face deeper into the straw, closed his burning eyes and waited, sleepless, for the dawn.

Thin daylight slanted into the barn through the open door, and somewhere a rooster strutted on a dung heap and crowed that he was king of the world.

McBride climbed to his feet and brushed wisps of straw from his clothes and hair. The pain was gone and only a vague anger was left. What Shannon had done to him was just another betrayal in a town where nothing ever was as it seemed.

But he vowed, no matter what, he would not betray himself. Donovan was expecting to score big from the sale of the girls from the orphan train. But McBride would not let it happen. Somehow he would stop it.

"Look at me," he'd told Dolly. "I'm only one man."

But if he's got sand, sometimes one man

is all it takes. McBride took some cold comfort in that thought.

He walked to the door of the barn and looked around. Dolly was standing outside the front of the house, rubbing brass polish onto the door knocker. She turned and saw him. She didn't smile. Bending, she put the can of polish and the rag at the bottom of the door and walked toward him. The hard morning light was unkind to her and did not allow a single line on her face to pass unnoticed.

"I thought you'd be back for your horse," the woman said. She glanced beyond him into the dark barn. "Where is Shannon?"

"She won't be leaving with me. Today or any other day."

It took a few moments for that to register. Then Dolly said, "You found out about her?"

"Yes. The hard way. She played me for a sap." There was sadness in his face, but the anger was stronger.

The woman nodded. "That's Shannon's style." Her eyes softened a little. "I'm sorry, McBride."

"So am I."

He felt he owed it to Dolly to tell her something, and he told her now. "I plan on being at the railroad station at noon today when the orphan train gets here."

"You're going to stop it."

"I'll try."

"I don't give two bits for your chances, McBride. Donovan will have plenty of gunhands with him."

McBride smiled. "Not so long ago you told me it was my duty to stop it. Have you used the woman's prerogative to change her mind?"

Dolly shook her head. "No, but I can see in your eyes that you've already died a little death. I'd just hate to see you die another."

"Trust me, the second will be a lot more permanent."

"Will it, McBride? Will it really?"

He had no answer for that question, knowing that Dolly was right. If he lived through this day, the hurt he felt right then would be with him for the rest of his life.

Dolly read the answer in his face and did not push him. She said, "Are you hungry?"

McBride forced a smile. "Believe it or not, I am. I could eat a steak and maybe six fried eggs."

"How about ham, potatoes and maybe three fried eggs?"

"Suits me just fine."

As they walked back to the house, McBride asked, "Do you still intend to leave the marshal?"

The woman stopped and turned to him. "I'll be at the station at noon, just like you. When the train pulls out again it will be empty and I'll ask the conductor to take me wherever it goes."

"I'm sorry it's working out this way, Dolly."

"Feel sorry for yourself, McBride. At least I'll still be alive."

He grinned. "You sure know how to boost a man's confidence."

"Uh-huh, learned that when I was working the line."

Dolly's kitchen was warm and steamy and smelled of cinnamon and stewed green apples. She waved McBride to a chair at the wooden table and took down a skillet from the pot rack.

"How do you like your eggs?"

"Over easy."

"Comin' right up."

The food was good and when McBride had finished eating he pushed his plate away and said, "That was an elegant meal, Dolly."

"Hardly elegant, but I hope it filled a hole."

"It did all of that." He nodded in the direction of Clark's bedroom. "How is he?"

"He knows I'm leaving today. He hasn't said anything."

"Want me to talk to him?"

"Lute won't talk to you. He's all through with talking. Now he waits for death to take him."

"A man doesn't have much of a choice on when that might be."

"I hope it's soon, McBride. For Lute's sake I do."

"Has he eaten anything this morning?"

"I took a breakfast in to him. He wouldn't touch it."

"Maybe I should talk to him."

Dolly shook her head as she brought her cup of tea to the table. "No. Lute has turned his face to the wall. He'll die very soon, I think."

McBride cast around in his head for something to say. He found only a useless scrap: "Silas Knowles is dead. Sean Donovan killed him."

Dolly's face was expressionless. "Silas wasn't much."

A tense silence stretched between them. Finally McBride said, "You may not see me at the station, at least not right away. I'll have to figure out how to go at it."

"Be careful, McBride. That's all."

"If I'm lucky, I'll kill Hack Burns for the

marshal."

"No, McBride, you won't kill Hack Burns. He's too fast, too good with a gun."

"I'll just have to figure out a way to go at it, that's all."

Dolly's eyes angled to the clock on the wall. "In another hour I'll say good-bye to Lute. Then I'll come to the barn and say good-bye to you." Her smile was fragile. "I'll be saying good-bye to dead men."

"Don't count me out, Dolly," McBride said. He tapped the handle of the Colt in his waistband. "I've gotten pretty good with this thing."

"You'll fire six shots. Then they'll kill you." The woman sighed deep and rose to her feet. "Better rest up now, McBride. You look tired."

As he was leaving, Dolly stopped him. "McBride."

He turned. "Yeah?"

"Good luck."

CHAPTER 30

McBride couldn't remember the last time he'd been in church, but he felt it right to pray a little. He had no illusions about what he'd be facing in less than three hours. He didn't have any kind of plan. All he could think of doing was to confront Donovan with his gun drawn and then let the chips fall from there.

But it was thin, real thin, and the outcome would be a very uncertain thing. If he raised enough fuss, others might hear and ask questions and the girls might be freed.

He shook his head on his straw pillow. It was all "might." Nothing was certain.

McBride did not sleep. Portugee had taken his watch and he judged the approach to noon by the sun. When he figured the hour was near, he rose to his feet, checked his gun and stepped out of the barn. Then he stopped. He'd forgotten about the mustang.

He walked back inside and threw the little horse more hay and a generous scoop of oats. He slapped the mustang on the shoulder and said, "If we don't meet again, pard, thanks for putting up with me."

The horse continued to chomp hay, as though McBride had not spoken. He smiled and walked out of the barn, into the sunlight.

To his surprise there was a large crowd on the station platform and he heard a brass band tuning up their instruments. He mingled with others walking toward the station and lost himself in the crowd. He asked an older woman at his side, "What's all the excitement about, ma'am?"

"Orphan train comin' in," the woman answered. "What larks! That nice Mr. Donovan, the new owner of the Golden Garter Saloon, says he's going to find good homes for all of them."

"That's true-blue of him," McBride said, keeping a straight face.

"They say it's all young girls," the old lady said. "I wouldn't mind getting one myself. At my age I need a servant."

It seemed to McBride that the whole town with the exception of miners who had left for the diggings was gathering to see the show. There had never been an orphan train in High Hopes and only a double hanging would have attracted a larger crowd.

He faded out of the throng and walked behind the station. Empty freight boxes were piled at the end of the platform, away from the crowd, and McBride stood beside them. From his place of concealment he had an excellent view of the entire station.

Sean Donovan was beaming, playing to the hilt his role of protector and benefactor of poor orphans to a crowd of admirers. He had his arm around Shannon's slender waist, but gone were the vivid silk dresses she wore in the Golden Garter. In their place was a somber day gown of russet taffeta. A small hat of the same color was perched atop her piled-up hair and she carried a yellow parasol against the glare of the noon sun.

Beyond Shannon and Donovan, the Allison brothers and Hack Burns stood together. Burns was wearing a coat, unusual for him, probably to conceal his gun from the arriving girls, McBride guessed. Donovan had made sure that nothing would alarm or scare the orphans when they stepped off the train. Even the half-dozen saloon girls who were distanced along the platform wore demure dresses, the better to convince the orphans that all was well and they were in kindly hands.

As yet there was no distant plume of smoke to herald the coming of the train. The expectant rails glittered in the sunlight, an inverted V of polished iron that vanished into a shimmering haze at the horizon.

The six-piece band finished an enthusiastic if ragged rendition of "Haste to the Wedding," then struck up "The Wisconsin Emigrant."

McBride watched Donovan turn his head, look behind him, then smile and nod to someone, but he couldn't see who it was. He left the cover of the piled boxes and walked to the corner of the station.

Portugee had stopped near the platform. It looked like he'd rounded up every spare freight wagon in town. In addition to his own three, there were another seven, drawn by mules, each covered with a bowed canvas. He and Ali al-Karim were up on the box of the first, Portugee at the reins, and his crew of ruffians were scattered among the others.

McBride drew back his head, then returned to the shelter of the boxes. Portugee must plan on driving the girls west to a station on the Union Pacific and then loading them on a train to carry them across the Divide. Thinking of his hat and money belt,

McBride knew a man who would rob an honest traveler of his few possessions would also make sure he disposed of the wagons at a handsome profit.

It seemed that everything Portugee touched turned to gold. McBride hoped to soon change all that.

The band was playing "Old Joe Clark" when a cheer went up from the crowd. McBride stepped away from his hiding place and his eyes searched the distance. He saw what had excited the crowd, a ribbon of black smoke emerging from the haze.

McBride drew back and checked his gun. But as he shoved the Colt back into his waistband, his elbow caught the edge of one of the empty boxes and it clattered, rolling onto the platform.

Donovan's head turned toward the sound and his face went black with anger when he saw McBride. Shannon was watching him too, but her eyes revealed a tangle of emotion, compassion knotted up with apprehension and a measure of fear.

Donovan urgently whispered to Burns and the Allisons. Burns smirked, the birthmark on his face like a bloodstain. Then he and the brothers walked slowly but purposefully in McBride's direction.

It had come. The fight was on. McBride

pulled his gun and held it at his side, thumb on the hammer, waiting, ready.

Burns got closer. He'd pulled back his coat, clearing his gun. The sun caught the star on his shirt and winked silver light.

At that moment, Dolly walked out of the waiting room, a carpetbag in her hand. She sized up what was happening, smiled at McBride and stepped quickly between him and the three gunmen.

It was a shrewd move and McBride appreciated it. If Burns and the Allisons cut loose, the chances were that a stray bullet would hit Dolly. At that time in the West, the Victorian ideal that a male should never abuse a respectable member of the fairer sex set a standard that was rigidly enforced. Killing a woman was a hanging offense, a fact that would not be lost on Burns and the Allisons.

McBride saw hesitation in Burns' face. He and the Allisons stopped where they were, but the confrontation was not over. All Dolly had given McBride was a few extra moments of time.

In the distance he heard the hoarse, smoky *chuff-chuff-chuff* of the approaching locomotive. The crowd was cheering and the band had stopped "Old Joe Clark" in midnote and was now robustly playing "The Dark-

Haired Lass."

The train was closer now. The locomotive's bell was clanging and thick, greasy smoke belched from the chimney. Blond heads were sticking out of every carriage window, all of them giggling. The girls were obviously amazed and excited at the size and scope of their reception.

McBride had to move. To remain where he was would put Dolly in even more danger. He picked up one of the empty crates and threw it at Burns. The gunman jumped to the side, cursing, and the box, splintering into pieces, bounded past his legs.

McBride turned and ran. He jumped off the edge of the platform and sprinted behind the station. He heard the thud of feet as Burns and the Allisons took off after him.

The train had come to a clanking, hissing halt and another cheer went up from the crowd. McBride ran directly for Portugee's wagon. The man was standing up in the box, yelling to his men to leave the wagons, get up on the platform and ride herd on the girls.

Portugee turned to say something to the Arab and saw McBride. His dark face twisted in shock and he reached down for the rifle leaning against the seat.

McBride fired at a run. His bullet hit Portugee dead center in the chest and the man screamed and toppled backward into the wagon bed. Al-Karim stood, his right hand flashing for the dagger in an ornate sheath he wore at his side. No mercy in him, McBride fired into the man, fired again and saw the Arab topple from the wagon seat and hit the ground with a thud.

A bullet grazed McBride's upper right arm and another split the air near his head. He heard the screams of girls from the platform, and panicked people streamed back toward town, away from the flying lead.

McBride ran past a wagon, then another. A bullet gouged the side of a wagon and threw splinters into his face. He got behind a huge, steel-rimmed wheel and snapped off a fast shot at Burns. A miss. But it had the effect of slowing the man down. More wary now, he and the Allisons came on at a walk.

McBride fired again, then ran for the platform, reloading as he went. People were streaming past him and the terrified orphan girls were milling around, uncertain of what to do or where to go. As he jumped onto the platform a fusillade of shots came from McBride's left and men were going down

— Portugee's men.

A stray bullet hit a tall girl in a white dress and she collapsed to the ground, sudden blood staining her left shoulder. Some of the other girls clustered around her as McBride ran past.

He was looking for Sean Donovan.

He pushed his way through a shifting sea of shrieking young females — and was stunned at what he saw ahead of him.

Detective Inspector Thomas Byrnes was standing on the platform, gun in hand, with a dozen of New York's finest around him, a motley group of detectives in shabby suits and plug hats. Several of Portugee's pirates lay sprawled on the ground. The rest had their hands in the air, looking seasick.

Byrnes grinned, waved to McBride, then staggered as a bullet hit him. His detectives were firing at targets to McBride's left. McBride turned and saw the Allison brothers, holding their ground, shooting steadily like the professional gunmen they were. But Hack Burns had turned and run, sprinting back toward town.

There was no sign of Shannon or Donovan.

Pushing his way through the girls a second time, McBride jumped off the platform and went after Burns. He pounded past the Allisons, fleetingly noted the startled expression on their faces and then was beyond them, running hard.

No bullets probed after him. The brothers were fully engaged with Byrnes and his men and didn't have time to spare for him.

Ahead of him, Burns reached the outlying buildings of town. He looked over his shoulder, saw McBride and thumbed off a shot. The bullet kicked up dirt at McBride's feet, but he did not slow, nor did he fire. He figured the range was too great for his dubious marksmanship.

Burns disappeared into an alley and McBride ran after him. He emerged into the street at the other side and quickly looked around him. The street was deserted, the good people of High Hopes obviously deciding it was safer indoors when a shooting war raged.

There was no sign of Hack Burns, but opposite McBride was the Golden Garter. It could be that Donovan had fled there with Shannon.

His gun up and ready, McBride crossed the street. He was halfway to his destination when the saloon's batwing doors swung open. A man stood there, his legs spread, looking at McBride with a cruel, mocking grin.

"You chased me, McBride," Burns said. "Well, now you've caught me."

The gunman was in no hurry. He had McBride flat-footed in the middle of the street, out in the open with no cover.

Burns' left hand slowly moved to his shirt pocket and he started to take out the makings. But then his right dropped to his gun and it came up spouting flame.

McBride raised his Colt and fired. He was fast, smooth and above all accurate.

He saw Burns take the hit. Then he stepped to his left and fired again. The gunman's expression changed from arrogance to shock. He stared in disbelief at McBride for several long moments before his knees crumpled and he fell facedown onto the boardwalk.

The gunman was still alive when McBride stepped onto the boards. He raised his head, looked up and whispered hoarsely through the blood that clogged his mouth: "You've learned."

McBride nodded. "Seems like."

"Gunfighter . . ." The last word Hack Burns ever spoke.

McBride walked around the dead gunman and stepped into the saloon.

He wanted Sean Donovan. He wanted him real bad.

CHAPTER 31

The only person in the saloon was the bartender. The man looked frightened, uncertainty bright in his eyes.

"Donovan?" McBride asked.

The bartender silently jerked a thumb in the direction of the office. The door was slightly ajar and McBride kicked it open and rushed inside, his Colt ready in his hand.

He saw only Shannon, who had changed into a shirt and a canvas riding skirt. She was kneeling at a small J. Watson & Son safe, a bundle of money in her hand. She looked up in alarm at McBride, then rose to her feet.

"Where is he?" McBride asked.

"If you're talking about Sean Donovan, I don't know," Shannon answered.

McBride looked at the woman he loved. "Shannon, it's over, but I didn't want it to end this way. I thought it would be so different. You and me married, having a family." He shook his head. "That's how I thought it would be."

The woman's beautiful mouth twisted into a sneer. She opened a drawer in the desk and dropped the money into it. "Mc-Bride, you're a fool. Did you really think I'd go with you back to New York and live on a policeman's salary? What did you think, that I'd be a dutiful little wife content to stand barefoot and pregnant in the kitchen of whatever hovel you could afford?"

"Yes, I thought that."

"Then you're an even bigger fool than I imagined. Once I had it in mind to make you my partner, that together we'd take everything Gamble Trask owned. But you're weak, McBride. I soon realized you didn't have the stomach for it."

"For what, Shannon? Murder?"

"Yes, if that's what was needed. Now all you've done is spoil everything. I won't have the hundred thousand from the sale of the orphans that I arranged with Sean Donovan, but there was enough in Gamble's safe to see me through. Besides, when I live with Sean in New York, I won't need money. I'll eventually take his."

"You arranged the orphan train?"

"Of course I did. Sean was doing business

with Gamble, but I wrote to him myself and set up the whole deal. I figured the girls would be my ticket out of here. And I was the one who contacted Portugee, an old friend of mine from my San Francisco days, and I had him get in touch with the Arab slaver. Then I made Gamble think it was all his idea. He was another fool."

"And the opium and the Chinese girls?"

"My ideas, my plans. I just got Gamble to carry them out, knowing that I'd eventually kill him and take it all. That's why I convinced him to hire the Allison brothers for his own protection."

"And in the end you did kill him."

Shannon smiled. "No, I had one of the Allisons kill him for me." She shrugged. "I offered to pay them more than Gamble was paying them."

"And it was you who had Leggett murdered."

"He was sniffing around, getting too close. I paid that fool cowboy to kill him."

"And me?"

"You were in the way. That was all."

"Recently I told someone that you played me for a sap, and you did, all along the line."

Shannon laughed. "McBride, you may not have noticed, but you are a sap. Did you really think I needed your protection? That was when I thought you might take care of Trask for me. I don't need you or any other man's protection. I was fourteen years old when I first worked the 'Frisco waterfront as a whore and I've been taking care of myself ever since. Hell, McBride, I'd killed two men by the time I was eighteen. I never let clients get rough with me, but now and again one of them would cross the line. It's amazing how a forty-four in the belly cools a man's desire to beat up on a woman."

Shannon took bundles of money from the drawer and stacked them on top of the desk. "It's been nice talking to you again, Mc-Bride. But now I have to be going."

McBride shook his head. "Shannon, you're not going anywhere except to the nearest law."

"I'm sorry you feel that way," Shannon said.

The gun had been in the drawer and it came up very fast. Shannon pulled the trigger and McBride felt like a club had crashed into his head. He was already unconscious, tumbling headlong into darkness, when he hit the floor.

McBride woke, aware that someone was lifting him into a sitting position.

"John, are you all right?"

It was Inspector Byrnes' voice.

"I've been shot," McBride said.

He saw the inspector nod. "I know, but the bullet only grazed you. Still, you're lucky you've got a thick skull."

McBride looked around, an effort that brought him pain. "Where is she?"

"Who?"

"Shannon Roark."

"Is she the one who shot you?"

"Yes. She pulled a forty-four on me."

"I don't know who Shannon Roark is, but I'd make an educated guess that she skedaddled with Sean Donovan."

"Where?"

Byrnes shook his head. "I don't know. I was kind of busy at the station."

"The Allisons?"

"Both dead." A shadow crossed Byrnes' face. "I lost a man too, Detective Sergeant Stanton."

McBride was shocked. "Bill Stanton?"

"Yes, Bill. But like the others from the detective department, he volunteered to come here. He knew the odds he was facing." Byrnes groped for something to say that would ease the fact of a good man's dying. "He went quickly, a shot to the heart. There could have been little pain."

Stanton was married and had three young

children. McBride felt his loss keenly.

"One of the Allisons kill him?"

"No, John. Sean Donovan did. He fired a couple of shots and then disappeared into the crowd. One of his bullets wounded an orphan girl. The other killed Sergeant Stanton."

McBride struggled to his feet, the room spinning around him. When he touched the side of his head his fingers came away bloody.

"How did you know about the orphan train?" he asked.

Byrnes smiled. "Good police work, John. Remember that? I got a tip about the orphan train from a railroader, a good company man, I guess. I arrested the train crew that had been paid by Donovan and replaced it with another. Then I asked for volunteers to come save your stubborn hide . . . and, well, you know the rest."

McBride looked at Byrnes. The left side of the man's coat was black with blood and he was obviously in considerable pain. "Better let the doctor take a look at that wound, inspector," he said.

Byrnes nodded, a wan smile touching his pale lips. "I'll be all right. When this is over I'll see a real doc back in New York."

McBride picked up his gun from the floor

and stuck it into his waistband.

"Where do you think you're going?" Byrnes asked.

"After Shannon and Donovan."

"No, you're not," the inspector said. "John, you're in no shape to go anywhere. I'll take care of Donovan."

"Can you ride a horse, Inspector?" McBride asked.

"No, but I can commandeer one of the wagons at the station."

"Too slow. Donovan has a head start — you'd never catch him." McBride smiled. "You can follow on behind me."

"In what direction?"

"That, I don't know. At least, not yet." McBride stepped toward the door, then stopped. "Inspector, you'll find a dead man in the box of the lead wagon. He's wearing my hat and probably has my Smith & Wesson, money belt and watch. Get them for me, will you?"

"All right, that's the wagon I'll commandeer," Byrnes said. He watched McBride walk unsteadily to the door. He said, "John, be careful. We'll be right behind you."

McBride nodded his thanks, stepped out of the saloon into the daylight and headed for Marshal Clark's barn.

There was a grim determination in Mc-

Bride. He intended to bring Shannon Roark
and Sean Donovan to justice.

The question was — where were they?

CHAPTER 32

John McBride was halfway to the barn when he saw a plump woman in a gingham dress striding purposefully along the boardwalk toward him. She stopped when she was a few feet away.

"Would you be John McBride?" she asked. Then she answered her own question. "Judging by the description he gave me, you must be." She smiled. "Lordy, you look all beat-up, but you're not near as ugly as he said."

"What can I do for you, ma'am?" McBride asked. He was irritated. This was no time for chitchat.

"My name is Lavender Coffin and I do for the marshal now that his . . . er . . . lady is gone."

By this time Dolly was probably riding the cushions of the orphan train. McBride felt a small sadness at her departure, which he could not fully explain.

"How is the marshal?" he asked.

Lavender shook her head. "Not well. He sent me to look for you, if you were still alive, like. He needs to talk to you."

McBride nodded. "I'll see him."

"Come back to the house with me," the woman said. "I'll wash that blood off your face and head." She gave him a sympathetic smile. "You poor thing."

Lavender had opened the curtains of Clark's room, letting in a stream of angled sunlight where dust motes danced. The room smelled of furniture polish, baking apple pie and the slow rot of the man in the bed.

"Mrs. Coffin said you wanted to see me, Marshal," McBride said. He shrugged an apology. "I don't have much time."

"I know. I saw Shannon Roark riding out of town with a man. I figured after all the shooting I heard earlier that you'd be going after them. That is, if you were still standing."

"In what direction were they headed?" McBride asked, his interest quickening.

"Northeast." Clark studied McBride's face. "She was smiling at the man. Didn't look much like a captive to me."

"She's not." McBride let the flat statement lie there.

The marshal understood and did not push it. "If I was a gambling man, I'd bet the farm that they'll stay west of the Picketwire, away from the rough, high-ridge country. They're probably heading for Las Animas on the old Santa Fe Trail, where they can catch a train east."

"Then I've got to be on my way, Marshal Clark. Thanks."

The man in the bed nodded. "Take care, McBride."

McBride stepped to the door, then stopped. He turned and said, "I killed Hack Burns. I thought you'd like to know that."

Clark's grin was wide. "Thank you, McBride. Now I can die easy."

McBride walked to the barn and saddled the mustang, trying to fend off most of Lavender's attentions. But the woman, a bowl of soapy water and a washing cloth in her hands, was determined. She cooed over him, dabbed blood from his face and head, then applied a generous amount of stinging stuff with a cotton swab.

"I know that must smart, poor dear," she murmured. "But we don't want a nasty infection, do we?"

It was with considerable relief that McBride swung into the saddle, told Lavender to let Inspector Byrnes know where he was headed, then took the trail to the northeast. After an hour he crossed Timpas Creek. The stream was dry, its rocky bottom bright with yellow, purple and red wildflowers.

Flat, rolling country lay in front of him, rising abruptly in the east to a rocky ridge that sloped away to the Picketwire. The sun had dropped in the sky, but the day was still hot and the land drowsed in a deep silence, the only sound the steady thud of the mustang's flinty hooves and the creak of saddle leather.

McBride was not a tracker, but he was enough of a detective to follow the trail of the two horses ahead of him. Confident that he would not be followed, and unused to riding, Donovan was setting an easy pace. McBride rode up on a small green meadow where underground water nourished a stand of cottonwoods. Someone, no doubt Shannon, had stopped there and picked wildflowers. McBride counted a dozen broken stems of buttercup, blue iris and corn lily and there were probably more he could not see.

A buttercup, wilted, had strayed from Shannon's hand and lay on the grass like a drop of gold fallen from the sun. McBride picked up the bloom and studied it for long moments. Finally he touched the flower to his lips, then carefully tucked it away in a pocket.

Grief and a dark sense of loss took hold of McBride and he let out a long, shuddering sigh that had its genesis deep inside him where the worst of hurts dwelled.

A flock of crows descended on the branches of the cottonwoods, wheeling like pieces of charred paper from out of the blue sky. They called out to one another noisily, for now ignoring the man who stood head bowed in pain, a gang of ragged ruffians who stood ready to mock him should he not quickly move along.

McBride stepped into the saddle and resumed his ride to the northeast. Behind him, the sun began its journey to the western horizon and the shadow of man and horse stretched longer across the prairie grass.

Three hours later, as the evening became night and the first stars appeared, McBride saw the light of a campfire ahead of him. He eased the Colt in his waistband and rode toward the camp . . . as around him the coyotes began to sing their requiem for the departed day.

McBride dismounted when he was still two hundred yards from the camp. He covered the rest of the distance on foot, trusting to the darkness to keep him hidden. When he was close, he saw Shannon and Donovan standing in each other's arms near the guttering fire. Shifting, scarlet shadows streaked the night around them and the wood crackled and snapped, sending up small showers of sparks.

Donovan kissed Shannon hard and long, then pushed her away from him, holding her at arm's length. He grinned and said, "I'll have a lot more of that later, but right now it's time for you to put some supper together."

"Don't bother." McBride spoke from the gloom, his voice hollow as a death knell. "You won't have time to eat it."

Sean Donovan was an affable, talkative man, but in that instant he realized the time for talk was not then. He turned, drawing from under his coat, his wild, angry eyes flashing ruby red in the firelight.

McBride drew from the waistband and his gun flared. Hit hard, Donovan staggered and tried to bring his Smith & Wesson Russian to bear. McBride fired again and the man fell heavily, his arm landing across the fire, throwing up a crimson fountain of sparks.

Shannon cowered among the shadows, her

horrified eyes on McBride. He stepped to the fire and kicked Donovan's smoldering coat sleeve from the flames.

Donovan's eyes rose to McBride's. "Damn you," the man snarled. "Damn you to hell, McBride."

McBride nodded. "Keep a seat warm for me, Sean."

Donovan's mouth opened to speak, but his lips pulled back from his gritted teeth in a death agony. He rattled deep in his chest, trying to kill McBride with his glare, and then his life left him.

Swinging his gun on Shannon, McBride said, "Let me have the bulldog, Shannon. I don't want to kill you."

The woman had an arm behind her back and McBride watched her closely. "Don't even try it, Shannon," he said. "I have others close behind me. Even if you kill me, they'll track you all the way to Las Animas and beyond if they have to."

"What will they do to me?" the woman asked. All of a sudden, she looked scared, unsure of herself.

McBride shook his head. "I don't know. Inspector Byrnes will take you to the law and then it will be up for a jury to decide."

"A jury!" Shannon almost spit the words. "They could put me away for years."

"Yes. A long, long time."

"I can't let that happen." Shannon stepped closer to McBride. She was smiling. "John, you can forget what happened between us. That . . . that was all a mistake on my part. We can leave — we can leave right now and be together just like you planned. I was wrong, I know it now. Please, John, give me another chance. I can make you happy, I know I can." Her smile was warm, wonderful. "I will make you a good wife, John."

McBride's smile was without humor. "A wife who did her best to kill me back there at the saloon?"

"I didn't try to kill you. I aimed wide on purpose."

"I'd say that's real good shooting," McBride said drily. He saw a small defeat in Shannon's eyes as she opened her mouth to speak, but he cut her off. "You made a sap of me once, Shannon. I won't let it happen again." He motioned with the barrel of his Colt. "Now, let drop whatever you're holding behind your back."

"There are no second chances with you, McBride," the woman said. "Are there?"

"Not tonight, Shannon. Or any other night."

"I thought so. Well, I can't allow you to let me rot in a prison for forty years."

The .44 bulldog came out quickly from behind Shannon's back. McBride hesitated, reluctant to shoot.

That was all the time she needed. Shannon shoved the muzzle of her gun between her breasts and pulled the trigger. She gasped and fell backward and McBride crossed the ground fast, taking a knee at her side.

"I'd die a little death every day in prison," she whispered, blood red against the paler pink of her lips. "I won't let that happen." She raised a hand and her fingers lightly touched McBride's cheek and she smiled. "You poor sap," she said.

She died, leaving a void in McBride's heart that he knew he would never fill, not if he lived for a hundred years.

He was still kneeling beside Shannon's body the next morning when Inspector Byrnes and another detective lifted him gently to his feet and led him away.

"Are you sure you won't come back to New York with us, John?" Inspector Byrnes asked.

They were standing on the platform of the High Hopes train station, surrounded by a hundred females that Byrnes had taken under his wing, vowing to find good homes

357

for all of them back along the line.

McBride shook his head. "No, Inspector, for me that life is over and there's no going back. The West has changed me. For better or worse, I haven't discovered yet."

"But surely you don't intend to stay in High Hopes?"

"With Trask and Donovan gone and the Golden Garter closed, High Hopes is finished as a town." He shrugged. "Maybe they can save it by attracting the cattle trade. I don't know."

"But what will you do, John?" The inspector's eyes moved to the end of the platform where the mustang was tied, a blanket roll behind the saddle. "Just ride here and there on that ugly horse?"

"That's about the size of it, Inspector." McBride smiled. "But first I have to find a home for four young Chinese girls I left behind me. That might take time."

"Huh, you think that's hard? Try finding homes for a hundred caterwauling females."

"Good luck, Inspector, and give my thanks again to the men who came here to help." McBride took off the money belt Byrnes had returned to him and handed it to the man. "There's around six hundred dollars there. Make sure Mrs. Stanton gets it."

"But, John, that's every penny you have."

"I'll make out," McBride said.

Later, after the train left with Byrnes and his girls, McBride swung into the saddle and headed west.

The sun had begun its climb into the sky, heralding the dawn of a bright new day.

HISTORICAL NOTES

Detective Inspector Thomas Byrnes created the first New York Detective Bureau on May 25, 1882. Byrnes hired forty detective sergeants at an annual salary of one thousand dollars and ordered them to use their powers of deduction rather than brute force to solve crimes. Something of a Sherlock Holmes himself, Byrnes later became a major dime novel hero who handily outsold his closest rival, Theodore Roosevelt.

In the late 1860s and throughout the next fifteen or twenty years, "orphan trains" were dispatched west from Chicago, New York, Boston, St. Louis, Cleveland and Cincinnati. Funded by charities and religious organizations, the trains were packed with hundreds of children under the age of fifteen, removed from overcrowded city orphanages. In most cases this worked out well for all concerned, but many kids fell into the hands of pedophiles, pederasts and other perverts. Many were beaten to death by cruel adoptive parents or by people who posed as parents but were truly little more than taskmasters.

Some readers, especially those familiar with film noir, might be surprised at the use of the word "sap" — as in fool or simpleton — in an 1880s context. The word was widely used in its present meaning as early as 1815, and probably grew out of the earlier word "sapskull," a thick or stupid person.

The railroad yard in the opening chapter of *West of the Law* is now the site of Grand Central Station.

Heroin was first synthesized from morphine (a derivative of opium) in England in 1874. By the mid-1870s it was being imported in fairly large quantities from Britain and Germany to the United States, where the drug was touted as a "safe, non-addictive substitute for morphine." It was then that the heroin addict was born.

The hypodermic needle was invented in 1853 by Scottish doctor Alexander Wood. By the late years of the War Between the States the needles were in widespread use to administer morphine to wounded soldiers. Morphine had been used as early as the War of 1812, but was given orally. One result of battlefield morphine was that many soldiers went home with an addiction, taking their needles with them.

The author is convinced that heroin was being mainlined in the West in 1882, but had not yet replaced the easier to get laudanum. When he researched what heroin was called back then, he hit a brick wall. It could be that the soiled doves and other addicts of Deadwood and Tombstone called the drug "heroic" or "heroic medicine." But it's more likely that it was already called heroin and that's the name that was later trademarked by the Bayer Company in the 1890s. Overall, the author feels comfortable portraying his Chinese doves shooting up heroin with hypodermics in 1882, and that they and their handlers call the drug by that name.

ABOUT THE AUTHOR

Ralph Compton stood six foot eight without his boots. He worked as a musician, a radio announcer, a songwriter, and a newspaper columnist. His first novel, *The Goodnight Trail,* was a finalist for the Western Writers of America Medicine Pipe Bearer Award for Best Debut Novel. He was also the author of the *Sundown Riders* series and the *Border Empire* series.

The employees of Thorndike Press hope you have enjoyed this Large Print book. All our Thorndike and Wheeler Large Print titles are designed for easy reading, and all our books are made to last. Other Thorndike Press Large Print books are available at your library, through selected bookstores, or directly from us.

For information about titles, please call:
    (800) 223-1244

or visit our Web site at:
    http://gale.cengage.com/thorndike

To share your comments, please write:
    Publisher
    Thorndike Press
    295 Kennedy Memorial Drive
    Waterville, ME 04901